Are You Trying To Seduce Me Mrs Daniels?

Don Bull

Published by Don Bull 2014

Thanks again to my wife, relatives and friends for their support as well as to other writers for their invaluable advice along the way. Finally to my characters for putting themselves forward in such a shameless way, I couldn't have written this without them.

A School Based Murder Romance, from the Pen of Don Bull.

All of the usual ingredients are here.

Teachers behaving badly.

A rich, selfish, headstrong and sexually overactive woman.

An unassuming, laid-back lover.

A gangster husband who speaks like Nigel Kennedy and acts like the O'Driscoll brothers.

A ménage a trois involving two lesbians and a straight man.

Three Irish navvies.

A recovering alcoholic.

A rich and reclusive artist.

An attractive trade union rep.

And a dog called Vernon.

What more could you ask for?

Some Other Writers Comment.

Steevan Glover.
Starts superbly and gathers pace really well. One of the more individual pieces of writing, it has its own voice and the writer is not trying to emulate another's style.

Bruce Brislin.
This is annoyingly good. I had to force myself to start reading and then damn me after the first page I actually wanted to go on. I detest these human relationship stories with a passion usually. You have no right to use such lousy material to make something so good, an Irish geek and a stunning forty something I ask you. To be serious for a moment this is really good writing. Definitely not the type of thing I'd choose to read but the skill and quality of the work shines through.

Maria McCurdie.
The pace moves along nicely and helps build the story, there is no unnecessary writing, each line has a purpose. I would recommend this book to anyone who enjoys a bit of a mystery with a splash of romance and sex.

Paul Krow.
The writing is effortless and snappy and the humour is almost always funny.

Elizabeth Xifarias.
A very appealing main character with an entertaining and convincing voice. A lovely light but literate style that is easy to read. The humour is gentle and well handled, I laughed out loud at times.

Chapter 1
School's Out – Alice Cooper

"Mr Wilson," The familiar voice causes me to hesitate and then as I hear. "Gerry," I stop and turn.

Victoria Daniels is hurrying towards me along a corridor that is rapidly emptying, as children dissolve into classrooms. I surmise that as Victoria's smiling at least I've done nothing to offend her. We are both teachers at St Winston's Comprehensive and despite her first name familiarity, until this moment I've barely registered on Victoria's radar. To be perfectly honest I've always been somewhat in awe and not a little nervous of our Mrs Daniels, hence my pathetic relief at her apparent good humour.

Victoria is quite tall for a woman, with rich auburn hair and while I've always wondered if the colour is entirely natural, I notice at close quarters that her eyebrows are actually dark brown. She dresses well, not a common trait in teachers whether male or female.

"Gerry, thank heavens I've caught you," she says, a little breathlessly after the exertion of hurrying after me along the corridor and then by the simple expedient of placing her hand on my arm she restores all of the anxieties that were beginning to recede.

"I like your new hairstyle," I say, instantly wondering why I've said it.

"Thank you."

"Not that there was anything wrong with the old one because that was nice as well but this one's even nicer... I think."

"Anyway enough of that," said Victoria. "I'm so glad I've caught you, tell me, are you going to the staff party tonight?"

It's the final day of term before the eagerly anticipated Christmas break. The pupils held their own disco last night and tonight is the staff's turn. I'm a little surprised by the question and can only muster a noncommittal "er," in response but then to er is human, after all.

"Actually I'm being a little disingenuous," Victoria continues. "I know the answer to that already. Sienna told me that you hadn't bought a ticket."

Sienna Lavender has assumed the mantle of un-elected social secretary to the staff and as such organises all of our communal activities. This is a fortunate eventuality, as no one else seems to have the energy or the inclination to bother. Tonight's bash involves eating, drinking and dancing at a Greek Taverna. I've cried off buying a ticket for two reasons, my only real friend among the staff Lyndsey, isn't going and just as crucially I'm temporarily embarrassed by a dire lack of funds.

"Have you anything else planned?" Victoria asks.

"Well I was going to re-label my collection of Albanian peasant caps," I say, aiming to sound both zany and flippant but sadly missing both targets.

Victoria looks puzzled and then realising that she's expected to laugh, does so, heartily if a little unconvincingly.

"I wondered Gerry," she pauses. "Would you do me the most enormous favour?"

I can't help thinking to myself that I'd tackle a Bengal tiger with a cocktail stick to do a favour for a woman like this, as my mind quickly scans the possibilities from the remote dog sitting to the more likely chauffeuring.

"Of course I will if I can."

"Oh good, you see I have two tickets for tonight's little *soiree*," she says fingering the *soiree* into inverted commas. "And *quelle surprise*, Lenny has an unavoidable business commitment. I was so looking forward to going but obviously I won't feel comfortable if I'm the only one to turn up without a partner." At this point she squeezes my forearm lightly, I suppose for emphasis. "Would you be an absolute angel Gerry, and be my beau for the evening?"

I only have a split second to weigh up my options. On the one hand I can accompany a glamorous, articulate woman, enjoy a no strings attached evening that will include all I can eat, plenty to drink and I feel sure, at least a hint of the dancing that will provide the cloud wrapping that seems a prerequisite of every silver lining life throws up. On the other hand lies a night in my dingy bed-sit with beans on toast, the telly and a couple of cans of lager.

"I'd love to," I say, perhaps a little too impetuously as the thought of my tatty old Volvo Estate hits me in the solar plexus of reality. Not quite what our Victoria is accustomed to. Her current set of wheels is a Mercedes Sports convertible, although she changes cars so quickly that if she smoked I'd suspect her of using 'the ashtray's full' excuse.

"Should I pick you up?" I venture a little more tentatively.

"No of course not it's a party and you'll want to have a drink won't you? To build up the Dutch courage to dance with an old biddy like me."

This time she really is being disingenuous, as Victoria is mid-forties at most and looks ten years younger. In the past I've heard lots of under the breath comments in the staff room, suggesting that she's all too aware of this. I start trying to construct a reply but realising the pitfalls involved after previous perilous expeditions into the dangerous territory of a woman's age, I merely stumble over a few false beginnings before giving up.

"We'll take a cab," she laughs. "There and back and I'll pay, after all you're the one doing me the favour."

I stand staring while trying to compose a reply. I have an unfortunate habit when nervous of trying too hard and can easily end up gabbling out a stream of dross. I know that silence is the best option but at times like these tend to experience difficulty reining in my mouth.

"People will start talking about you two if you stand there staring into each other's eyes for much longer." This is Lyndsey as she bustles past us.

"Right," I say, stunned into action by the interruption. "I'll book a taxi and call for you at about seven then. You're sure your husband won't mind?"

"It's only a meal with colleagues, what is there to mind?" Victoria said in a business-like manner before purring. "Or have you other plans for me?"

I can feel my face redden. "I'll see you tonight then," I say, and make to hurry away. Did she think I was implying something more?

"Gerry," I turn again. "Don't you think that you ought to have my address?"

She scribbles it down and I scurry off, tucking it into my pocket.

∞

I'm taking my own year eleven form for the morning and for what will be an abbreviated afternoon. Last day of term as usual is winding down time and the class are amusing themselves. I don't have to over emphasise the need to keep the noise down as most of them are nursing hangovers from last night's alcohol free disco. The girls are talking clothes, make up and whatever extravagant gifts they're receiving for Christmas. The boys are discussing football, music and how far they got into whose blouse the night before.

The Red Hot Chilli Peppers 'Californication' CD is playing at a volume decided by multilateral negotiations. I'm pleased that at least some of the kids still have taste in music. A lot of the lads tend to go for 'gangsta rap' or whatever nom de plume it masquerades under at the moment, while the girls seem to be into boy bands. I try to enjoy modern music and not criticise their tastes, even indulging in a little hubris that the kids in my class think that this is 'cool' and haven't started to call me the oldest swinger in town yet. Not to my face anyway, despite the fact that I'm rapidly approaching the big three zero.

Notwithstanding the laid back mood that prevails, I'm unable to relax because I now have time to consider the evening ahead. But what do I think is going to happen, why am I worrying? Victoria has the sort of looks any red blooded male drools over and the sort of strong personality that a wuss like me has nightmares about. I hail from a small market town in rural Ireland and my parents moved to England when I was twelve, to improve their financial outlook. I still mirror their placid, unassuming personas. When they returned to the homeland five years ago I remained here, in what I now regard as home. As a teenager, while making return visits to see relatives I was always referred to as a Brit by the local kids. This was never done in a nasty way but nevertheless always served as a reminder that I was an outsider. Strangely enough at school in England I was called Paddy. Is it any wonder that I've grown up with a refugee mentality?

A day with my class is probably the best antidote I could have to worrying about squiring Victoria tonight. They are on the whole, much scarier and that's just the girls. I consider my year elevens to be one of the success stories of my teaching career to date. Our paths first crossed when they were in year eight, an ill disciplined, barely educated rabble. Under my guidance they progressed through year nine and year ten, before attaining their current dizzy heights of year eleven, an ill disciplined but slightly better educated rabble. Along the way we've reached an accommodation of each other's needs. For their part they don't interrupt my teaching and in return I don't interfere too much with whatever it is they're doing while I attempt to teach them.

At mid-morning break I volunteer for the generally detested playground duty, hoping that the keen air might clear my head of the worries that were forming an orderly queue there. It also keeps me away from the staff room and any possible encounter with Victoria. There isn't too much going on and I only need to be careful not to catch the young smokers huddled in their usual corners. Lyndsey bounces towards me full of her usual bonhomie. Ninety nine per cent of the time she's bubbling over with fun and good humour while the other one per cent she could depress for England. Luckily today is a ninety nine per cent day, everything is hunky dory between Lyndsey and her partner Violet at the moment and little else is going to be allowed to affect her cordiality.

"Aren't you bloody froze?" I enquire politely.

While I'm weighed down with every layer of clothing that I have access to, topped off rather raffishly with the donkey jacket bequeathed to me by Uncle Barney as my inheritance, Lyndsey is wearing a thin, short-sleeved pullover, her only concession to the weather being a fluffy scarf and hat that matched.

"It's absolutely gorgeous out here today," she positively glows with a healthy redness. "It's so crisp and vibrant it's shouting out at you that you're alive."

"That's if it doesn't kill you first" I said miserably. "I see your nips have certainly come to life or are you just pleased to see me."

"Mind your own business, they're no one's concern but Violet's and mine," she says crossing her arms over them. "And don't try to distract me from what I came over for. I've just heard the goss'. What's the gig you've got going with Cruella De Ville?"

"I haven't got a gig going, I'm taking her to the staff do tonight but it's not what you mean by a gig. I'm only going as her escort for the evening, I get a free night out and she gets someone to talk to."

"That's cool, I'm always saying you need to get out more and a quick shag will do you the world of good."

"What are you talking about?" I say. "Don't go there, not even in jest. She's a respectable married woman."

"Yeah and I dress as a nun when I go to see the Sound of Music."

"What do you mean?"

"Oh nothing, do you want me to pop round and act as your unpaid dresser tonight?"

"No thank you," I say, sounding more than a little stroppy and instantly regretting it but too proud to renege.

I often go shopping with Lyndsey and she's assumed the mantle of being unofficial style guru to Gerry Wilson and rarely gets it wrong. I seldom receive compliments when I wear clothes that I've chosen myself as opposed to the Lyndsey Francis collection. When we first became friends Lyndsey had broken the news to me, fairly subtly by her standards, that I possessed all the dress sense of Des O'Connor.

"What's all this talk about shaggin' then?"

The broad Brummie tones of Dave Stack, PE and sometime geography teacher, signal that he's materialised behind us, remarkably quietly for such a big man. I'm unsure just how much he's actually heard.

"I was just offering to sacrifice my virginity if Gerry's desperate for a shag," says Lyndsey, winking at me.

"You can't do that, you bat for the other side," says Dave, looking a little piqued and once again proving what a loss he's been to the diplomatic corps until suddenly he sees the light. "Ohhh I see, you think you might like to give life on the right side of the bed a go. You should try a real man if you're up for a conversion job. No offence Gerry but I mean, she's not bad looking for a er..."

"Ooh, do you mean that David?" Lyndsey swoons. "I didn't dare dream of setting my sights so high."

Dave is beginning to visibly preen himself. He automatically flexes his muscles in an unselfconscious mockery of some primitive courtship ritual. Dave is about six feet two and eighteen stone of solid muscle, including a shaven head that you wouldn't expect to encounter outside Easter Island. It's hard to believe that he has no inkling that he's being sent up. I suppose that in the land of the vain, flattery provides a blind to most things.

"Look doll, I'd be only too glad to oblige, any time," Dave smiled before realising a drawback. "It'll have to fit in around my training though."

"Can I feel your bicep?"

I drift away, leaving them to it. If I didn't know Lyndsey as well as I do, I could almost have been convinced that she was serious. The rest of the day passes in a series of calm moments interspersed with panic attacks over what I've agreed to do tonight. What option did I have though? After all she's only expecting a dance partner and I can dance. Thanks to Alison my ex-wife, she'd taught me during our marriage. My mind just keeps regurgitating, 'you need a good shag.' True as this may be I doubt I'm ready for a smart, confident, 'woman of the world'. Anyway what am I getting hot under the collar about? Victoria is married to a rich man and could have easily selected a suave, debonair companion. She's picked me to avoid any gossip. Who in their right mind would imagine Victoria and me together and with that thought I almost relax.

After arriving home I lose my nerve and take up Lyndsey on her offer to select my outfit, but only after trying on almost every garment that I own in every conceivable combination. Lyndsey arrives to find me clad in a black, velvet Paul Smith jacket. Even in the half-price sale it had been ridiculously out of my price range. I have teamed this with a white shirt that has a raised embroidered pattern and elaborate fold over cuffs that Lyndsey had once picked out for me. A pair of John Rocha jeans completes my ensemble.

"You're not going out like that are you?"

"What's wrong with it?" I demand a little abashed.

"Oh nothing," she says matter of factly. "Well, not if you insist on living up to your ethnic stereotype and don't mind being mistaken for a Daniel O'Donnell tribute act."

After holding out for at least another thirty seconds I give in and Lyndsey leaves my top half alone but puts me into a pair of black trousers, telling me that my look is now one of understated

quality and that I should proceed to knock them
dead.

Chapter 2
Taxi – Harry Chapin

I arrive at the address Victoria had furnished me with. It's on a small exclusive looking estate in the countryside on the fringe of Bewdley. We're about thirty miles from our destination in Birmingham and twenty from my flat in Lye.

"Posh gaff," says the driver.

I've taken an instant dislike to this man, anticipating it'll save time later. He's one of those 'nudge nudge, wink wink,' know it all's, a bit of a man of the world and speaks in the condescending manner of one who's seen it all before. Victoria has arranged the car through one of the private hire companies her husband's firm uses, I'm not sure if he may even own it. I think her nerve failed at the thought of leaving the taxi booking to me. I get out and approach the door but before I reach it Victoria emerges, perhaps she doesn't want her husband to meet me.

I hold the car door open for Victoria to get in before getting back in the other side. It's a large Ford with leather seats. After making herself comfortable she settles her gaze on me and I realise that I'd planned to compose a list of emergency conversation topics but never got round to it. The smell of her perfume mingles with the leather of the seats and the pine air freshener.

"Is that Chanel you're wearing?" I ask.

"What a pleasant surprise, a man that not only notices a lady's perfume but recognises it as well."

"It was one of Alison's favourites. One of the things I really miss about being close to a woman, is smelling her perfume. Well not just the perfume but all of the other scents that men don't seem to have."

"Were you very much in love with her?"

"Yeah, probably."

"What do you mean probably?"

"Well I did love her but it was never really down to me, I didn't have much say in it, Alison sort of picked me. Actually I think that might be the case with most couples, the women lay the ground rules and make the decisions but most men don't realise what's going on. The woman lets the man think that he's the boss because it suits her to. Anyway in the end Alison also made the decision that I'd outlived my usefulness. I don't think I ever quite lived up to her expectations."

"And I think that I may have misjudged you too. At school I always thought there was less to you than met the eye, now I'm thinking that perhaps there's a little more, quite the philosopher Mr Wilson."

"You often see an intelligent man with a dumb woman," I said. "But you rarely see a clever woman with a stupid man."

"That's rather good actually, I may steal it from you."

"Not me its Clint Eastwood but I don't suppose he'd mind."

"You said you've missed being close to women since your divorce. Surely there have been others?"

"No, not really, I've never been much of a ladies man you see, I'm too shy and when I took up with Alison it sort of removed the need to make the effort. Since the divorce I've just drifted really, I go out with the lads and with Lyndsey and Violet but not on any proper dates."

I catch the driver's eye in the mirror as I say this and I can guess that he's smirking. I realise that my nervous state has led me to talk too much. I would have clammed up there and then had Victoria not taken over the conversation. After guiding it onto school matters the rest of the journey passes pleasantly enough.

∞

I help Victoria out of her coat and check it in. She's wearing a matching top and trousers in some sort of floaty material. It's neither fashionable nor unfashionable but possesses the effortless style that quality clothes seem to enjoy. It could have looked good on an eighteen year old or an eighty year old but on Victoria it looks stunning, the sea green hue perfectly complements her red hair. Most of the others are already here and our party is seated around a large table. Victoria has Colin Burley, the school letch and his wife to her right. Dennis Sheary and spouse are to my left.

As we sit down Colin leans across us and asks. "What do you think of Vicky's toy boy then Den?"

Before the answer is spoken, Victoria says, sotto voce. "If you want to discuss staff relationships Colin, carry on. I'll have such fun going over your school dirty laundry with Jean."

"Just a joke Vicky, no harm intended," said Colin, the smirk gone from his face, replaced by a nervous twitch.

"Same here Colin," replies Victoria, then changing tack. "I say, Jean."

Colin visibly blanches.

"Oh hello Vicky," says Jean, as if she's just noticed her presence. "Christine and I were just discussing the children. Of course you don't have any do you?"

She must know this and I sense Victoria stiffen slightly at what is obviously delivered as a put down.

"No I don't," she replies

"My three are all at school now," says Jean with a smug smile.

"What do they teach?" This is instant revenge served very cold indeed. Jean most definitely looks older than her years.

"Did you know that our Dennis is standing as a Liberal Democrat candidate at the next election?" Colin interjects quickly, obviously worried where this exchange might be heading.

"Typical," says Victoria. "A bloody political science teacher who's a Liberal, what does a Liberal know about politics? I vote Tory because I have money and they look after the rich. If I was poor I'd vote Labour but just look at how many car workers and miners must have voted for Maggie. She spent years shitting on them and yet most of them seemed to say, 'it's what we needed,' and carried on voting for her. You don't need to teach the great unwashed politics when they vote, just math's, to count the money in their pockets. Still, you're not going to bother the returning officer too much as a Liberal are you Dennis?"

Both couples fill the shocked silence by politely starting conversations on their opposite sides.

"Weren't you a bit hard on them?" I ask.

I know Colin Burley is a gossiping, woman chaser and Dennis Sheary's a sanctimonious, two faced waste of space, in fact ideal politician material but I think what shocked me more was the brutality of Victoria's attack rather than any sense of unfairness.

"It served its purpose anyway," she said. "I hate bloody Jean Burley, she's a pompous bitch and I have to listen to Colin and Dennis wittering on all day in the staff room. I really don't want to hear it all again tonight. I'm here to enjoy myself."

"You have to listen to me at school," I said.

"That's an exaggeration, I think you've probably spoken more to me tonight than you have in entirety previously."

"I'm sorry, I tend to gabble when I'm nervous."

"Don't be silly I'm enjoying our conversation. I'd be disappointed if you weren't talking to me and anyway, why should you be nervous?"

"I'm sort of…" I hesitate, daring myself to reply. "Well a bit frightened that I might do something to embarrass you."

"Am I really that much of an ogre?"

"No, you're really much nicer than I expected."

"Thank you. At least I think that was a compliment. Come on you can earn your corn by dancing with me before the food arrives."

We get up and Shania Twain's 'That Don't Impress Me Much' is playing. Victoria dances close enough to maintain our conversation.

"Tell me about yourself?" Victoria asks.

I explain my arrival from rural Ireland. "It was so behind the times where I came from that even Blue Peter was in black and white." A terrible old joke but it raises a smile. "When I first arrived here the other kids at school presumed that because I was Irish I must be from Belfast and ergo a tough streetwise boy steeped in violence. They'd seen it all on the TV news, which was as close as I'd ever gotten to it myself. They took my quietness for brooding menace and I quite enjoyed the cachet it gave me and didn't attempt to disabuse them of their wayward fancies. It was a while before they realised their mistake and by then I was accepted. Actually my mother is a Catholic and my father is a Protestant. I think that's what gave me the sense of humour you need to live with the Papist doctrines and the stoicism to survive the pig headedness of the Church of Ireland"

"And are you very devout either way?"

"I gave up on both churches after coming to England. It's one of the things that I love about this country, the English are too civilised to take religion seriously. I flirted with Buddhism a few years ago until someone explained to me that it wasn't really a religion, but a way of life and I decided I didn't need anyone telling me how to live my life. I'd avoided the IRA and the UDA not to mention the Fascists and Communists. On top of that Buddhists wear orange and Lyndsey always says orange is a fashion no-go area and Sean and the lads would tar and feather me on political grounds if I dared turn up wearing orange. Sorry I'm talking rubbish again, aren't I?"

"You're very funny," Victoria laughed. "Sometimes when you're not trying to be."

The record comes to an end and as the food is now being brought to the tables we resume our seats.

"I see Shara has her husband in tow," says Victoria, nodding to where our deputy head is seated. "That explains Mark's absence, I'd wondered why he's not here as this sort of thing is just his cup of tea as a rule. A chance to show that he's one of us and press the flesh as he'd say or smarm around as I'd put it"

Mark is our headmaster and Shara his deputy head. I'm not sure what I make of Mark but I know exactly my feelings for Shara Merchant, she's a nasty ambitious cow. Although she's of Indian origin, her skin is so pale that it's not immediately obvious. This however hasn't prevented her from using the race card to further her career in our highly PC environment. One of the other Indian teachers at school Jack Chakravarty told me that she looks down on him because he is of a lower caste. Hypocrisy rules.

"Why, does Mark not get on with Shara's husband?" I ask.

"Are you serious, you really don't know?"

"Know what?"

"I thought everyone knew that Mark and Shara are having an affair."

"I didn't."

I knew these things went on, but I could never imagine those two at it. I help myself to a piece of crusty bread.

"I could never work out what Mark saw in her," Victoria whispers conspiratorially. "Until one day in the school dining hall I saw her eating corn on the cob."

I give a blank look until suddenly the penny drops. I can't hold back my shocked laughter, even though I'm embarrassed by it. This in turn causes a piece of the crust that I'm eating to fly onto Victoria's plate. Should I retrieve it or just pretend that I haven't noticed. She solves my dilemma by picking it up on her middle finger and with a smile in my direction puts it in her mouth, although I'm not sure that sucking the whole finger is entirely necessary.

"Sorry did you want that?" Victoria asks innocently. My mouth works wordlessly, trying to find a reply that won't sound entirely stupid. "Come on one of us needs a lot more lubrication and I think it's probably you," she adds while filling up my wine glass.

I attempt to cover my embarrassment with conversation, nearly always a mistake.

"Did you notice Shara's jeans? They're so tight I don't know how you'd get into them."

"I've heard a gin and tonic usually does the trick."

I'm close to losing control and decide the best way to stem Victoria's saucy badinage would be to stop laughing at it. Unfortunately she's as funny as she is rude, which combined with the drink stymies my plan to keep a straight face. The meal comes to an end and I'm not only stuffed to bursting but more than a tad squiffy. The waiters clear the tables quickly and efficiently before three of them return to the tiny dance floor. The music changes to a cheery Greek bouzouki tune and our showmen embark on some intricate ethnic steps. The waiters are very good and a spontaneous ripple of applause naturally evolves into clapping out the beat of the music. All three are beaming widely, a testimony to their inherent good nature, as I assume that they go through this ritual most nights.

"Thank you but we didn't come out to do all of the hard work by ourselves. We would like some volunteers on the floor to help us out."

No one seems inclined to make the first move until Victoria jumps up dragging me with her. This is the sort of thing I'd normally run a mile from, yet whether it's the drink, Victoria's high spirits or a combination of both, I find that being here with one arm on the waiter's shoulder and the other on Victoria's, extremely exhilarating. Sienna soon joins us on the floor before others follow suit as we clumsily ruin Greek folk dances for about twenty minutes. Eventually the waiters make good their escape amid much backslapping and applause and I head back towards our table.

"Oh no you don't," says Victoria. "We're dancing the night away, it's Christmas and I'm enjoying myself."

We dance to 'Agadoo.' We dance to 'Hi Ho Silver Lining.' We dance to 'Young At Heart,' 'Baggy Trousers,' 'Come On Eileen,' and rather aptly,' Dance The Night Away.' I'm surprised as Victoria always so aloof at school lets her hair down with such abandon. The effect of this helps me to do the same. The party swingers reach their natural seasonal conclusion with Slade's 'Merry Christmas Everybody.' My shirt has come adrift of my trousers, unfettered cuffs flap around my hands and the buttons are undone almost to the waist, I think Victoria may have had a hand in this. One of two things has occurred. Either I've developed a love of dancing or I'm well on my way up the ladder of drunkenness without realising I've left the first rung.

Spandau Ballet are bringing the evening to an inevitable conclusion with 'True.' I'm not a fan of these smoochy type of dances. I found them okay when I was with Alison and it was my duty to joust closely with her but as a free agent I'm always wary of being thought either too standoffish or even worse a groper.

"Come on you can hold me tighter than that, I won't break," laughed Victoria.

"I'm sorry I didn't like to, I'm a bit hot and sweaty."

"So am I silly, we've been dancing for an hour or is it that you think I'm too cold a fish to sweat?"

Feeling a little pathetic I move closer. I must be about half a head taller than Victoria and as I look down, her green eyes glitter back at me, satisfyingly yet uncomfortably close. Her mouth entertains the sort of smile that suggests butter has never even considered melting in it. At the same time a very firm breast presses into me and all of this generates a pang of desire that worries me more than a little.

"Have you had a good time?" she enquires.

"Yes, much better than I'd have thought possible. It's not really my sort of thing but you've made it special," I add quickly in case she assumes this to be a slur on her company. "What about you?"

"Yes, actually I have and like you, much better than I'd hoped for. It's been a lot of fun."

Tony Hadley utters his final 'ha, ha ha, hah, hah,' and everyone engages in cheek kissing, hand shaking and bucketfuls of bonhomie that will evaporate with the passing of this evening's festivities, not to be heard from again until next year's Christmas party rears its ugly head. All a little false but nice I suppose in a way, if you ignore the fact that they all hate each other. Most of the older male staff are going out of their way to hug and kiss Victoria although I don't think that I've ever heard any of them have a good word to say about her before.

While this is going on I've collected Victoria's coat and now help her slip into it.

"Very gallant, I can see that I'll have to ask you again."

"The taxi should be outside by now."

The one that had brought us had also been booked for the return journey. I'm not looking forward to renewing my acquaintance with 'Black Cat Bill.'

"We can hail a cab," says Victoria. " I've cancelled the contract car, the driver was such an obnoxious little prick, don't you agree?"

"Yes," I concur enthusiastically. We're out on the pavement now. "We could call a private hire car it'll be cheaper," I suggest, thinking of my dwindling finances.

"Lenny's paying, he can afford it," she says, putting her arm out and bringing a black cab to a screeching halt.

We climb in and to my surprise Victoria snuggles against me in the corner of the back seat. I put it down to Christmas spirits and put my arm around her shoulders, careful not to let my hand rest anywhere too intimate while wondering what to do with the arm I have left over. Although my nerves are still a little on the wracked side I'm finding the close contact with a woman very enjoyable. Lyndsey was right, it has been too long and I decide that my number one New Year's resolution should be, 'get girlfriend.' We remain in each other's arms all the way back to Victoria's house, neither of us breaking the silence that has developed and taken on its own aura, like a magic spell. As we pull up outside the house Victoria starts to open her purse. "It's okay, I'll pay when I get home," I say benevolently, considering that I'm not even sure that I have sufficient cash.

"No, I'll pay but surely you're coming in for a Christmas nightcap? I can call you another cab later."

I acquiesce with good grace and not a little relief. It would be rude to say no and as I don't really want the evening to end yet, another drink in Victoria's company suddenly seems a very pleasant idea. It's only as we approach the front door that I'm struck by the sudden thought that Lenny may have arrived home early. I cling to the hope that if he has then my coming in will merely confirm my innocent intent.

Chapter 3
Let's Spend The Night Together – The Rolling Stones

We enter through a large front door and the house is in darkness. If Lenny is home he's decided on an early night. Victoria flicks a switch and we're bathed in light. The entrance hall would swallow my entire flat comfortably. As we enter the lounge I reflect that it wouldn't be out of place in Dynasty except that it's much more tasteful. It's just as I'd have it furnished it if I had the money.

"Wow, this is a lovely house," I said.

"I'll give you the grand tour sometime when my feet aren't killing me. Have a seat Gerry, oh hang on why don't you pour some drinks first? I'll have a large Bailey's, make it on the rocks and don't spare the ice. Help yourself to whatever you want, the drinks cabinet's over there next to the stereo. Why don't you put some music on as well? I must change out of this underwear it works wonders with your tits but it's cutting me in half."

I'd been about to say something devastatingly witty but the casual mention of tits and underwear strikes me dumb. I pour the drinks and after drinking wine all evening I settle on a long weak spritzer. When nervous I have a tendency to gulp down my drinks and my current state of anxiety is a sure path to drink induced oblivion. I peruse the music collection but it's not exactly to my taste, mostly middle of the road schmaltz. Stowed away almost ashamedly at one end though, are some impressive jazz albums. I crack open a Miles Davis that I've always been partial to, albeit not sufficiently to part with hard earned for.

I'm stooping down trying to fathom the workings of the Swedish sound system, which as they tend to be is much more straightforward than those at the cheaper end of the market. This model is far better than anything I've ever aspired to own and probably cost more than my car. Envy isn't a sin that's entirely a stranger at my door. Rising to my feet I turn and find to my surprise Victoria is leaning against one of the large cream coloured sofas watching me. She's wearing the same clothes but has obviously removed the offending garment. It may well have 'worked wonders with her tits,' but they're not making a bad stab at things on their own.

"You'll never know just how good that feels," she says.

I notice she's also barefoot and minus her high heels the trouser legs crumple over her feet.

"Is that for me?" she asks and taking the drink downs half of it in one go. "Mm that gives me such a warm feeling deep inside. I do love the feeling of something warm inside me," she says, so innocently that I'm not totally sure that she realises the double entendre.

I gulp my drink, trying to maintain an air of calm. The fabric of her top clings to her body, probably no bad thing as there are a couple more buttons undone than there had been earlier.

"This is one of Lenny's,' she says.' I can't stand jazz, do you really like this sort of music?"

"Yeah, they're nice," I say as my mind Freudianly slips to other things. "The records I mean, er they're really good."

"Pardon?"

I'm flapping about trying to take my mind off the situation I'm in but to no avail. Victoria has flopped down on one end of the settee. She stretches her arms back catlike over her head and the almost sheer material of her top pulls taut over her breasts leaving virtually less than nothing to the imagination.

I'm trying through my drink-fuddled senses to decide if she's enjoying some colossal practical joke at my expense or is she actually flirting with me. I wish I could find a way to ask her. I decide to attempt lightening the tone with a little humour and try my famously bad Dustin Hoffman impression.

"Are you trying to seduce me Mrs Robinson?"

She stops mid-stretch and deliberately turning her head stares into my eyes. "Would you like me to seduce you Benjamin?"

I'm in too much of a state even to admire the fact that not only has she immediately picked up on the allusion but has fired back the riposte almost word perfect. Unfortunately I'm no further forward in my quest for enlightenment, its worse now in fact because I've embarrassed myself even more.

"Do you mind if I change the music?" Victoria asks, as if the last exchange had never taken place.

"No of course not, I really ought to be going home though. Your husband could be back soon."

I notice that she replaces Miles with 'The Crooners Sing Love,' and I'm not sure that she's heard my suggestion.

"Come and dance with me," Victoria says.

I do as I'm bid and we pick up where we left off at George's *Taverna*, except that Victoria is even closer now and rubbing against me intimately as Nat King Cole eggs us on.

"No need to worry. Lenny's not coming home tonight."

"But I thought you said he was only at a business meeting."

"That's right, it's in Stuttgart. He won't be back until Tuesday but I thought you might not come back if I told you the truth. I so hate the idea of being stuck here alone, especially after such a lovely night out."

I say nothing. I know there are a thousand things that could be said but at this moment I can't compose a sentence around any of them.

She looks up at me. "I like that you're tall, it's so nice being with a man I can look up to, morally as well as physically."

"What do you mean?"

"Well Lenny's shorter than me physically but he's morally stunted as well, I suppose what I really mean is that you have standards and that's not common these days."

"I'm with a married woman and I'm in her house while her husband's away for the night, so they're obviously not very high standards."

"Well he is a shit but it's got nothing to do with that. I mean that you have a sense of duty to your friends. Lenny doesn't do friends, he's only interested in anyone if they can further his interests. You respect people and try to do right by them."

"Bit of a wuss you mean."

"I did think that at first but it's been a little like the Road to Damascus thing. Who knows perhaps I've seen the light? Perhaps the life I've been leading's not all it's cracked up to be," Victoria paused for a moment. "Or then again perhaps I'm just very pissed."

She buries her face into my shirt and in a very quiet stifled voice says. "Please, stay with me tonight."

I'm not sure that I've heard properly and my lack of a reply seems to be taken as an acceptance speech. The drinks are abandoned, the lights remain on and Dino croons to a vacant auditorium as Victoria aborts our dance and taking me by the hand leads me upstairs. The bedroom is on the same scale as the rest of the house and the bed must be king size, assuming the king in question is Henry VIII.

"The door opposite is a guest bathroom," says Victoria. "I've laid out a towel and a toothbrush for you. Come back in when you're ready, don't bother knocking."

Chapter 4
Love Cats – The Cure

My mind is spinning as I'm not the sort of person that things like this happen to. I clean my teeth and wash all the bits I'm half hoping and half dreading might see action. I do all of these things automatically as Alison's almost clinical obsession with cleanliness has turned me into a bathroom robot. Finally I can postpone it no longer, I leave my safe haven and despite the instructions I tap softly on the door.

"Entrée," purrs seductively from within.

I push the door open and enter a room that's a tribute to subdued lighting. To my consternation Victoria is already ensconced under the duvet, she's lying on her side, head propped on her hand and one very naked arm on top. I stand at the side of the bed, not confident enough to take the next step.

"Can I assume that you intend taking your clothes off?"

"Yeah, er yes," I stammer, and start unbuttoning my shirt.

The first two buttons seem to each take about ten minutes. I can feel my hands shaking and inelegantly opt for the over the head option rather than struggling with the rest. The shoes and socks offer no such resistance and neither do my trousers as I'm left standing there with only my Calvin Klein's between me and my destiny. I decide to act before I receive the royal decree to remove them and I dive under the duvet.

"You spoilsport," laughs Victoria. "I was hoping to see what teachers hide under their kilts."

I remember a joke that Sean had told me. "A woman asks a Scotsman, 'what's worn under the kilt?' He replies, 'nothing it's all in perfect working order.'"

Despite the weakness of the anecdote, Victoria dutifully giggles and while kissing me puts her hand on the front of my boxers.

"Hmm, it all appears to be in perfect working order," she murmurs.

This action seems to release me from my self-inflicted inertia. I return her kiss while exploring her right breast with my now steady hand, a little like a gunfighter in a corny old Western overcoming his nerves once the action begins. Victoria has manoeuvred me out of my underwear and I can feel her heart pounding.

"Do it now," she pants breathlessly. "Please. I've been waiting all night, no more messing about just do it."

As soon as we start Victoria emits a loud moan while wriggling about all over the place and I appreciate the need for the oversize bed as I do my best to remain onboard. Victoria makes continual adjustments, pushing me first this way and then that, nuzzling and biting, ordering me to slightly change position, to go faster or to slow down. Suddenly, out of nowhere it starts, a long drawn out moan that increases in volume. I'm almost unnerved by its intensity but then she starts screaming at the top of her voice.

Alison was my only other significant sexual partner. She'd had two fairly substantial relationships behind her at the time whereas I was virtually a twenty-year old virgin. Our lovemaking had been quite energetic but as in all things 'Alison,' it was controlled and governed by her rules. Her lovemaking volume would be decided by what could be heard by the neighbours. The nearest neighbours to Victoria's mini mansion are at least fifty metres away but I still wouldn't bet against their having a disturbed night.

The outcome of Victoria's energetic and noisy efforts is that I'm deprived of the luxury of worrying about my own performance. Her tumultuous climax releases me to do the same; after all a true gentleman always comes second although I can't match her in the volume stakes.

I lay there on top, bathed in roughly equal quantities of sweat, exhaustion and shock.

"I'm not going to run off," Victoria says.

"Pardon?"

"You can get off me now, unless you were planning an encore that is."

I hurriedly and clumsily roll off and lie on my back, wondering what I should do next, now that the deed is done. I've reverted to my normal gauche, thirty year old adolescent. Victoria turns onto her side and starts tracing a long dark red fingernail around my lips.

"I could do things with you, you show real promise. Definitely more than meets the eye."

"Can I ask you something?" I say.

"Ask away, as long as it's not to do it again straight away. I'm wrecked."

"No nothing like that," I suddenly feel relaxed enough to laugh. "Why did you choose to take me tonight? I mean someone like you would have men queuing round the block."

"Well it had to be someone from school or it really would have set the tongues wagging and men on the staff are in the minority and most of them are married anyway. So the odds aren't good to start with and some of the goods are decidedly odd. Of all the unattached males and I suppose the attached ones as well, you're about the only one that doesn't look like an identikit teacher. You're a little bit different."

"When I was married Alison used to choose my clothes and I really did look like a teacher then, even before I was one. It was all chinos and polo shirts. I was that 'man at C&A.,'" I said indicating the exclamation marks. "Lyndsey helps me to choose my clothes now and she's got really good taste."

"Ah your little lesbian pal, I don't suppose we could interest her in a ménage could we? Now that would be interesting?"

"No!" I almost shout. I think she's teasing me but the thought of sex with Lyndsey seems almost incestuous and the idea of two women at the same time, terrifying. "She's in a very settled relationship." I add quickly.

"Oh well, just a thought."

"Anyway, how did you know that she's a lesbian?"

"It's hardly rocket science is it, I'm sure most of the staff know," she says laughing. "I could name you all of the homosexuals in the school."

"You mean there are others?"

"Of course, you didn't think Lyndsey was the only gay in the village did you? Take Tony Price and I wish someone would take him but that's beside the point. Don't let that big motorcycle fool you, he rides that as much because he likes stomping around in black leathers as anything else. They always say that a red sports car is the straight man's penis substitute, well I think a powerful motorcycle is the gay equivalent or at the very least the closet gay equivalent."

"So it was only my dress sense and the fact that I can't get a girlfriend that made you decide to choose me?"

"Well, be reasonable it was hardly going to be your conversational prowess was it. I don't think you've ever said more than two words to me before today."

"I'm sorry, I've always been a bit scared of you and I could never imagine having anything to say that would interest you."

"You're creeping back into ogre territory."

"I'm sorry but you always seem so glamorous, sort of from another world."

"I do all the normal things you know, watch TV, go to the supermarket, pick my nose and despite what you may have heard in the staff room, I am not nor ever have been a nymphomaniac. I enjoy sex a lot and yes I've been known to use it to my advantage but I don't need it or crave it. To be honest most of my relationships have been short flings either when I'm bored or to get what I want, all except for Ben that is."

"Who's Ben?" I ask without thinking. "Oh sorry you don't have to answer that, I didn't mean to be nosey."

"It's okay it was all a long time ago now," Victoria flops onto her back. "Ben Roberts is an artist. You may have heard of him, he's become quite well known recently although he's a little reclusive. We were an item when we were at teacher training college together oh it must be twenty odd years ago now, back in the days when he had lots of talent and no money. He wanted to go and paint in Tahiti like his hero Gauguin, even if it meant living on rice in a mud hut. He asked me to go with him but I was Madonna's original 'Material Girl' at that time and I just wanted all the things that money could buy. Ben went off to follow his dream and I stayed, I ended up with all the things that I thought I wanted only to find out that what I really wanted was on an island in Tahiti. So there it is in a nutshell, hoist on my own capitalist petard."

"Could you not have found him? I'm sure he doesn't live in a thatched hut any longer."

"Sorry, I don't do sackcloth and ashes. Anyway that's enough talk, I need my beauty sleep and I find I need it more with each passing year."

"You must have had plenty already then." The success of the lovemaking emboldened me to this attempt at flirting.

"I must try kissing more frogs. Good night Benjamin."

Chapter 5
Breakfast In Bed – UB40 and Chrissie Hynde

I wake up to the sound of music, not 'Let It Be,' but what sounds like a British Airways commercial. My first thought is that I've dropped off to sleep at home with the TV on and I open one exploratory eye. Victoria Daniels is staring back at me from a distance of about six inches. Have I dozed off in the school staff room? It wouldn't be the first time. I risk opening the other eye and unless she's pushing 'dress down Friday,' to the very limit it's definitely not the school staff room. Reality dawns and a maelstrom of emotions surge through me, shock, elation, pride, satisfaction, terror, even a little embarrassment.

"I've been watching you sleep," says Victoria. "So innocent, almost childlike."

"I hope I wasn't snoring," I joke

"You were and you've dribbled on my pillow."

"I don't dribble."

"Yes you do but I'll forgive you."

"Is the television on?" I ask.

She looks puzzled.

"The music," I add.

"Oh no, no it's the stereo, Delibes. I love classical music in the stillness of the morning, it's so romantic."

"I like a bit of U2 myself."

"Philistine," she says. "Jump in the shower while I make us some breakfast, we can eat it in bed, it still feels so decadent."

I wait for Victoria to go downstairs before entering her bathroom. There are twin washbasins and I wonder if rich people feel the need to wash both feet at the same time. The walk-in shower is large enough to entertain the Dagenham Girl Pipers in full marching order. The overhead rose looks about a foot in diameter and as I turn the water on the effect is akin to a tropical monsoon. I could happily spend an hour in this shower; it's so very like the one over the bath in my own flat, where a contortionist would struggle to become fully suffused under the ferocious dribble. Eventually I drag myself out and after drying myself on a large, white, fluffy bath sheet I wrap another around my waist before re-entering the bedroom. Victoria lies propped on one elbow on the bed. She's wearing a filmy, coffee coloured dressing gown and the tray is in front of her.

"Come on," she says. "You can have some breakfast and then you'd better get going. My 'lady that does,' usually arrives at around nine."

The tray is well loaded with croissants, tea, and what smells like freshly squeezed orange juice. I notice that while I'm hungrily tucking in, Victoria nibbles at a croissant like a mouse, and drinks only water. I feel the need to get last night into a little more perspective.

"You know you said you more or less only chose me because of the way I dress. Have I been a disappointment?" Okay, I'm doing a little angling for compliments as well.

"No, I don't think you were. I like the fact that you're very gentle for a man and while I could tolerate a little more roughness, after what some of the so and so's I've been with have done to me. Well I'll happily settle for gentle."

"You mean they've hurt you?" I ask incredulously.

"You're such a divine innocent. Yes some have gone further than that. Oh I suppose it's my own fault I seem to be attracted to bastards."

"Does Lenny hit you?"

"No bless him. He's hurt me in a thousand other ways but not physical pain."

"When you asked me, did you think I might be a bastard?"

She snorts a convulsive laugh. "Oh Christ no and that's part of what I'm finding so compelling about you, you're so blissfully naïve. Sorry I'm not laughing at you. Well I am, but only at the idea that I could have imagined you'd be a shit. Actually, you've been something of a project and although it's taken some getting used to, I've quite enjoyed being treated like a lady."

A raucous voice from downstairs rudely interrupts my testimonial.

"It's only me Mrs D."

I nearly shoot through the ceiling but Victoria looks totally relaxed.

48

"It's only my cleaning lady, Mrs Brimble. She'll make herself a cup of tea first and then start on the kitchen. When you're dressed I'll go and distract her while you disappear."

And that's exactly what we do, simple as that.

Chapter 6
Venus In Furs – Velvet Underground

I wend my weary way home via the local bus network. It costs almost as much as a taxi would have done; the difference is probably only a couple of quid in money but about two hours of my life I'll never get back. I've barely been home twenty minutes when the doorbell rings and as I open the door Lyndsey bounces past me.

"Good night last night?" Lyndsey asks.

"Yeah, it was okay."

"Is that it, just okay?"

"No actually, I had lots to eat, lots to drink and a bit of a dance. It was phantasmagorical."

"That's not a real word is it? You've made it up. Anyway what time did you get home?"

A rapid mental calculation on my part results in. "About midnight."

"I called round at about half twelve and there was no answer."

"I must not have heard you."

"I rang your mobile."

"I switched it off when I went to bed. I was tired and didn't want to be disturbed."

"Okay," Lyndsey savoured her impending triumph. "So why are you wearing the same clothes that you went out in last night?"

"They were the only things handy when I got up this morning," I say, before noticing the pile of clothes on the table that I'd tried on yesterday.

"You spent the night at Castle Grayskull with the evil queen didn't you?"

"No, of course I didn't," I knew I'd lost but determined to go down fighting.

Lyndsey puts her hand on my heart. "I'm going to ask you a question and if you lie your heart will beat faster."

"Okay I did stay the night but I slept in the spare room."

She puts her hand back on my heart.

"Look I'm not talking about this anymore. It's none of your business."

"I knew it, you shagged the old bunny boiler, fantastic. I can't wait to tell Violet."

"Alright but just don't tell anyone else okay and tell Violet not to either. Victoria's a married woman you know."

"Okay but on one condition, I want to know everything. The lot."

"I'm not telling you what we did."

"Oh yeuk gross, I don't want to know any of that, I'd feel sick. I want to know about the house, how it was decorated? What was the furniture like? How many rooms? Has it got a swimming pool?"

Lyndsey makes some tea while I change my clothes and regale her with all I can remember of Chez Daniels.

"What are you doing today?" Lyndsey asks when she's extricated every detail.

"No plans, I'll probably have a dinner time drink with the lads and then if I can stay awake, listen to the football this afternoon while I go over some prep work for next term, I know if I leave it then it won't get done."

"What about tonight?"

"It'll have to be a night in I'm afraid, I've hardly got two ha'pennies to rub together until pay day."

"Come out with us," Lyndsay says. "Violet has purloined freebie invites to a new club in Brum. The first drink's free and we'll sub you after that."

"I'm not that bad, I can afford to stand my round."

"We'll meet you in the Railway at eight o'clock then. We can get the bus into Birmingham and a taxi home."

Having organised my life for the immediate future, Lyndsey happily decamps. I make a start on washing up the breakfast dishes when the doorbell rings again. Without thinking, I scan the room for whatever it is that Lyndsey's left behind and seeing nothing, open the door. In front of me on the unprepossessing and rather threadbare landing is the incongruous vision of Victoria Daniels looking a million dollars in a fur coat. I blink my eyes twice but she's still there.

"Warm as this coat may be there's still a wicked draught out here," she says. "Aren't you going to ask me in?"

I have no alternative. Despite Lyndsey's quick tidy up done while listening to my version of 'Through The Keyhole,' the place still isn't at its best and when it is at its best it's hardly 'Home and

Gardens.' I still have the washing up sponge in one hand.

"You may be domesticated as well as being a thoughtful lover but you're never likely to be voted 'The Hostess with the Mostest.'"

"Of course come in, I'm sorry about the mess. It was a shock because I thought you were Lyndsey come back for something."

Victoria steps inside and closes the door behind her. I can't help notice the involuntary look of horror. At least Lyndsey has put on the gas fire and the room is warming nicely.

"May I take my coat off?"

"Yeah I'll hang it up for you."

She slips her coat off and as it falls to the floor the reason she was feeling the draught becomes obvious. Apart from high-heeled black boots she's only wearing a bra, stockings and a thong, needless to say, very classy and expensive looking bra, stockings and thong, but only a bra, stockings and thong nonetheless.

My mouth hangs open, like a letterbox with a broken spring. I'm deciding whether it's ruder to stare or to look away. Staring wins the day as Victoria stands there for a moment holding the pose before collapsing on to the settee in fits of helpless laughter. Yet she still looks amazingly sexy despite the ungainly posture.

When she finally regains control Victoria holds her arms out wide and asks, "what do you think?"

"What about?" I reply, no longer knowing what I think.

"Dur, global warming lump head, about me of course?"

"You're very nice."

"You can be such hard work at times. When I think about what we were doing last night and now you're looking at me as if I'm your maiden aunt."

"I'm sorry, it was such a shock. I'm not really used to this sort of thing."

"Would you like to get used to it?" Victoria askes as she stares into my eyes.

I remembered once seeing a film; I think it was Dudley Moore whose conscience was troubling him. There was a little white angel Dudley Moore on his one shoulder and a little red devil Dudley Moore on the other. The angel me is wagging his finger and saying, 'you work with her, she's a married woman and she shows all the signs of being ever so slightly unhinged.' The devil me prods me with his pitchfork and prompts my reply, "I think I would."

Victoria comes over to me and putting her arms around my neck kisses me. "That will have to do to be going on with. I've got a dress to put on in my bag. I'm on my way to pick up Lenny from the airport. His meeting was cut short but I wanted to surprise you."

"You've certainly done that."

She wriggles into said dress and says. "Zip me up would you?"

I feel like Cary Grant as I'm too stunned even to fumble the zip.

"I'll see you Tuesday evening," says Victoria. "I'll pick you up at around seven thirty and we'll go for a meal. I'm going to be out of the country for the Christmas hols, Lenny's taking me to Gstaad. Ciao."

With that she's gone. The door closes behind her and I'm left standing there more than a little nonplussed.

Chapter 7
The Boys Are Back In Town – Thin Lizzy

After my morning encounters with Lyndsey and Victoria, I seek out Shaun and the lads at 'The Bricklayers' in Lye, an old fashioned workingmen's pub. Wreathed in cigarette smoke and maleness, it suits their aspirations to a tee. They're already settled around the pool table, as I knew they would be, bickering away as I suspected they would be. Brendan and Aiden are playing and doing most of the arguing. Shaun looks on benevolently, dropping in the odd comment to keep the embers fanned.

Shaun is the main reason I'm a part of their social circle, he's a bear of a man, naturally affable but with an impish sense of humour. We first met when I was getting over Alison. I was drinking alone at a bar; I think it may even have been this one, when Shaun picked up on what remained of my Irish accent. He more or less adopted me and introduced me to the other two members of his clique. Aiden is a small, wiry terrier of a man with ginger hair and a temper to match. His disposition allows him little in the way of tolerance and my being a teacher doesn't impress Aiden much either. Brendan sports a thick mop of black wavy hair and what always seems to me, a distant, dreamy quality around the eyes. Brendan has never made any effort to conceal his complete indifference to me.

Shaun once revealed to me that he regretted not having had a better education, one that would have enabled him to follow a worthwhile career such as teaching or medicine. This revelation is typical of the man, as is the fact that he seems to harbour no resentment over it; rather he sees it as his own fault. Brendan has always been aloof, neither friendly nor hostile. He is fiercely loyal to the other two but I feel that like Aiden, he's never really taken to me but wouldn't dream of going against Shaun's wishes.

The one thing that the three of them share and that makes me a little uncomfortable is their fervent nationalism. They all hate the English to varying degrees. Shaun does so in a passive, half-hearted manner, Aiden in a blinkered, unthinking way but Brendan I find the most disturbing, he's almost fanatical. Brendan has listened to and absorbed everything the propaganda machine has churned his way. I've tried on numerous occasions to get over to them the fact that generally England has given us a good living, and been a benevolent landlord, only to be met with the horrors of the potato famine and what Oliver Cromwell and King Billy did to Ireland. My argument that all of this is history and not current affairs falls on very stony ground.

As is the norm Shaun greets me like the returning prodigal son. The other two acknowledge me but not to the extent of interrupting their game.

"I thought you'd have been in last night celebrating the end of term," says Shaun.

"I got an invitation to the school shindig. It was all gratis and as I'm fairly stony at the moment I couldn't turn it down."

"You've found a rich benefactor then?" Shaun asks.

"A benefactor with a rich husband away on business, she just needed a dance partner as she didn't fancy going alone."

"I suppose he was away on business, raping and pillaging the poor proletariat," mutters Brendan, in his strange Marxist, Trotskyist mode of speech that surfaces whenever he mounts his soapbox.

"Never mind that, did you plough his wife's lonely furrow while he was away?" Aiden leers.

I'm about to answer non-commitally when Sean intervenes.

"It's none of your feckin' business, you dirty minded little bleeder," he says, laughing. "Anyway, what are you doing with the rest of your day?" Shaun asks me.

"I've some school stuff that I want to get out of the way this afternoon and then I can put the place right out of my mind. I'm out with Lyndsey and Violet tonight, Violet's blagged us freebies for some new club in town."

"Are you still trying to get into that little les's knickers?" sniggers Aiden. I don't suppose political correctness will penetrate building sites in the next hundred years or Aiden's brain in the next thousand.

"Is it any wonder that we don't get near any women with your attitude," says Shaun.

"I get my share," says Aiden.

I've never seen any evidence to back this up. I've witnessed Shaun enjoy plenty of liaisons with women, while Brendan's romantic dreaminess seems to act as a candle to the gentler sex's moth-like tendencies. Perhaps it's his lack of success with the fairer gender that fans Aiden's jaundiced outlook towards them.

"The last pair of real tits you got close to Aiden were your own Mammy's," says Shaun.

"Now that brings to mind an interesting fact," says Aiden. "One that I hadn't realised 'til the other day." Aiden is a philosopher of the 'School of the Inconsequential.'

"Did you realise," he carried on. "That every woman you ever meet is totally naked underneath her clothes." He gives us a second to absorb this startling revelation and for our part we just stare in disbelief. "Yes, there you are sat next to a girl in the pub and under her clothes she's as naked as a jaybird, whatever jaybirds might be when they're at home. Yeah when that big blonde lass at the dentist's with the gap in her teeth and the black framed glasses leans over the counter asking you if you pay for your treatment, well her as well, totally nude under that white uniform as she flaunts her tits at yer. Although I'm not sure when I think about it if a uniform might be even better than naked, I need to give that one a bit more thought."

"Let's get this right," says Shaun, barely disguising his incredulity. "You've reached the grand old age of twenty eight and you've just realised that women are naked under their clothes."

"I'd always just thought of them as people with clothes on before but can't you see how great this is? It turns every situation you're in with a good looking girl into a sexual encounter."

"Are you sure you've thought this through?" I ask.

"Come on then Carol fuckin' Vorderman, why don't you explain it to me."

"Well it's just that if every girl you sit next to is naked under her clothes. So is every old granny you look at on the bus and when you're up at the bar for last orders fighting your way to the front of a crowd of blokes. They're all naked too."

"Oh sweet baby Jesus, Isn't that just typical. I make the best discovery of my life and some sick fucker has to go and ruin it for me."

"Never mind Aiden me old virtual naturist mucker. Better someone tells you now rather than the next time you see Mrs Atkinson in the wages office," says Brendan, who is laughing too much to finish his game.

When eventually they tear themselves away from the pool table to venture out for an afternoon of Guinness and Sky Sport in the lounge bar, I'm tempted to tag along. I know only too well that if I succumb, then at their rate of drinking I'll be unconscious by teatime and good for nothing tonight. I politely but regretfully decline the invitation to join them.

Chapter 8
Little Man – Sonny And Cher

I head for The Railway, not a great distance for either me or the girls, it's our normal rendezvous point and another of Lye's galaxy of timeless old working men's pubs. As I'm about to enter the front door a large dark coloured BMW with smoked glass windows pulls up outside. I experience a strange feeling that it may have been following me and quickly make a mental note to curb my paranoia. I carry my drink from the bar and settle down to await the inevitable late arrival of my evening's dance partners. As I sit down so do two other men, at what I had assumed up until that point to be my table. The room is bereft of customers apart from us and I'm a little unnerved by their apparent display of unspoken sociability.

The first to break the silence is an individual who is short and stocky but in a podgy way. The piggy nature of his eyes isn't even rescued by the thick magnifying lenses of his rectangular, designer spectacles. He's decked out in what even my sartorially stunted fashion sense identifies as a very expensive suit. He sports the shade of bright orange tan that shouts out that whatever product he's using, it does exactly what it says on the tin.
"I'm Lenny Daniels and I believe you're Gerald Wilson," he says, catching me unawares.

He delivers the information in a strangely well-enunciated cockney accent. In a momentary flash of lucidity I realise that this must be Victoria's husband. Suddenly my heart begins to beat a little bit faster.

"That's right, my friends call me Gerry," I smile.

"Well Gerald, I believe you were kind enough to accompany Victoria to the school social last night while I was away on business." My input is obviously not a requirement, as he doesn't wait for a reply. "Wasn't that good of him Harry?" This is directed to his companion. Harry is almost a dead ringer for Mike Read; the comedian from EastEnders that is, not the Radio One DJ, except that he's bigger, more rugged looking, and where Mike's face would crease into an infectious laugh, Harry's doesn't.

"This is Harry Brown, an associate of mine," Lenny says.

My mind races through the possibilities. 'How much does he know?' 'Has Victoria told him?' Surely not and as I ponder the merits of acknowledging Harry, a third party arrives with three drinks. This one is much younger than the other two, probably early twenties. He's of mixed race and his skin is almost golden, perfectly complimenting the chiselled features of his face. I register an air of male beauty about him right up until the moment he turns his eyes on me. There is no beauty in those eyes, just a frightening cold hardness that chills me to the marrow.

"And this is another of my associates, Jermaine Etienne. Mr Etienne and Mr Brown work for me.

They look after my interests and possessions but I'm sure you're not tempted by anything that belongs to me, are you Gerald?"

"No, I've got my own car," I say, feigning all of the innocence that I can muster at such short notice. I know that one of Lenny's business interests is a car-leasing firm and pathetically hope the mention of it will add a little authenticity to my probity.

"I'm so glad to hear that Gerald." Since he'd opened the conversation I'd had the feeling that I knew Lenny from somewhere. I was trying to pinpoint where, when suddenly it came to me. It's Mike from the TV comedy the 'Young Ones.' He doesn't look exactly like him, it's more in the, 'little man in a big suit,' attitude that oozes from him. Harry also sports a well-cut suit but unfortunately it's been well cut for someone of totally different proportions. Jermaine's suit is inevitably immaculate, as is his shirt, tie, shoes and everything else about him. He looks as if he's probably got creases ironed into his underpants, Alison would have loved him.

"Is he the school teacher?" Jermaine suddenly joins the conversation making no effort to hide the sneer in his voice.

"Yes Jermaine," Lenny affirms.

"What sort of job's that for a man?" At last, I'd found a soul mate for Aiden.

The sheer hatred in Jermaine's eyes unnerves me but even when terrified, I'm cursed with a stubborn pride that can't bear to let others see it.

"When I was young," I said. "I always aspired to be an errand boy with an effeminate name but somehow I just got stuck in teaching, and had to make do with a man's name."

A little puerile I know but the best that I can manage on the spur of the moment. Anyway my feathered barb finds its target as Jermaine jumps to his feet.

"What's that supposed to mean?" Jermaine demands, eyes instantly upgrading from mere hatred to bloodlust.

"Not here Jermaine, leave it. He's just trying to wind you up, don't rise to the bait." With this Lenny knocks back his drink, followed by the other two. "Much as I've enjoyed our little *tête a tête* I must go. I had no idea places like this really existed and I have no desire to repeat the experience so I do hope it doesn't become necessary come back. You're not Victoria's type, *comprende*."

Ah, Mike with a dash of Del Boy I muse as they get up to leave but for health reasons keep the thought to myself. I realise as they depart that Harry hasn't uttered a word all the time they were here, he just sat there staring at me as if he'd take great pleasure from snapping me in two with one hand and looking more than capable of doing it.

The girls witter their way in and Violet says. "What horrible creepy looking men, I can't remember seeing them in here before."

"I didn't notice them," I reply.

"They looked as though they were going to a fancy dress as the O'Driscoll's from 'Only Fools And Horses,'" says Lyndsey.

That was it! The comparison I'd been searching my brain for, the perfect summation of the Lenny Daniels gang.

"Come on Gerry," says Lyndsey. "We haven't time to hang about, it's half price drinks for women from nine to twelve and I intend being bladdered by midnight."

We find the club and Violet spirits us in without any problems. She's from a wealthy family and has a good job in PR. Although she's a bright girl, Violet admits that the job came as a result of family contacts rather than her academic prowess. Lyndsey was wrong about the half priced drinks as Violet procures free drinks for all of us until midnight. The result of this is three individuals all well-lashed long before the witching hour, a blessed relief as the music is the usual pounding, screeching rubbish, championed in these places, although I find the foam party unexpectedly enjoyable.

Lyndsey and Violet like having me in tow on these nights out. Apart from the obvious benefits of my sparkling wit and personality it saves them a great deal of hassle from predatory blokes. They're both very attractive girls and I'd once rather tentatively broached this fact with Lyndsey, not that she was in the slightest embarrassed by the topic but I was. After my initial probing the conversation went along the lines of.

'You mean that you want to know which one of us is the bloke,' Lyndsey had cut to the chase.

'No, well it's not really that as much as the fact you're both really good looking and I always thought that one half of the couple should be, well, sort of more manly.'

'You mean you want to know which of us is the bloke.'

'Yeah, I suppose so but it doesn't sound very nice when you say it like that.'

'Well the answer is neither,' she'd said. 'It's a popular misconception among straights that sapph couples are always made up of one butch and one girlie but it doesn't work like that. We're all people and we just fall in love with other people. Violet and I are just very much in love and that's the only thing that matters. It's just a total coincidence that we're both eye candy as well.'

Which is true I suppose except for the fact that they seem to spend much more time falling out than looking like they're going to end up as Joan and Joan fifty years from now. I suppose the making up is probably a lot of fun though.

Lyndsey is one of those naturally big boned, healthy looking girls and is usually full of joie de vivre. She has small breasts and big shoulders, her dark hair perfectly setting off an open, attractive face. Were it not for her predilection, I could easily have fallen in love with her myself. Anyone seeing the girls together would jump to the conclusion that Lyndsey is the strong one of the partnership but they'd be totally wrong. Under the veneer of confidence lurks a mass of insecurities. Violet on the other hand is blonde, heart-achingly pretty with an ample bust and personality to match. She's a real one hundred per cent girlie girl, nothing of the tomboy that still lurks in Lyndsey just pure satin and lace but again the conundrum. Under the flounces and frills hides a core of steel. If anyone messes with Violet they do so at their peril.

As the fingers on the clock approach one thirty, I calculate with no little difficulty that we've been paying for our drinks for almost one and a half hours. We decide to steal a march on the two o'clock rush for the cab rank.

"Why don't you come back and sleep on our futon?" Lyndsey asks me.

I mull over the possibility of the O'Driscolls lying in wait for me and decide that the futon may have added health benefits. Apart from that consideration, it's been a great night and I don't particularly crave the anti-climax of a cold empty flat.

"I'd love to but you're sure you don't mind."

"If you were a girl," says Violet, a little the worse for wear. "You could share our bed."

"Yeah, why don't you anyway? After all, you are our best mate," pipes up Lyndsey, sounding like the archetypal drunk into the bargain.

"Yeah, go on, we won't molest you," giggles Violet.

"No the futon will be fine thanks."

We return to the flat and pick up where we left off with the drinking. Eventually we decide that although the spirit's willing the flesh is decidedly debilitated and as we're all tired, decamp to bed. I head determinedly for the futon in the spare room where lying in the dark I ponder the offer to share their bed. I know that they're both straight as it were, and as such are quite revolted by men's dangly bits, as Violet so endearingly calls them. I also know they're both fairly uninhibited, especially when drink has been imbibed. Had I accepted the invitation, what would be the polite thing to do if they became amorous toward one another? Would it be rude to watch or perhaps, even ruder to look away? Perhaps one just pretends it isn't happening, like the Queen when one of the corgis does a poo on the red carpet. I realise what a ridiculous train of thought this is and decide to clear my mind and get some sleep.

The flat is one of a modern block and the wall between the bedrooms must be paper-thin as I realise that for some time now the girls have been in earnest conversation next door. Although I can't hear what they're saying, it's interspersed with giggles. Deciding that I'm probably the butt of the joke, something not entirely unknown to me, I drift into sleep.

I wake in a strange bed for the second day running and with a hangover for the second day running. Today's experience is much more relaxed than yesterdays. I've woken in this strange bed many times before. The sound of pots and pans resonates from the kitchen and I quickly wash and dress before making my entrance. Lyndsey is sitting at the table wearing an oversize rugby shirt and playing with the cutlery. Violet is busy at the cooker and wears a bra and knickers apron over a very pretty pink and white nightie.

Lyndsey looks up. "We're bringing you breakfast in bed, go back."

"I get indigestion from breakfast in bed," I whine, thinking back twenty-four hours.

"Sit at the table, "says Violet. "I'm sure you'll enjoy it more anyway. Would you like juice?"

"Yes please," I answer too late, as Lyndsey has already half-filled my glass as well as sloshing some on the table.

Violet puts the plate in front of me and then kneels on a chair at one side of the table as she leans on her folded arms and with a cherubic smile proceeds to watch me eat. Lyndsey is sitting opposite and having tired of playing with the cutlery, is also smiling at me. A little unnerved by all this smiling I keep my head down and tuck in heartily.

"What are you doing at Christmas?" Violet asks. "Are you going over to Ireland?"

"No, I thought about it," I reply. "Both of my sisters are going and it would have been nice to see the whole family but I'm a bit financially embarrassed. I'll just have a quiet Christmas, the lads usually book up at a pub for a Christmas dinner so I'll go with them."

In truth I've overspent on presents. Without Alison's steadying hand on the purse strings I'm hopeless with money.

"Come and spend it with us," says Violet. "We'll have a traditional Christmas, loads of food, watch the telly, play party games and get legless. You can be Dad and carve the turkey."

"I'm not sure that two lesbians and a straight bloke exactly constitutes a traditional family Christmas and being vegetarians you don't have a turkey."

"Well you can carve the nut roast," says Lyndsey. "We'll have loads of vegetables and plenty of stuffing. You know what a brilliant cook Violet is and we'll have streamers and crackers and guzzle wine and beer and sherry and port and watch the Great Escape on the box. It won't cost you a thing it's our treat, all you need to do is turn up. What do you say?"

There's only one thing I can say. I've grown as close to these girls as I am to my own sisters and this invitation has turned what would have been a fairly sterile festival into one I was already looking forward to.

"I'd really love to, thanks."

"Great," said Lyndsey. "We'll pick you up at lunchtime on Christmas Eve. You can come shopping with us in the afternoon and then we'll come back here and have the odd drink or seven in the evening."

Chapter 9
What Are You Doing New Year's Eve – Vonda Shepherd

I'm not really expecting Victoria to put in an appearance. I suspect Friday may by now be just an embarrassing memory for her, never to be spoken of again. Despite this I'm sitting here waiting in my suit, spruced up to my dapper best and feeling not a little foolish. At seven thirty and forty seconds the doorbell rings. I jump up as if I've been sitting in the electric chair and the warders have forgotten to tighten the straps. Standing in the hall is Victoria, her mode of apparel even more shocking than last time she stood there.

"I thought we were going for a meal?" I ask as she stands in front of me, dressed in a very chic, grey and pink tracksuit and pristine white trainers.

"We're still going; my clothes and make up are in my bag. I'll change and put my face on in your bathroom," Victoria announces as she breezes past me. "I'll leave the door open and we can talk as I dress, the table's booked for eight."

"Have you been to the gym then?"

"It's rather charming that you think I look this well groomed after a session at the gym but no. The gym is where I'm supposed to be tonight, with the girls. Jenna will cover for me with Lenny should he check up on me."

"Who's Jenna?"

"Jenna's my best friend and like me she's married to a very rich, very obnoxious man and also like me she gets very bored."

"I didn't realise you were bored," I said.

"Well, I would be if I allowed myself that luxury. Jenna says she doesn't know how I put up with going to work and mixing with those horrible snotty little urchins but to be honest I sometimes think it's the only thing that keeps me sane. Well that and my little adventures."

"Have you got everything you need in there?" I ask timidly.

I've seated myself on the settee with my back to the bathroom door. The fact that she's a married woman makes it seem strangely improper to look in that direction.

"That's it," she says, emerging from the bathroom and looking as though she's spent the day in a beauty salon rather than fifteen minutes in front of a cracked mirror. "Let's get going."

I'm surprised to find that Victoria has driven here and say as much.

"I always take the car to the gym and it would have looked strange if I hadn't tonight."

"You won't be able to have much to drink then?"

"I'll be okay as long as I don't go mad. If I get pulled over and can't flirt my way out of it, Lenny will fix it with the Chief Constable at the Lodge."

She gives credence to this statement by driving at about half the speed of sound. We park outside a little Italian restaurant on the outskirts of Kidderminster and as we enter, a waiter greets Victoria by name. The room is lit in a very subdued manner and we're shown to a booth that is even dimmer. This is only slightly improved when the waiter puts his lighter to the candle. It's a very romantic setting and the flickering flame emphasises Victoria's fine bone structure.

"Your usual wine Mrs Daniels?" The waiter asks.

She raises an eyebrow in my direction and I nod.

"That will be fine thank you Tony, we'll order now as well please."

Having ordered, Victoria looks at me. "What have you been doing with yourself since I last saw you?"

I'd been waiting to broach this topic but wasn't sure of the right moment, I take my chance and dive straight in. "Your husband came to see me on Saturday night."

I expect fear, shock, disbelief or at the very least surprise. What I receive is mild indifference. "Did he really? That must have been rather tiresome for you."

I'm amazed, not to say a little worried. "How do you think he found out about me?"

"I told him."

"You told him? How much did you tell him?"

74

"Just that you'd taken me to the meal, he'd have been even more suspicious if I'd told him I went alone and he found out later that I hadn't. He can be quite paranoid at the best of times where I'm concerned."

"I think it's only paranoia when it's a delusive fear."

"Oh please, don't go all English teacher on me. Did he threaten you?"

"Only in a veiled way but he spoke in a very strange accent. It was sort of cockney but not cockney."

"Ah, therein lies a tale. You see he's not the self-made man he'd have people believe. His real name is Lionel and he reinvented himself as Lenny when he left public school and took over the family businesses. The main part of it is the vehicle leasing company that you know about but there are numerous other smaller subsidiaries. He's always craved street cred and started trying to nurture a Brummie accent but could never quite master it and just sounded daft. Then he saw an old clip of that violinist on TV, another upper class Brummie with a posh accent. The realisation dawned on Lenny that at some point he must have adopted that rather unconvincing cockney enunciation and for some reason decided to follow suit and he hasn't looked back since."

"He had two men with him. The older one just gave me the cold stare but the young bloke looked as though he really wanted to kill me."

"Oh dear, I'm afraid that may be my fault indirectly. I took a fancy to Jermaine a while back, he's very easy on the eye and I had a little fling with him. Big mistake on my part because unfortunately Jermaine took it far too seriously and proceeded to prove that beauty is very much in his case, only skin deep. He's a nasty piece of work and not even very good in bed. I think he loves himself too much to be a good lover, anyway he turned nasty when I dropped him and threatened to tell Lenny."

"What did you do?"

"I laughed in his face, I knew he wouldn't dare do any such thing. Jermaine is terrified of Harry and Harry is devoted to Lenny, misguided fool that he is. You see Lenny took him on when he was at rock bottom, fresh out of jail for GBH and without a friend in the world. Lenny can be unexpectedly nice sometimes, although I suppose there was a little self-interest involved. Anyway, that's enough about Lenny, I've come out to get away from him not to talk about him. Tell me more about yourself?"

"I told you before about moving here from Ireland as a youngster. I did okay at school once I settled down and I married Alison when I was twenty and she was a couple of years older. We met at the bank where we both worked. Two years later and very much against Alison's wishes, in fact I think it was the only time that I ever dared to stand up to her, I enrolled at teacher training college. I think it was the beginning of the end for our marriage. I was going nowhere fast at the Bank, I didn't really have enough interest in the work but Alison was convinced I was destined to become a branch manager. The relationship meandered on for another four years but the inevitable end had nothing to do with me or with teaching. It had everything to do with Alison meeting Dexter Gaunt at work. He was everything I wasn't, Dexter worked in Corporate Accounts, owned a nice house, drove a Vauxhall turbo and had a good physique as well but the deciding factor was his matchless wardrobe of unchallenging casual leisurewear in pastel shades."

"You'd already started teaching at St Winston's by then hadn't you?" Victoria asked. "I seem to remember someone mentioning your divorce in the staff room."

"Yeah, the marriage had already gone into under-drive by the time I started teaching. My first memory of school was being introduced to my beloved year eight. All of the flotsam and jetsam seemed to have washed up and settled there, I think they were the reason my predecessor moved to pastures new. I told them I was their new form master and would be taking them for English. Mark Widgeon a cheeky, podgy lad wearing glasses that made him look like an owl asked me in a broad Birmingham accent, 'how can an Irish bloke teach us English?' I said to him 'It's possible to teach anyone anything, as long as you know more than they do.' 'What's the capital of Uzbekistan then?' he challenged me. I racked my brain but I knew

77

that I hadn't a clue with all of those new Soviet republics. 'I don't know,' I admitted. 'U,' he smirked in triumph. I knew that if I left it there, I'd lose them. 'Alright,' I said. 'Who was Joan of Arc's father?' 'How should I know?' 'Noah,' I said and enough of the class were sufficiently smart to get the joke and laugh. From that moment we seemed to hit it off. We've had the usual ups and downs but I get a lot of satisfaction from the improvement they've shown and I'm very proud they're so loyal to me."

"You'll soon have all of that enthusiasm knocked out of you."

"Do you think so?" Gerry asked, surprised. "I think it's the kids that keep me going. I rarely go into school happy and come home miserable but quite often I'm depressed going in and they cheer me up."

"I wasn't referring to the children, I meant management. Between them the Ministry of Education and the likes of Mark and Shara can drain your enthusiasm and squeeze the goodwill out of you more effectively than any boa constrictor and they crawl much closer to the ground."

"Yeah, I suppose you might be right."

"I know I'm right, it's just that you haven't been doing it long enough yet to realise what leeches they are. Anyway, I stopped talking about Lenny to talk about something interesting not Mark bloody Shadwell."

"In that case can I ask you a personal question?"

"Fire away," Victoria laughed. "Jenna always says I'm unembarrassable, I think that I may have just made that word up."

"You told me that you've had relationships with quite a few men and I wondered why? I mean, now that I know you a bit better I think you're really nice. I can't imagine that if I was married to you I'd risk losing you."

"It's a nice thing to say but the answer is probably down to me. I have a very low boredom threshold and I need the excitement of new challenges. To be honest I sometimes wonder what I do want. Whenever I think I'm close to finding it I realise that I want something different."

"Have I reached that stage yet?"

"Don't flatter yourself, you haven't even approached the stage of being something that I want, never mind growing tired of you." Her mood has changed suddenly, as this isn't said with humour but delivered with a degree of vitriol.

I realise that I've overdosed on casting for compliments.

"I'm sorry, I didn't mean that to come out the way it did" I hastily dissembled. "I honestly thought you would have gotten bored with me by now."

"Don't have such a low opinion of yourself Gerry," she says, mellowing a little. "Or I will start to think that way about you, try to be more confident in yourself and stop worrying about everything.

79

When I get tired of people I don't waste time dropping hints, I'll just tell you outright."

"Are you staying in Gstaad for Christmas and the New Year?" I ask.

"No, I'll be back for the New Year. Gstaad is Lenny's sop to me so that I can get some skiing in. Lenny doesn't ski but he'll drink a lot, eat a lot and brag a lot to anyone who'll listen. He's meeting up with the brothers grim for New Year and they're off to Hamburg on 'a business trip,'" she says, indicating the inverted commas with her fingers. "It'll be monkey business if you ask me, down the Reeper Bahn, or some other equally seedy place."

"Oh," I said. I don't want to sound as if I'm fishing again by asking what she'll be doing for New Year but at the same time not quite sure what to say to someone who has just intimated that their husband will be away 'a whoring for the hols.'

Suddenly I remember. "I've bought you a little present for Christmas, it's not much."

I wasn't sure about getting a present and was doubly unsure what to get the woman who probably has everything, Lyndsey had suggested penicillin. Anyway the upshot is I've spent most of what was intended to last me over the holiday period on a dress ring from an antique jewellery shop. It's probably something she won't give houseroom to and I'll end up feeling stupid when she laughs at it.

Victoria's face turns suddenly serious as she unwraps it. I'm sure I've put my foot in it again and

I'm steeling myself for the storm, when suddenly her face breaks into a sort of wonky smile and she looks as if she might cry.

"It's lovely," she says. "You shouldn't have, I haven't got you anything."

"It's okay," I reply and only for the briefest guilty second does it cross my mind that I could have conserved my Christmas lifeline. The pleasure of giving presents is something I've always enjoyed and this one, which by Victoria's standards must be a fairly mundane trinket, seems to have given disproportionate pleasure.

"I can't believe that you bothered to go out and buy something for me. Did you choose it yourself?"

"Yeah, I'm glad you like it."

"What are you doing New Year's Eve?"

"I don't know, I'm spending Christmas with Lyndsey and Violet but they're off to a gay club on New Year's Eve and I don't really fancy singing YMCA and Auld Lang Syne while holding hands with a load of gay men. I'll probably end up getting roaring drunk with some Irish lads I know and regretting the hangover that will last until February."

"I have two tickets to a party at the Copthorne, why don't you come with me? I guarantee you won't regret it, hangover or not."

"What if someone you know sees you with me?"

"Ah well, therein lies the beauty of my plan. You see, it's fancy dress and the theme is masked characters. Even if we're seen we won't be recognised, are you up for it, it should be great fun?"

After the brief show of pique a few moments ago, Victoria is smiling again. I'm melting in my shoes and harbour no desire to make Mrs Angry return. Once again the angel me is standing on my right shoulder stamping his feet, hollering for all he's worth in my ear and saying, 'don't do it, make an excuse, any excuse will do, even the Albanian peasant caps.' At the same time, the devil me is chuckling and confidently drawling in my left ear as he emphasises his point by prodding me with his pitch-fork and saying, 'you know you've always fancied cutting a dash as Zorro.'

"Yes I'd love to come."

"Good that's a date then, I'll pick you up at about eight. Come on we need to get back to your place, I have to change and get home we don't want Lenny paying you any more visits, do we?"

∞

As we enter my flat Victoria says. "Put the fire on full while I get changed, we need it hot in here," before disappearing into the bathroom again.

By the time I've coaxed the cantankerous old gas fire into life, Victoria emerges from the bathroom decked out in a little tennis skirt and polo shirt. Coming over to me she unbuckles my belt and after unfastening my trousers, eases them over my hips. "Make love to me."

"Shall we go to the bedroom?" I ask while trying to hide my astonishment.

"Definitely not," Victoria smiles. "There's a reason for all of this. One of Lenny's favourite sayings is, 'remember the seven P's.'"

"What are the seven P's?"

"Prior planning and preparation prevents piss poor performance. Just in case he looks in my bag I need the gear to look convincingly sweaty and can you think of a nicer way of achieving it?"

Victoria pulls me towards her so that her back is against the wall. Putting her arms around my neck she hitches her legs around my waist. Despite her height she's unexpectedly light and seems to carry no spare weight. We set to with a vengeance and I find powers of stamina I hadn't realised I possess, a good thing as she's almost kicking me on, I thank my lucky stars that Tuesday's badminton and not horse-riding night or spurs and a whip might have been the order of the day. Eventually Victoria climaxes but thankfully much more quietly than last time. I know it's not exactly what you should be thinking about at a time like this but I couldn't help worrying what old Mrs Mendoza in flat five might make of it all.

"I need to use your shower before I go," she says, almost immediately. Not exactly my idea of impassioned, post coital discourse but then I'm still very much the novice in these matters.

"Yeah, of course," I reply as she disappears into the bathroom, pulling off the polo shirt en-route.

I go into the bedroom to clean myself up. When I come out the bathroom door is open, the shower's running and Victoria is singing Kylie's, 'Can't Get You Out Of My Head.' I'm in no doubt that after the earlier rebuke I shouldn't take this too literally and I resume my self-censoring posture facing away from the bathroom door. The shower stops.

"I've just realised." I wrongly assume that she's going to tell me what she's just realised but she doesn't, so I ask.

"What?"

"We've made love twice and you still haven't seen me naked."

Strangely this hadn't occurred to me until now. I realise that knowing what Victoria looks like in the nude would feel bizarre, almost to the point of scary when we next met in the mundane environs of school, something akin to Aiden's 'we're all naked under our clothes' discovery. Totally illogical considering that we've enjoyed sexual congress on more than one occasion but the machinations of my mind have always been a mystery to me where sex is concerned. I clear my mind to reply.

"Well, I am a bloke and you know what they say."

"No tell me."

"You've seen one woman naked you want to see them all."

Her laughter tinkles. "Clint Eastwood by any chance?"

84

"I don't think so. It may even be original but I doubt it, it's too good to be mine."

"I don't know? You can be quite droll. Perhaps you should try your hand at stand-up comedy."

"I'd never have the nerve."

"If I'd told you on Thursday that you'd be making love to me on Friday what would you have said?"

"I'd have run a mile, no sorry that sounds terrible. I didn't mean it in that way at all, I meant..."

"Do be quiet, I know exactly what you mean," says Victoria as she stands in front of me, tracksuit back in place, sports bag on shoulder and wet hair plastered back making her more alluring than ever. I can't explain it but wet hair has always had this effect on me. I quickly get to my feet, before hormones could take over and make the manoeuvre much too embarrassing to execute safely.

"I must run now, don't forget about New Year's Eve and don't let me down, Make sure you get a good costume and don't forget, it's masked characters. Oh and enjoy your Christmas with the boiler suit brigade." She hesitates long enough to deliver a peck on the cheek.

"And you," I say as the door bangs behind her.

Chapter 10
Sweet Dreams – The Eurythmics

Christmas Eve finds me in the mad house that is Merry Hill Shopping Centre. I'm still trying to fathom the reason for my inclusion on this expedition. We've picked up a couple of grocery necessities but the girls tell me they already have the bulk of the Christmas feast so I'm not really being utilised as a packhorse which was my first thought for being here. In fact all I'm really doing is getting under their feet. We seem to be spending an inordinate amount of time in women's boutiques where undue emphasis is being placed on my opinion. The strange thing being that my fashion sense is usually derided whereas today it's being treated with the utmost deference. To my embarrassment, I'm dragged to the outskirts of numerous women's changing rooms and it's here the girls model the clothes they've selected. While they're getting into them I receive more than the odd quizzical glance from the other denizens of this exotic territory. Eventually I persuade them to get changed singly, while one remains as my chaperone.

Being a very girlie sort of girl, Violet looks good in svelte, elegant, slinky garments. One of these causes me to avert my eyes. The blouse in question is sheer enough that I can see clear as daylight that she's left her brassiere off. This isn't exactly new ground, when I first became friends with the girls they would parade around their flat in various states of undress until they realised that it discomfited me not a little. Lyndsey because she's more solidly built can't carry off the pretty style of clothes that suit Violet so well but in the more classically cut designs looks stunning. The fact that Lyndsey has come out in heels and a skirt indicates that this is no normal shopping trip. She is invariably encased in trousers and flat heels. Although muscular her legs are shapely and the high heels emphasise this, I don't comment on this as I'm not sure how she'll take it.

The final part of my trial by shopping is the underwear department at Debenhams. This really puzzles me, as I can't possibly imagine what sort of input I can have. Despite this the girls sort through the most exotic fripperies on offer and ask my opinion of bra and knickers sets on mannequins, seeking out my thoughts on which ones I find most arousing. I do my best to offer sound advice through tightly closed eyes.

∞

Back at the flat Violet prepares the evening meal while Lyndsey plies the three of us liberally with wine. After eating we settle down to watch a film, 'Sleepless In Seattle.' I'm surprised at the choice as the normal fare is of a more robust genre, 'Alien' or 'Driller Killer Zombies,' the types of film that give me nightmares. Despite the fact that I'm enjoying the movie a lot, the food, the wine, the warm room and the cosy armchair all conspire to deliver me into the 'Land of Nod,' long before the happy if slightly predictable ending of the film arrives.

I wake to find Violet perched on the arm of my chair and Lyndsey curled up on the floor against my legs with her head on my lap. As I become a little more *compos mentis* Lyndsey breaks the silence.

"Gerry, Violet wants to ask you something."

Violet leans over and slaps her arm. "We both want to ask you something, don't we Lyndsey?"

"Yeah but you're doing the asking, you're much more persuasive than me."

I blink, trying to clear my fuddled senses.

"Lyndsey and I want to start a family," Violet announces.

"But you can't," I say without thinking, but pull up short of saying, 'you're lesbians.' Instead I bluster out. "I mean how?"

"Well that's where you come in," Violet continues.

"Me?"

"Yes," says Lyndsey. "Even you must have worked out that we need a man and just as obviously that we don't know all that many men."

"Well not men we like or that we could ask to do something like this," adds Violet.

"So we want you to be the Daddy."

"You want me to be a sperm donor?"

"Daddy sounds much nicer."

"And which one of you is going to be Mommy?"

"Ah your analytical mind has instantly pinpointed our dilemma," says Lyndsey.

88

"Violet earns more money than me but my job is more secure than hers."

"And what was your final decision."

"Well that rather depends on you," says Violet. "It's the reason we're asking you now, so that you can think it over."

"Yeah, it's like this. If you agree, there are two ways we can go, you could supply us with the sperm in a jar and we could go down the turkey baster route but that would be a bit clinical and nasty," I have no idea what Lyndsey's talking about. "Or the preferred option from our point of view is," she buries her face in her hands and blurts out quickly. "That you sleep with us," a stunned silence envelops the room until Lyndsey breaks it again. "I know what you're going to say, that it will be hideous for us doing it with a bloke and it will but it won't be half as bad if the bloke is you. 'Cause you're a mate and you're not a big macho, hairy bloke." Lyndsey issues forth, in a verbal stream.

"And because we couldn't come to a decision about which of us the mother should be we decided that we would both have a go. It'll be like Russian Roulette," says Violet, sounding equally excited.

"What if you both became pregnant?" I ask before realising that I'm making it sound as though I'm agreeing.

"Even better," replies Lyndsey. "We can both have maternity leave together and then decide who's best suited to looking after them. It will be like having twins."

All of this is so surreal that it makes my unlikely affair with Victoria seem as normal as having your breakfast.

"And when did you decide all of this?"

"The germ of the idea's been around for a while but we only talked seriously about it last week. We've been building up to asking you," says Violet.

"And you really are serious. This isn't some elaborate practical joke?"

"Coming into contact with men's dangly bits is no joke to us Gerry," says Lyndsey. "We couldn't be more serious,"

I'm gobsmacked. "Can I think it over?" I ask.

"Of course you can," says Violet. "We wouldn't expect you to make a decision like this on the spur of the moment. Take as long as you want, we know it's a big thing to ask of someone and if you say no it won't affect our friendship."

"I'll go and sleep on it but I'll definitely let you know tomorrow. I wouldn't want to keep you hanging in the air over something like this."

"It would be the best Christmas present in the world ever," says Lyndsey. "No pressure though."

I go to bed and lie there, trying to co-ordinate my thoughts which are behaving like a drunken Italian motorist negotiating Spaghetti junction for the first time. What are the problems? I need to list them.

Question One. Can same sex couples become good parents?

Answer. I had got my class to debate this thorny issue only last month. From a distance it's all too easy to be objective and the result was an almost overwhelming vote of no despite my acting as Devil's advocate. But when the people involved are two kind and loving friends, objectivity isn't arrived at so glibly.

Question Two. Is it fair on the child?

Answer. We extended the debate to cover this and decided that people said similar things about mixed race marriages at one time but they were now accepted, as were the children of these matches.

Question Three. Could I effectively give my child over to someone else's care?

Answer. Being practical, I would be able to stay in touch, I'd be able to enjoy the best parts of fatherhood by proxy, while missing most of the downside.

Question Four. Is more of a practical consideration than a moral one but could I have sexual relations with two friends? And if I did would the friendship survive this?

Answer. They're both attractive girls whose main problem may be to stop giggling long enough for us to do the deed. Besides that, if I said no then what sort of friend would I be anyway?

Eventually I must have drifted into a fractious slumber. Suddenly I'm awake, at least I think I am but I have that eerie feeling of a presence in the room with me. I try to move my arms but they're pinned to my sides as if some great force is subduing me. I've heard of people having supernatural experiences when a spirit or entity prevents them from moving. I realise that I can move my arm just enough to wriggle a hand from under the duvet and tremulously switch on the bedside lamp. I don't know whether to be relieved or not as the light reveals Violet and Lyndsey sitting on either side of the bed, attired in very fetching underwear. I click the switch off again.

"Put it back on," says Lyndsey.

I do as I'm told and stare determinedly at the ceiling.

"What time is it?" I ask noncommittally.

"Twelve fifty seven," answers Violet.

"I've only been in bed an hour."

"We were too excited to sleep and started trying the things on that we bought today. Then we thought that as it was gone midnight technically it was already tomorrow, so we could ask you how the thought processes are going," says Violet.

"And that seeing us like this might help things along," adds Lyndsey. "It's why you had to come shopping with us today."

"At least look at us," says Violet. "Or won't you look because we're a couple of repulsively butch dykes?"

"No of course not, you know you're both drop dead gorgeous," I say, looking at them and wondering why I'm procrastinating on what would be most men's dream scenario. "It's just that it's too important a decision to be made entirely on carnal grounds." I continue, unable to believe just how priggish I sound.

"I suppose you're right," says Violet pouting.

"Yeah, come on Vee," said Lyndsey, smiling seductively at me. "Let's leave Gerry to his thoughts."

"Sweet dreams Gerry," says Violet, and holding hands they make for the door.

Lyndsey blows me a kiss and then putting her head back around the door asks. "Are we really drop-dead gorgeous?" Before she's hauled out and the door closed.

I return to a fitful sleep, knowing that there can only be one answer. These girls are my best friends and when Alison chucked me they had more or less adopted me, they were my pillars of strength then, my support system and have been ever since. I decide to delay giving them my answer until the morning. Not to be cruel but to avoid looking as though the underwear has swayed my decision. There's also the little matter that if I say yes now they may want to make a start right away and I am after all rather tired.

Chapter 11
Christmas Wrapping – The Waitresses

I'm woken by a symphony being played on an orchestra of crockery, cutlery and saucepans that sounds like the opening bars of World War III. On entering the kitchen it doesn't take long to deduce the reason for the bellicose sounds. In the intervening hours since our last rendezvous, hostilities have broken out and the kitchen is now a combat zone. I've experienced this situation many times and as usual it's a deadly serious business.

"Would you like some breakfast Gerry?" Violet asks pleasantly.

"I'll do it," offers Lyndsey, even more pleasantly.

"You don't want a bad stomach on Christmas Day do you Gerry?"

"He'll get one anyway looking at your sour face all day."

"I'll just have some cereal," I say, deciding that I might starve if I wait for the outcome of the S.A.L.T talks.

After breakfast we open our presents. I've bought Violet a very delicate filigree silver necklace from an antique jewellery shop, the same one that I got Victoria's ring from. I knew it was just up her street. Lyndsey had been easier, the box set of The Soprano's on DVD. My present buying errs on the extravagant side of the line. It's the reason I'm always broke from December to February. The girls have bought me a reclining armchair. I protest that it's too expensive but Violet says she got it for a very good price from one of her contacts and that anyway there are prison cells that are better furnished than my flat. The girls gush over their gifts from me while barely muttering an acknowledgement for the piles of lovely presents they've given each other.

It's approaching three o'clock and Violet's dishing up her homemade leek and potato soup for starters. I feel sure that they'll opt for Channel Four's alternative Christmas message but although fervently anti-royalist they both insist on The Queen's Speech, as it's traditional, they then mock her delivery all the way through. The cold war shows no sign of thawing and I make an executive decision as the soup and the Queen come to an end simultaneously.

"I'm not going to touch more any of this lovely food and I'm going to go home and sit on my own in a cold miserable flat if you two don't make it up this very minute." I almost sound like a character from Charles Dickens.

They both stare at me a little surprised and then look at each other.

"She started it," says Lyndsey, pouting like a three year old. "Saying that I'm too immature to look after a baby and that I still need someone to wet nurse me."

"Only after you called me a hard faced cow."

"That's because you are sometimes."

"That's not fair it's because I always have to make the difficult decisions."

I put my table napkin down and begin rising from the table.

"What are you doing?" Lyndsey demands.

"I told you my conditions, I'm going home," I say in a surprising bout of authority.

"I'm sorry," says Violet.

"Who to?" Lyndsey jumps in.

"Sorry to you for what I said and to Gerry for being the most ungracious host in the world."

"Well I'm sorry too then," says Lyndsey, the wind suddenly removed from her sails although I wouldn't have been surprised if she'd challenged Violet over the right to be considered the most ungracious host in the world for the same reasons.

"Good, now you've both behaved like little children or even worse, like Premier League footballers and therefore you must be treated as such. Shake hands."

They earnestly shake hands, before giggling and hugging each other. The meal continues and proves every bit as sumptuous, as well as every bit as alcoholic as they'd promised. After dinner Lyndsey washes up as a further penance while Violet dries. I'm made to sit and watch television until they come and sit either side of me.

"Well," says Lyndsey. "You've slept on it and you've made us kiss and make up, so what's your decision?"

"I've fretted about it all night but I've weighed everything up and the one thing that I worry about above all else is that it could affect our friendship. But I've decided I'll do it, I don't know if it's the right thing but if it makes you two happy how could I refuse."

"Turkey baster or rumpy-pumpy?" shouts Lyndsey.

"Well I think I'd be more embarrassed handing over a jar of sperm than the other way, although it's a close run thing."

"Thank you so much Gerry," says Violet, looking serious. "The thing is, after our row this morning I think we've decided to take a rain check on the idea for at least a few weeks."

"Yeah we decided to give some more thought to whether we're ready for the responsibility but don't look so relieved, you're not off the hook yet," said Lyndsey. "If we decide to go for it you've said yes now."

But she's right, I am relieved. Despite my decision I still have grave reservations about the whole thing. On the other hand I'm still honest enough to admit to myself that their decision is tinged with a slight regret. I know deep down that I'd harboured a covert fascination over the whole concept of the conception.

Chapter 12
Millennium – Robbie Williams

After a lovely Christmas Day I stay over with the girls for the night and Boxing Day morning as well. I could have happily enjoyed another week of their slightly eccentric hospitality but decide they need a little quality time to themselves. I spend a few days pootling about my flat, engaging in light but overdue household chores as well as some schoolwork. I also fit in a visit to the Rag Market in Birmingham to track down the missing ingredients of my Zorro costume. I find a pair of second hand riding boots at a ridiculously low price and purchase a black mask from a fancy dress stall. The entire outlay for my costume is less than twenty pounds. The black shirt I already own, along with a pair of black cords that I'd stopped wearing for safety reasons after the washing machine rendered them to be on the dangerous side of tight. The black hat is borrowed from a teaching colleague I know to be a closet line dancer, while one of Violets posh chums comes up trumps with the sword that turns out to be a genuine competition rapier. I must waste at least two hours every day carving imaginary Z's with it.

Seven forty five December the thirty-first finds me sitting in full fig, feeling rather silly again as I wait for Victoria and again I'm fully expecting a no show on her part. What if she'd been kidding about the fancy dress? What if she'd forgotten that she'd asked me? What if she'd had a better offer? At least I'd made provision for the last two contingencies by laying in a DVD of Con Air, some comfort food and a pack of Rolling Rock beer in the fridge.

My 'depression in a teacup,' is rudely interrupted by a scratching sound at the front door. It isn't unknown for cats to get into our building and I decide it's prudent to check that there's no one about rather than step straight out into the hall dressed as a masked avenger. However when I attempt to look through the spy-hole, I knock my hat off and can't see anything there anyway. I open the door slightly but just as I decide the hall is empty, Catwoman suddenly leaps out in front of me, giving vent to a throaty miaow that would make Eartha Kitt sound like Mary Whitehouse.

"What do you think?" purrs said feline, leaning nonchalantly on the doorframe.

It's one of those questions that mere words can't do justice in answer.

"You make Michelle Pfeiffer look like Catwoman's dowdy little kitten sister. What about me, will I do?"

"The Lady from Del Monte she say yes," she declares, after doing a lap of me, (no pun intended.) "Where did you get it from?"

I explain all of its disparate origins.

"How quaint but wouldn't it have been easier to hire one?"

"I suppose it would, but it wouldn't be as much fun would it?"

"I'd never have thought of it as being fun, what a strange person you are. Anyway you'd never have got trousers that tight from a fancy dress shop would you? I can't wait to get my hands on them later."

"Which fancy dress shop did you get your outfit from?" I ask in an attempt to cover my confusion. "It's fantastic."

"I had it made by a little woman that I use for alterations and the like. I gave her a photo from the film and she did the rest. I wanted it to fit like a second skin and I couldn't face wearing anything that's had someone else's crotch sweating in it, it's too tight for underwear. Come on let's go and show off."

Victoria drives us to the Copthorne and after pulling up outside the front doors she gives the car keys to a uniformed doorman.

"Would you get it parked and have the bags taken to the cream suite," as she says this I notice that a five-pound note accompanies the keys.

"How do I look?" Victoria asks while smoothing creases that aren't there due to the PVC's close fitting qualities.

"Va va voom," I reply, in the style of the great Alfred E Newman of Mad Magazine.

"Come on then, let's go and let the new century in with a bang."

We enter a room that's full of more masked characters than you could shake a stick at. I don't feel that any of them put us in the shade and unlike some of the more elaborate ones ours won't grow too uncomfortable with the passage of time. The meal is about to begin and we find our designated table and sit down at the same time as our companions for the meal. The Lone Ranger and what is either Marie Antoinette or a very close friend, greet us. The Lone Ranger's pale blue suit is a trifle snug and his pale blue stomach bulges over his gun belt. He sports a moustache that is brown verging on ginger. Marie Antoinette carries a mask on a stick but is overshadowed by a huge powdered wig that even wins its own personal battle for attention with an audacious cleavage.

"I think we may be fighting it out for the best costume prizes," says the Lone Ranger in a Yorkshire accent that sounds strangely familiar.

"Yes, although I've seen a lot of other good ones here as well," I reply.

"Oh you're from the Emerald Isles, what line are you in?" The Lone Ranger asks.

"He's a doctor at Kidderminster General," interrupts Catwoman, using an Irish accent that puts mine to shame in its enthusiasm.

"That's interesting and what's your speciality?" Although the question is addressed to me Victoria dives in again.

"Obs and gobs," says Catwoman. "He's very good and I'm an X-ray technician. I knock 'em out and he pops 'em out, we're quite a team."

"I'm headmaster at a school in South Birmingham." Like a bolt from the blue I'm stricken with a blinding realisation. Victoria has turned into Dana because she has cottoned on to the fact much quicker than I have, that the Lone Ranger is none other than our own Mark Shadwell. Although he's changed the location of the school, his pride in his position allied to the fact that he doesn't expect to meet anyone that he knows has obviously proved too much of a temptation.

"Wow that's a big responsibility," gushes Dana. "And what does the little woman do?"

"The little woman has a voice," hisses Shara, rising to the bait as Victoria had, no doubt anticipated.

"My wife's a PA, at the local education authority."

"Do you have children?" Victoria's question is directed at Shara, obviously by way of appeasement.

"I have two, they're both at the same school."

"And what do they teach?"

"Pardon," splutters Shara, looking at least as affronted as Marie Antoinette could have managed. I instantly forgive Victoria for recycling her barb, if only for the effect it has on Shara.

"Sorry, just my little joke," laughs Victoria, now veering towards Galway in her tour of the Gaelic dialects.

Mark has removed his white Stetson and now that she's cast aside her mask to eat, it isn't difficult to recognise Shara. I'm just praying that corn on the cob isn't on the menu. I've discarded my hat but the black bandana I'm sporting, covers my hair and this in conjunction with the black moustache that Vicky insisted on giving me with an eyebrow pencil has obviously kept my identity incognito. Most of Victoria's features are hidden by her costume and the Irish accent would even have thrown Lenny off the track.

The talk miraculously returns to the difficulties of running a school and inevitably Mark's expertise in overcoming them. Along with the change of location, Mark has now become Michael to Shara's Sharan. I can sense Victoria tiring of Mark's self-adulation and the free flowing alcohol is loosening her self-control. We're finishing our main course and having listened to SuperMark conquer the fourfold problems of budget, the education authority, the pupils and now getting stuck into troublesome teachers, Victoria slams down her knife and fork.

"If it's such a bloody awful job why don't you..."

Luckily as her blarney seems to have slipped, she's interrupted by a commotion from a nearby table.

"Is there a doctor in the house," shouts a man's voice. "My wife's choking to death."

I'm looking around the room, to see if anyone will respond when Marie Antoinette proclaims. "We have a doctor here," and gripping my arm thrusts me forward.

"I'm not fully qualified," is the best I can come up with, as the blood in my veins suddenly turns to ice.

"That doesn't matter, Christ it's an emergency man," says the Lone Ranger.

The sweat is running from under my mask and staining my black shirt even darker. All of the stored data from my first aid course is deleted from my brain as sheer panic sets in. I will myself to dematerialise, a la 'Dr Who,' but to no avail, as the whole room seems to have frozen while staring in my direction. Victoria strides towards the woman lying on the floor who now appears to be turning blue.

"Can you two men lift her upright and support her there," she says to a couple of bystanders.

They do as they're told and Victoria calmly walks behind the woman who is wildly attempting to draw in a breath. Putting her arms around the woman's midriff Victoria gives a sharp tug. It's at this juncture that Mark chooses to stand in front of the lady, announcing, 'she's not looking right well...' He's cut short by a ball of half masticated turkey, which despite the protection offered by his mask knocks him over backwards. The crowd breaks into a cheer which I assume is for Victoria's rescue act as none of them could have known what a piece of work Mark is.

Victoria melts away from the action as the chokee is fussed over, and grabbing my hand Catwoman leads me towards the foyer.

"What about the rest of the meal and seeing the New Year in?" I enquire as we head toward the lifts.

"If we hang around here people will want to thank me and they might just ask why the young doctor froze," she says and smiling adds. "And I couldn't have eaten any more in this costume without splitting a seam. Anyway I hate all of that Auld Lang Syne shit, it's so false."

"Where are we going?" I venture to ask as the lift speeds upward.

"I took the liberty of booking a room, is that okay?" I can't believe that I'm seriously being asked this question but answer 'yes' anyway.

We enter what I expect to be a normal hotel room but instead I find myself in a luxurious suite that has a separate lounge and bedroom. As a child, this would have been my idea, mainly gleaned from Hollywood movies of what hotel rooms are always like but until now have always found to be a major disappointment. I notice Victoria's overnight bag placed on a table and realise that I've only the clothes I stand up in. I voice my misgivings over the unsuitability of my attire when the time to return home arrives, if only to prevent myself from making a puerile remark about the surroundings,

"I've just realised that I'll need to go home dressed as Zorro in the morning."

"Don't panic, I took another liberty and bought you some clothes. They're hanging in the closet, go and have a look."

I follow her bidding and look at the clothes in the wardrobe. They bear the obviously understated style of quality garments.

"I can't afford these." I say, looking at them enviously.

"They're a gift," she laughs. "Remember, I didn't get you a Christmas present."

"I didn't expect anything like this. A book token would have been fine."

"Don't be so ungracious, you'll spoil the pleasure of giving for me."

"I'm sorry, they're fantastic. It was a lovely thought, it just came as such a shock."

"What do you think of the room?"

"I've never been anywhere so luxurious, apart from your house that is, it's like another world. How did you manage to book a place like this for tonight? I'd have thought it would have been snapped up months ago."

"Friends in high places, when money talks it usually shouts. Find some music and I'll order the dessert that you missed downstairs. Are you fussy?"

"Not really, I like most sweet things."

The television has cable and I tune in to VH1. Number sixty-seven of the 'One Hundred Greatest Anthems' is playing, it's 'Whole Lotta Love' by Led

Zeppelin. Surely, I think to myself, a classic like this should be much higher. We settle onto one of the sumptuous sofas to await the remainder of our meal.

"What would you be doing now if you weren't here?"

"I'd be in a scruffy pub somewhere with Sean, Aiden and Brendan. I'd be trying to avoid drinking as much as them in order to avoid oblivion and hangover hell."

"Do you wish you were there?"

"Are you joking?"

"Don't you have any friends that don't drink so much?"

"I don't know how it happened but somehow during our marriage Allison got rid of all my friends from my single days without me realising it. When we divorced she seemed to get custody of our new friends along with the house and most other things. I wasn't all that bothered really, most of them weren't my type anyway."

"Are you bitter about your divorce?"

"Not really, Allison was good for me in a lot of ways and I think she loved me at one time. It was probably all my own fault, I should have put more effort in."

"You're such a doormat Gerry don't always reproach yourself for everything. Blame her, call her a bitch, hate womankind in general, curse me while we make love."

"That's not my way, I really don't think I could do that."

I'm rescued from this uncomfortable line of questioning by a knock on the door.

"Shall I go?" I ask. "Zorro might be less of a shock than Catwoman."

"No, let's give the waiter a treat," she says, donning her headgear.

A young waiter wheels a trolley into the room.

"Happy New Year," purrs Victoria, delivering a kiss on his cheek. I notice that a five-pound note changes hands again as he leaves, although God knows where she produced it from in that suit.

"Will trifle do?" Victoria asks.

"I love trifle."

Victoria ceremoniously carries over the large bowl.

"Are you not having anything?" I ask.

"I'll help you out with this," she says, kneeling astride my legs on the sofa.

She digs in and puts a loaded spoonful into my mouth. Some of it misses and goes around my mouth, I'm about to wipe it with the back my hand. "Leave it," Victoria says stopping my hand. "I'll do that," she says and leaning forward licks my mouth clean.

"Thanks," I say.

"You're impossible," she says, laughing. "Haven't you seen 'Nine and a Half Weeks? Try for erotic, rather than polite."

"Sorry, I think you're probably the first person to feed me for about twenty odd years."

"And I'll be the last the way you're going."

I dip my finger into the whipped cream and after smearing it over her PVC encased breasts I lick it off.

"By Jove he's got it, I think he's got it."

We finish the trifle and after overcoming my initial embarrassment I found it a lot of fun.

"What's the time?" Victoria asks.

"Seven minutes to the next century."

"Open the champagne and charge our glasses."

I bounce the cork off the ceiling, bringing forth an excited squeal from Victoria before flooding the coffee table but just about manage to get two glassfuls."

"What would you like to do to see in the millennium in style and I do mean anything, go on let your imagination run riot?"

"Well there is something but you might think I'm a bit weird."

"Go on risk shocking me, I did say anything and I meant... Anything."

"I noticed that the patio doors to the balcony face Birmingham," I say. "I thought it might be nice to move the sofa over there and watch the big firework display."

"Well you've certainly shocked me but I did say anything."

There are fireworks going off whichever direction you look but the big display in Birmingham is truly spectacular, possibly more so viewed from this distance. Victoria snuggles up to me, sipping her champers.

"You've surprised me again," she said. "Mainly at myself, I wouldn't have dreamed that I'd enjoy something so simple."

"I've always been a sucker for fireworks."

Getting up Victoria starts to push the end of the sofa around.

"What are you doing?" I ask.

"I'm testing your love of fireworks," she says, as she steps onto the rug in front of the fireplace. "You can choose whether you'd rather carry on watching the fireworks, or me."

Victoria starts gyrating sensually to Guns n' Roses 'Paradise City,' that is number nineteen. By the time the zip on the suit starts to come down all thoughts of fireworks are a distant memory. When the costume is finally discarded I'm no nearer to finding out if Victoria is a natural redhead but this is a very minor setback when balanced against the reason I'm none the wiser. This is because despite having an aversion to coffee and loving both their football and samba dancing, I have to admit that Brazilians have bequeathed a gift to mankind that is even greater than either of these.

Clad only in mask and high-heels Victoria stalks over to the bedroom door. "Bring some drinks in," she purrs. "When you get tired of your fireworks."

Chapter 13
McDonald's Girl – Barenaked Ladies

It's a Baker day as these training days are unofficially known and therefore my presence isn't required at school. It coincides with the lads being off work due to their site undergoing a spot check from the health and safety people and we're spending our windfall time at the Merry Hill Shopping Centre. They're not great ones for the shopping but the threadbare state of their wardrobe has forced them into this hated place. I've been press ganged into attendance as a sort of style guru because by their standards I'm something of a dandy. The dread deed is now complete and festooned with plastic carrier bags we head hungrily for a midday meal at McDonalds. A shout from the other side of the mall heralds the presence of Lyndsey and Violet. They've met the lads before but aren't exactly close acquaintances.

"We're going for a burger, want to join us?" I ask.

Violet surprises me by saying. "Yeah, that's great."

As we join the queue Aiden sidles up to Lyndsey, she towers over him by about four inches and probably a couple of stone. Displaying his natural diplomacy he leers, "I really like big girls you know. I'd love to shag you."

This is Aiden testing Lyndsey out but he's picked the wrong target.

"Well if you do and I ever find out about it there'll be big trouble."

111

Shaun roars, Brendan chuckles and even Aiden smiles a rueful acknowledgement but he's never been one to give up when he's on a losing streak.

He turns his attention to the young girl behind the counter. "Hiya sexy, why don't you hit me with a whopper," he shouts.

Unimpressed she looks him in the eye. "Okay you're a good looking bastard with a great personality," this in a broad Black Country accent teamed with perfect deadpan delivery.

Everyone enjoys another laugh at Aiden's expense.

"I like you love, you might not be the best looking girl in the world but then beauty's only ever a light switch away isn't it?"

"Who are yo then? Brad Pitt's younger brother Cess," she fires back and putting Aiden's whopper on the counter averts any possible retort by yelling. "Next."

We make our way to the seated area upstairs. To everyone's amusement not to mention amazement, Aiden announces he's sure the girl fancies him. I suppose it's not really that much of a surprise, as he believes most of the female population have secret designs on him but thus far they've enjoyed great success at reining in these desires. The conversation grows desultory as we tuck into our food.

A few minutes later, Aiden's waitress appears, busily cleaning tables and all the time getting closer to ours. As she squeezes into the space between the next table and ours, Aiden strikes with another of his dire chat up lines.

"Excuse me love, I could get you into modelling. I don't think I'd find much work for your arms but I'd like to find your legs a part." As the rest of us cringe his smirk suddenly changes to a howl of pain, "I think you've broken my foot, yer big clumsy mare."

"Ooh you men are such babies, I haven't even got any heels on these," she says without breaking stride in her polishing.

"Babies nothing, I'm in agony."

"Come here I'll rub it better. You blokes have such a low pain threshold, it's a good job yo doe 'ave to have the babbies."

"Another typical piece of feminist propaganda," grimaces Aiden. "You pick on the only thing that we can't possibly contradict you on as a comparison. It can't be that much worse than having a good shite can it?" Everyone else appears to be unconsciously trying to distance themselves from Aiden although his waitress seems totally unconcerned by his comments as he continues. "And that can be one of the best feelings in the world. In fact I sometimes think it's better than sex."

"I dare say that's probably another thing you haven't experienced," she says turning to the rest of us. "When Cess here was born and the midwife held him upside down to smack his bum, did his brains drop out by any chance?" But it's delivered with a smile.

"You could look good in a certain light darling," said Aiden. "A total eclipse, now how about us going out together sometime?"

"I think yo must be suffering from delusions of adequacy but goo on then, I'm a fool to miself sometimes. I finish me shift in half an hour if you can wait that long."

"Course we can, can we not?" Aiden said. "Then we can all go for a drink somewhere. What do you say girls?"

"Yeah, whatever," replies Lyndsey.

"I'm sorry, I'll have to cry off," I say.

"Why?" Aiden asks.

"I'm meeting someone."

"You're not still seeing the Wicked Witch of the West are you?" Lyndsey asks.

I don't need to reply and, I feel my face burning as they all let out a dirty cheer and I sense that everyone in the place is looking at me. Since New Year I've managed to keep our meetings quiet and everyone assumed that the affair had fizzled out. After mumbling my farewells I leave them all laughing at my discomfort.

∞

While driving over there, my confidence is bolstered by Victoria's assurance that Lenny is away and won't return until late evening. She answers the door looking devastating as usual, although she's achieved this effect merely by wearing a T-shirt, flat shoes and faded jeans.

"Come in," she gushes. A relief, as her moods can vary erratically and aren't always this good. "And what have you been up to this morning?"

"I've been shopping with the lads. We bumped into Lyndsey and Violet and most surprising of all, Aiden managed to chat up a girl."

"Why is that such a shock? Is he as timid as you?"

"No he's the opposite. He tends to frighten them off but this one seems more than a match for him, even though she's only a youngster."

"I'm almost sorry to have missed out on all of this merriment."

"Are you really?"

"Don't be silly of course I'm not." Despite the rather sharp answer I have my doubts. Victoria has everything she wants materially yet at times can seem both lonely and unhappy, hence I suppose her interest in me. "Come on," she says, softening. "Time we relaxed a little."

I follow her through the house to reach the pool complex at the back. The blue reflecting water of the swimming pool looks so cool and inviting that I could fancy a dip if only I'd brought a costume. Music permeates the warm air as Frank invites us to, 'Come Fly With Him.'

"Jump in the Jacuzzi while I make some drinks."

"I've no trunks, you didn't tell me to bring any."

"Don't be so silly. There's only the two of us here, be a devil and do without."

As soon as Victoria is out of the room I undress as quickly as possible and leap into the Jacuzzi. I almost jump out again, as it's hotter than I'd run a bath. Victoria returns with a tray and sets it down on the side.

"My you're eager, is the water warm enough for you?"

"Yes," I say, sweat trickling down my face.

Victoria dispenses with her normally exaggerated mode of undressing and after kicking off her shoes more or less throws off her jeans and T-shirt, before climbing in and sitting next to me.

"Mm I adore being immersed in water. I've been looking forward to this all day."

"It's really nice once you get used to the temperature."

"Sorry is it too hot?"

Before I can answer, the doorbell interrupts.

"Ignore it I'm not expecting anyone, it's probably a Jehovah's Witness."

The ringing continues.

"It couldn't be Lenny could it?"

"Don't be silly he's old enough to have his own key. I suppose I'd better go and get rid of them," she says, getting out and slipping into a robe.

I agonise over my desire to jump out and get dressed but don't want to appear silly and immature. I remain in situ and hear voices, both reassuringly female. Victoria comes back in followed by a slightly younger blonde, dressed in the de rigueur designer tracksuit in lemon.

"Darling, Jenna's here, do you remember me telling you about her? She's my best friend in the whole world, we're soul sisters. She's married to an even bigger shit than Lenny, but he's richer too. There seems to be some sort of correlation between money and repugnance, anyway Jenna this is Gerry, I've mentioned him to you before."

"Excuse me not standing," I try to smile in a confident, relaxed manner and despite the bubbles I still can't stop my hands from covering my embarrassment.

"Don't worry, any friend of Vicky's is a friend of mine."

"Come on Jen, get your kit off and join us."

"I'd love to but I have to meet Simon and I need to go home and get changed first."

"What can I do for you then?"

"He wants me to wear the diamonds tonight," says Jenna. "I'm being shown off to some boring business colleague."

"Have I got them?"

"I bloody hope so, don't you remember when I picked up that gorgeous waiter that I didn't trust. I gave them to you to look after them for me?"

"Oh God yes! I remember now, I put them in the safe. Chat to Gerry while I fetch them."

I hope Jenna will go with her but instead she lays a towel out at the side of the Jacuzzi, and sits on it, giving every appearance of appraising me.

"How well do you know Victoria?"

"We work together at St Winston's'."

"Do you share a Jacuzzi with all of your work colleagues?"

"No I just dropped round and er…"

"It's alright," she laughs. "I know all about your relationship, Victoria and I have no secrets from each other."

"Ah, Victoria's Secrets."

"Pardon."

"The underwear firm." I answer, as if this explains everything.

"Oh," she replies. "Yes."

"I'm sorry, that was a stupid thing to say. I'm just a little embarrassed at being naked with someone I don't know and who's fully clothed."

"Are you asking me to get undressed?"

"No of course not!" I say hurriedly. "I mean I'm sure that would be very nice but I'd never ask you to do that."

"It's okay I'm just teasing again, it's very naughty of me. Let's change the subject, have you met Lenny?"

"Yes." I briefly relate our close encounter, which makes her giggle.

"I'm sorry I shouldn't laugh but that's so Lenny. Simon can't stand him he calls him Sinex."

I look perplexed.

"You know, a little squirt that gets up everyone's nose." Jenna explains.

I laugh.

"Don't be fooled though,' she says. "He may be a bit of a joke but he has some nasty friends. Simon thinks he may be involved in the drug trade with the Russian mafia."

I don't know why this hasn't occurred to me before, as this house must be worth a mint. Does a small businessman, no pun intended, really need hired help like Harry and Jermaine? They're hardly likely to be much help with the VAT returns. It all seems so obvious now. As this is fermenting in my brain Victoria returns.

Swinging the necklace round her finger she then dangles it under my nose saying. "Feast your eyes on those Gerry."

Even to my untrained eye it's obviously a serious bit of gear.

"I've earned every last carat of it," says Jenna. "Putting up with an arse like Simon for all these years."

"It's only been seven years," Victoria says. "But hear, hear to the sentiment."

"Thanks Vic and I hope I'll be seeing more of you in the future Gerry but it'll have to be some other time, bye," and with that she's gone.

Victoria has cast her robe aside and re-joined me in the tub.

"She seems nice," I say.

"She's the best, I'd trust her with anything. We've had some good times together and she keeps me going at times, sometimes it seems she's the only thing that does. Come on, let's have a swim and a shower then go to bed."

And that's just what we do. It's the first time I've swum naked and the feeling of freedom is unbelievable, especially in the company of a lithe female although I've no plans to repeat the exercise at the public baths. As we climb the staircase I catch our reflection in the ceiling to floor mirror that dominates the mezzanine landing. Victoria's hair, still wet and slicked back makes her look gorgeous while mine sticks up like Vivian from the Young Ones having a bad hair day.

We always utilise one of the spare bedrooms and this in turn comes as a relief because the bed is more of a normal size and acts as a brake on Victoria's carnal athleticism.

"Are you happy?" I ask as we lay there post coitally.

"What do you mean?"

"It just set me thinking when you were talking to Jenna. You both seem to hate your husbands so much, how can you be happy with your life?"

"I don't know... Who is? At least I'm rich and miserable, that's far better than being poor and depressed. Are you happy with your life?"

"No I don't suppose I am although you've brought some fun back into it. I enjoy our time together but I'm not in love with you and you don't love me, we're just friends who give each other pleasure. I think I'm in a sort of transient period, waiting to see what turns up whereas you're in a place that you don't really want to be."

This is fairly daring for me, it isn't my style to confront things head on and I'm a little worried that I've gone too far.

"I don't want to talk about it," Victoria snaps but then mellows. "I don't want to talk about it because you're right and I don't know what to do about it. What I want to do right now is make love again because then I don't need to think of anything else."

And so we do exactly that and afterwards she seems to be trying very hard to appear happy.

Chapter 14
The Irish Rover – The Pogues

Sitting alone at my desk in the classroom, I'm awaiting the imminent arrival of my year elevens when Victoria unexpectedly makes an entrance.

"Top of the morning to ya and a happy St Patrick's Day," I say, in my best Terry Wogan brogue.

"Gerry, you dropped this by the pool yesterday," she says, handing me my video shop rental card. "Lenny found it."

"Oh Mother Mary and Jesus," I reply, plunging into deeper Hibernia than even Terry would get away with.

"Don't worry, I had a hell of a job but I convinced him that you'd brought me a letter from Mark Shadwell. Fortunately I had one he'd given me the day before regarding my contract, so when Lenny asked to see the letter it seemed quite convincing."

"Are you sure?" I asked, totally rattled.

"Well you can never be one hundred per cent with Lenny, he's such a duplicitous bastard but I think I've calmed things down."

"Thanks."

"It's the least I could do isn't it?" Victoria said. "After all I got you into this and I've become quite fond of you along the way. Are you out celebrating tonight?"

"Yeah I think we might be having the odd pint or seventeen."

"Enjoy yourself Gerry and be careful."

∞

I'm driving Aiden to Merry Hill to pick up Emm from Macdonald's at teatime. It turns out that Emm is not short for Emma, but Emmeline and again, not as I'd expected after the Hot Chocolate ditty but Emmeline Pankhurst as her dad's a strong socialist and a shop steward. Emm likes to play the part of a thick Black Country wench but in reality she's very intelligent and is working at MacDonald's to pay her way through University. Emm is a little on the plump side, probably puppy fat but she's vivacious and quick to break into a hearty laugh. What's really obvious to me though is the change she's brought about in Aiden. Since meeting her he's become a totally different person and none the worse for that.

Emm spots us as we come in and shouting. 'Oi'll get mi coat,' disappears through a door at the end of the counter.

At the same time that she reappears, two men come down the spiral staircase that leads from the upstairs seating area. To my total surprise one of them is none other than Lenny and he's in the company of a swarthy man clad in a black leather jacket.

"Hello, er Mr Daniels," I volunteer hesitantly.

Giving me a withering look he pushes past us without speaking.

"Who the hell does he think he is?" Aiden asks, making to go after him. Emm has also worked a positive effect on his vocabulary.

I stop him and explain our connection.

"I suppose that's fair enough then seeing as how you're tupping his Missus."

"It's just that it's such a strange place for him to be," I said. "I mean, he's loaded, he can afford to eat anywhere."

"Perhaps he likes burgers," Aiden suggests.

"No he doesn't," says Emm. "He comes in every week, same day, same time. Whoever he meets they always have a coffee and sit at the same corner table upstairs."

"Have you ever noticed what they talk about?"

"No, cleaning tables isn't really my job but if it's quiet I do it to keep busy. Anyway if ever I go near their table they always clam up. The one he meets is always a foreigner, usually that one."

"A foreigner, where from?"

"I don't know but somewhere in Eastern Europe would be my guess."

∞

Conveniently St Patrick's Day has fallen on a Friday and we have tickets for the Irish Centre in Digbeth. After I left the lads yesterday, invitations had been extended to Emm, Lyndsey and Violet and they'd all graciously accepted. While the rest of us have settled for a sprig of shamrock, Lyndsey and Violet are clad from head to foot in various shades of green including green hair. We enjoy a great night to the accompaniment of a non-stop supply of bands, contemporary and traditional, electric and acoustic, mostly amateurs thrown together for the night. We dance to them all and drink to them all as we pay our annual homage to the country that has turned us into refugees. In the spirit of the occasion everyone quaffs pints of Guinness, including the girls, who match us drink for drink. By the end of the evening, although my judgement may be a little blurred I think I'm probably the worse for wear of the seven of us.

The minibus we've booked to take us home duly turns up. The girls are dropped off first followed by the other three at their digs and finally me. I pay the driver and as he pulls away I wobble towards my front door. There's something familiar about the car parked outside my flats and the figure that emerges I recognise immediately although I'm in no condition to take evasive action. Harry Brown throws me into the back of the car as if I'm a feather pillow, a feather pillow that has disturbed his sleep. He climbs in after me, crushing me against a leering Jermaine.

Chapter 15
Up On The Roof – The Drifters

I recognise the back of Lenny's head in the passenger seat as his red neck bulges over the collar of his shirt. The driver is unknown to me and as we pull away no one breaks the silence. I'm not sure about making a tentative enquiry but decide it may be better not to know where we're going. Eventually we reach Wolverhampton town centre and pull into a multi-story car park, not stopping until we reach the open air of the top level.

The car screeches to a halt and all of the doors are flung open. I'm dragged out and pushed over to the small wall that looks out over the street a long, long way below us. A drunk tacks his way along the opposite pavement and a couple of young girls give him a wide berth as they hurry on their way. No members of the constabulary are in evidence as Harry and Jermaine take post either side of me and Lenny stands in front, wearing a camel coat, black leather gloves and lighting a fat cigar. The driver stands slightly behind him.

"Paddy," says Lenny sounding encouragingly amiable, despite the deliberate use of the wrong name but I realise I'm clutching at straws. "I don't know if you suffer with amnesia Paddy but did I or did I not take the trouble to warn you before Christmas to keep out of my affairs?"

"You did and I've never had trouble sleeping thanks."

"And were you or were you not at my house yesterday?"

Having realised that my attempt at levity was probably misplaced, I'm quite pleased that he's either missed the joke or ignored it.

"I was," I say feeling suddenly very sober.

"And then I bump into you again today. Are you bloody stalking me?"

"No, that was pure coincidence, I was picking someone up."

"Let's throw him off boss."

"Shut up Jermaine, I'll ask the Mick for advice before I ask you."

I make a mental promise to myself that if the leap into infinity becomes the chosen option I won't go alone. I'll reveal everything I know about Jermaine's fling with Victoria.

"That's it then boys," says Lenny. "I'll see you around Paddy or to be accurate I won't if you know what's good for you."

"It's Gerry not Paddy," I say helpfully, as he climbs back into the car leaving me thinking that I may have gotten away with it.

At that very moment I experience the most excruciating pain I've ever known as a fist connects with my kidneys, courtesy I presume of Harry Brown as he was on that side. I hit the tarmac and find myself looking at Jermaine's expensively shod feet as he lays into me. After the sickening agony of the initial blow these kicks seem fairly mild, almost a convenient distraction and I force myself to smile up at him, until he aims a kick at my head. It's at this point that Harry pulls him away.

"Leave it. We're not supposed to kill him."

As they get back into the car, the front window glides down.

"Keep your nose out of my business arsehole and your dick out of my wife or you will go flying," says Lenny and the nub of his cigar bounces off my head as the car pulls away.

I lie there for a while unable to convince myself that I really should confront the increase in pain that I know any movement will bring. Eventually I manage to get to my feet and hobble over to sit on the wall. My mobile seems to have survived the kicking and I punch in Lyndsey's number. After an age a listless 'hello' slurs down the airways.

Once I've established that she's *compos mentis* I outline my situation.

"Stay right where you are Gerry, we'll get a cab and be there in half an hour."

∞

I'm being treated in the Accident & Emergency Department of Wolverhampton General when the police arrive. A tired looking young doctor has just finished his examination and a pretty West Indian nurse is helping to prop me up on the bed. I realise I'm getting old as the Health Service appears to be in the hands of people little older than my year elevens.

"Are you comfortable luv?" she asks, flashing a lovely smile that contradicts the tiredness around her eyes.

"Well I've got two hundred pounds in the Post Office." I receive the old fashioned look that I probably deserve until the penny drops and she dissolves into one of the most fantastic laughs I've ever heard.

"Yo should be on the stage," she says in a broad Wolverhampton accent.

"The next one out of town?" I ask.

"Ar that's the one but no it's nice to have a laugh ennit? Especially at this time of night when we should really be tucked up in bed."

"Thanks for the offer but I don't think I'm up to it just now."

"Cheeky sod."

The girls had called the police and are in the process of outlining the story to a uniform constable, one in each ear. Eventually when he's had enough he puts a hand up each side and firmly says. 'Shut up,' which amazingly, as they're both still a little worse for wear they do.

"Are you Gerald Wilson?" The PC asks me.

"Well its Gerry Wilson actually."

"As soon as they discharge you from here I'll take you back to the station. We need you to clear up some facts."

"Can we come with him?" Lyndsey asks.

"You'll have to make your own way there," the PC said. "Do you know where it is?"

"We'll take a cab."

∞

The constable leads me to an interview room and abandons me there. After about twenty minutes of twiddling my thumbs, an overweight man with a florid face and creased suit enters. I've never been anti police as such but there's something about this one that I don't like. The way he's looking me over suggests that we've already found some common ground.

"Right first things first, the name's Cartwright, D.S. Cartwright or God as far as you're concerned."

I struggle to contain a giggle. Not only because it hurts when I laugh but because this egomaniac obviously has no conception of how ludicrous his last statement makes him sound.

"Is something amusing you Sonny Jim?"

"No, my ribs are just giving me a bit of gyp."

"I understand that some friends of yours alerted us," Cartwright said. "Claimed that you'd been beaten up by a Mr Lenny Daniels and three other men."

"That's right, only he didn't personally do any of the beating it was two of the others. I can give you the names of the two that beat me up but Lenny Daniels just gave the orders."

"And why would he do that?"

"Shouldn't you be taping this or something?"

"Not until I decide there's a case to answer. Until then I'LL ask the questions and you just answer them, starting with that one."

"He thinks I've been seeing his wife."

"Seeing?"

"Having a relationship."

"Oh I see," said Cartwright. "It just so happens that my wife left me after 'seeing' another bloke. A bleedin' landscape gardener would you believe, anyway that's beside the point I'm strictly impartial in these matters. Were you, 'seeing his wife?'"

"Sort of but it's not the way you think."

"I know I'm only a thick copper and not a University educated school teacher but I believe that I'm capable of deciding what I think, thank you very much."

"I'm sorry, I didn't mean it to sound like that. Anyway it doesn't alter the fact that I've been beaten up... and kidnapped as well. I was forced into a car outside my flat and driven to a car park in Wolverhampton."

"Do you have any witnesses?"

"No."

"Well funnily enough I've already spoken to Mr Daniels tonight and very interesting it was too. You see he called us at eleven thirty-seven, said that you'd been drinking in his club all night, the Purple Flamingo, do you know it?"

"I know of it but I've never been there."

"Oh that's interesting because he said you'd been in there tonight, celebrating St Paddy's Day and

131

partying like there's no tomorrow. Then you picked a fight with a gang of lads and it was only the intervention of the club's security men that stopped you getting a really bad beating. Mr Daniels said he couldn't really blame the other lads as you'd started it, in fact you'd been a nuisance all night and the only reason he didn't throw you out was that you work with his wife. He also told me that when you were ejected you shouted, 'I'll drop Lenny Daniels in it, I'm going to tell the police that he did this to me'. Now what do you say to that?"

"I'm guessing you believe him and not me."

"What do you think? On the one hand we have a sober, respectable businessman who can provide a number of sober witnesses. On the other we have an Irish teacher who has imbibed rather too freely and comes up with an episode of 'The Soprano's.'"

"It's a waste of time coming to the police. I might as well have taken care of it myself."

"I will just make a note of that," said Cartwright. "Now, should anything untoward happen to Mr Daniels, we'll know where to come won't we? Is there anything sensible that you'd like to add?"

"Yes it's all a pack of lies. What about security cameras? All the clubs have them now, let's see this so called altercation."

"They're waiting to be repaired."

"I've got witnesses that I was in the Irish Centre all night from eight o'clock until two thirty, you've got to believe me."

"Are these witnesses by any chance friends of yours?"

"Yes."

"Well Mr Daniels can produce a couple of dozen witnesses who will say that you were in his club causing trouble. So put yourself in my shoes, what would you do?"

I don't know whether Cartwright's bent or not but then I can't put up a compelling argument either. I'm tired, hung-over and hurting like Billy-O. I decide to cut my losses and get out of this place. Lyndsey and Violet are outraged when I tell them but after I explain things they understand my plight and want to take me home with them to nurse me back to health. I thank them but decide to go back to my own flat, preferring to suffer in splendid isolation, the wounded animal in its lair. I've been well and truly done up like a kipper by Lenny Daniels.

∞

I go to the doctor Monday morning and he signs me off work for a week. The girls are being diamonds doing my shopping as well as cooking and cleaning for me. The lads had visited me on Saturday afternoon but I heard no more from them until Monday evening when Shaun turns up.

"How are you boy?" Shaun asks.

"I'm fine. Well I'm on the mend anyway thanks."

"Here's something that might make you feel better," he says although he has no bag that might contain grapes. "Some of the boys got together and paid your friends a visit."

"What do you mean?"

"When word got round about what happened we could have had an army, we were turning people away. The crew we picked dressed in black, ski masks, camouflage jackets the works. A vanload of us jumped the fella and his mates Saturday night. Mad Jimmy Callaghan did the talking you know how he's always boasting that he was a runner for the Provo's when he was young, anyway he seemed to have all the lingo off pat. So we just tickled them up a bit with pick axe handles and hinted that if they as much as looked funny at you again then they could wave goodbye to their kneecaps. The boss and the half caste were shiteing themselves but that big fella's a hard bastard, he just kept snarling at us, never bowed his head at all."

"This is terrible, the police will think I organised it."

"Don't worry, they won't dare go to the police."

"I just wish you hadn't done it, I mean what if you'd been caught?"

"Listen, we were all volunteers and anyway I did it because I don't like bullies. You're a decent bloke Gerry and you don't deserve that sort of treatment. And I suppose if I'm honest, deep down I enjoyed it. So that's it, never worry about things that you can't change Gerry."

"Sorry Shaun, I didn't mean to sound ungrateful."

"It's alright, have you seen 'Her Ladyship' since it happened?"

"No, I'm sort of hoping it'll put her off and things will cool down a bit."

∞

I carry the hope that Victoria's ardour has been dampened until Friday afternoon when the Ladyship in question turns up with chocolates, fruit and flowers.

"Darling I'm so sorry," she says, kissing me on the cheek. "I gave Lenny the mother and father of all dressing downs as soon as I found out what had happened. Your little friend came and told me off at school. How are you now?"

"I'm pretty much A1 now."

"Good I've got some news that should cheer you up." I offer a silent prayer that she hasn't got a gang of her friends together to give Lenny a kicking. "Believe it or not Lenny and the gruesome twosome got beaten up themselves on Sunday. He said it was some troublemakers at the club that did it but anyway its poetic justice isn't it? What goes around comes around or whatever it is they say."

This is good news. If Lenny hasn't told Victoria the truth then he's unlikely to go to the police. I decide to leave well alone and keep her in the dark.

"You're coming out with me tonight," Victoria informs me. "I'm going to cheer you up."

"I don't think we should," I say hopefully.

"Oh don't worry about Lenny, he's off to Jersey on business tomorrow and he's staying the night at wherever it is they catch the plane from. I'm meeting three of the girls for an evening out and they're all bringing an escort, so you're surely not going to make me look a saddo by being the only one without a date are you?"

I know it's playing with fire but the nice thing about playing with fire is that at least it keeps you warm. Life since Alison has been fairly cold, there's been no romance and my only real friends are Shaun and the girls. Being a builder, Shaun might well move on at any time to follow the work. The girls frequently speak of getting out of 'this lousy country,' by moving to LA, Sydney, Barcelona, New York, Paris, Rome, Madrid or anywhere else that takes their fancy on 'A Place in the Sun,' or 'The Holiday Programme.'

"Where are we going?" I ask.

"Just for a drink, smart casual. I'll pick you up at eight thirty."

Chapter 16
Girls And Boys – Blur

The Hummingbird Hotel is a small, cosy establishment by today's standards and is situated next to a posh housing development on the edge of the greenbelt. We pull onto its car park.

"Jenna must be here already," says Victoria. "That's her little lemon Carrera over there. She has a thing about lemon, definitely not yellow has to be lemon."

As we enter the bar I see the other three couples seated around a table at the far end of the room. Even from this distance it's easy to tell that the blokes are all good looking, well groomed and smartly turned out.

"I'm out of my depth here," I whisper to Victoria. "They all look like off duty movie stars."

"Don't worry you're a much better person than any of them."

Despite the advice I worry anyway, and that's before I've had time to take in the women. Jenna looks stunning, not surprisingly she's arrayed in a little black number with a tasteful hint of lemon. The other two wouldn't have been out of place in 'Footballers' Wives' and give me a look that makes me feel very Sunday League.

Introductions are made for my benefit, as the others already know each other. The hunks are John, Mark and Freddie although I'm not sure in which order. Tanya and Chardonnay actually turn out to be Serena and Diana. As the chatter develops we drift into a male-female divide.

A dark haired Adonis with designer stubble asks, "What do you do?"

I consider subterfuge but decide that he probably knows the answer anyway.

"I'm a teacher."

"Oh yes... and how old are the kids?"

"My own class are sixteen year olds but I teach a range of ages."

"Boys or girls."

"Both."

"You must get lots of offers then, you know nubile young Lolita's with a crush on teacher. 'Don't stand so close to me,' and all that," he croons the song and smirks as the other two seem to take a sudden interest.

I know I'm on a loser here, as whatever I say will make me sound prim and holier than thou.

"It's not like that when you're there," I say.

"You must have had offers though?"

"Of course I have but I'm not a paedophile and I don't fancy being out of work and in jail. Anyway what do you do?"

"I'm an accounts manager."

"That must be interesting," I say automatically but before I can qualify this, his face tells me he's taken offence. Stifled laughs from the other two confirm this.

"*Touché*," says Mark. "And you only got the job because it's the family business. You're as thick as two planks really, aren't you Freddo?"

"Well it's better than being a pimp or a gigolo which is all you are Mark."

"I run a *bona fide* escort service. Believe me tonight is purely gratis, I don't mix business and pleasure."

While this petty squabbling is in full flow the ladies get up.

Victoria throws me a key saying. "If you're longer than fifteen minutes I'll start without you," causing much laughter from the others.

I've taken to John more than the other two and as the ladies leave, he brings over a round of doubles. "Come on lads, bit of Dutch courage before we do our duty. It's a dirty job but someone's got to do it."

As we head up to the rooms, John points mine out and after a little fumbling with the lock I go in. Victoria is already in the bed and the room is only illuminated by a very dim wall light. I undress quickly and slip between the sheets.

"Am I glad to get away from them?" I ask, rhetorically.

"Including that bitch Jenna?" A teasing voice that I immediately recognise as belonging to Jenna replies.

"I'm sorry," I say jumping backwards out of the bed. "I must have come into the wrong room."

"No you didn't," she says, throwing open the bedclothes. "Please, come back to bed. Vicky and I did a swap, do you mind?"

The only possible answer without the risk of causing great offence, could be 'no,' so I give it.

"Oh good, Vicky said you might well storm off in a huff. I'm glad you didn't."

"It's just that I'm still a bit of an innocent abroad. Where I come from people don't do this sort of thing."

"Vicky told me all about your past. She said you're shocked when she suggests anything in the least bit kinky but that your *naïveté* is infectious and it makes her feel like a teenager again."

"I think I'm losing my innocence fast but can I get something clear. What you're saying is that Victoria offered me to you as a sort of sex toy."

Jenna stifles an involuntary laugh. "I'm sorry about laughing and about not consulting you but Vicky said you'd run a mile otherwise. It's just that we share everything, we have no secrets from each other and she wanted to share you with me. Can you ever find it in your heart to forgive us?"

"Of course." I answer without thinking.

"So you'll stay."

"Yes." I have no alternative really and then wonder why on earth I would want one. She's beautiful and the only attachment I have at the moment is Victoria, who has arranged all of this anyway.

Jenna kneels over me on the bed and slipping out of her bra, takes my hands and places them on her breasts.

"Do you like them?"

They're large for someone with such a sylph like figure and feel a little too firm, as well as seeming to defy all natural forms of gravity but again there's really only one possible answer.

"They're very nice."

She laughs. "Is that the best you can manage? They cost over twenty grand but I know what you mean though, I'd rather have Vicky's real ones."

We make love twice and it becomes even more obvious that she and Victoria share all of their secrets. Afterwards we lie on sheets, soaked in sweat and mutual satisfaction. Jenna sings quietly and quite beautifully, it's a Keane song although I can't remember the title.

I decide to broach something that's been bothering me since our last meeting.

"You know you told me last time we met that Lenny might have connections with the Russian Mafia?"

"Yes."

"How do you know?"

"Oh Serena told me and Diana has mentioned it too."

"What about Victoria, or your husband have they told you?"

"Vicky says she doesn't know or care where he gets his money. Simon goes out of his way to avoid

Lenny if he can but he has said that he doesn't know where Lenny keeps finding the money to expand his business.   As I told you before, he supports the gangster theory.   Lenny started off with the family car leasing business, it was a good solid going concern but it was all he had.   Now he has car sales pitches, a driving school, a nightclub and some other things that I can't remember but Simon did mention some dodgy imports and exports.   I assumed he was talking about drugs, although most of this is still only hearsay."

"So you don't know any of it for a fact?"

"No of course not, Serena and Diana can be a pair of malicious bitches.   I wouldn't worry too much about it though, let's get some sleep."

The following morning we shower.   While Jenna is putting her face on and I'm dressing, a tap on the door presages the arrival of Victoria.

"How did you find it with a younger model Gerry?"

"It was in just the same place as with you Gran."

"You cheeky sod, you'll pay for that later.   Can I have him back now Jen?"

"Of course, how was it for you Vic?"

"Oh you know John, he's a nice fella and he bangs away like a steam hammer but his conversation leaves a lot to be desired."

"I know, still you can't have everything can you?"

"Why not, I want everything but that's me all over isn't it?   Anyway we're off now, I'll see you for coffee on Monday and we can pick over the bones of Gerry's performance."

"Bye Vicky, bye Gerry and don't worry you were very good."

Chapter 17
Hanging On The Telephone – Blondie

I eat a hearty breakfast, while Victoria almost polishes off an entire croissant before we return to Chez Daniels. I'm still a little uneasy about Victoria's reassurances that Lenny won't return at any moment, as she seems to thrive on taking risks but as the decision to stay is seemingly out of my hands I do my best to relax and go with the flow.

"How did it go last night?" She asks brightly.

This is very dodgy ground. Too complimentary would suggest Victoria pales by comparison while not enough enthusiasm will no doubt be relayed back to Jenna.

"It was good. I was shaking but she was really nice to me."

"As nice as I am?"

"Er, different." I thrash around as suitable words elude me. "She thinks the world of you she talks about you a lot."

"The feeling's mutual, I'd trust Jenna with anything, men, money, secrets, especially secrets. But I notice you've very cleverly sidestepped my question. So if it was different was it better or worse?"

"You know the answer to that already. You've spoilt me for anyone else."

"You're a sycophant but I forgive you."

"What are we going to do today?" I ask.

"Well I've spent a very boring night with John, as I said he's very competent but very earnest when it comes to sex. I need a bit of fun, a little variety."

"Oh bloody hell, not the chandelier?"

"You know I'd never be that obvious, come with me."

We go up to the usual spare bedroom.

"Undress and lie on the bed," she says.

"What, everything?"

"The lot."

While I strip, Victoria unlocks a bedside cabinet and as I lie on the bed she produces two chiffon scarves and a pair of handcuffs.

"I've a very low pain threshold."

"I'd never hurt you," she says as she cuffs my hands to the headboard. "Not unless you ask for it anyway."

"What then?" I ask as she ties my ankles to the bottom of the bed. Apart from feeling very silly I don't think I've ever felt so vulnerable.

"Let's see what we've got," she says and delving into the cupboard produces a feather, a jar of edible chocolate body paint, a state of the art vibrator, a bottle of baby oil and a torch.

"What do you use the torch for?" I ask, puzzled.

"To find the fuse-box if we have a power cut," she replies matter of factly.

"Have got a conveyor belt and a cuddly toy in there as well?" I ask, trying to cover my growing embarrassment.

145

"I've got the most erotic sex toy known to mankind or womankind come to that and it can't be bought in any shop."

"A fondue set?"

"My imagination." She says as she gets up and clicking a switch on the phone, leaves the room.

I lie there, wondering what I should do. I settle on twiddling my thumbs as it's about all I can manage at the moment.

The disembodied voice of Victoria filters through the telephone's speaker. "It's terribly hot in here, I'm so glad that I'm alone in the house it means I can slip out of my clothes." The sultry tones describe the removal of each item in far greater detail than I'd have thought possible. "Mm that's better, think I'll lie down on the bed."

"My breasts are just…" A door slams. Bugger me I'm impressed, she even does her own sound effects.

"Vicky! It's me." The unmistakeable mockney twang of Lenny violates the ether.

"Darling! What a wonderful surprise!" I see Victoria, clad in a dressing gown flash past the door to my bedroom as it's been left ajar.

'Shut the door you witless trollop.' I mentally shout at her, unable to utter any actual words.

"You couldn't resist coming home so that I can drag you off to bed for a day of unbridled passion could you?" She gushes as she skips down the stairs.

Even in the dire situation I find myself, I can't help but be impressed by her nerve.

146

"No I'm not staying long, you can fix me a drink though. I've a call to make but I'll do it in the bedroom."

"Here use my mobile."

"I'll use the house phone, its long distance and I don't want to risk losing the line."

"What happened to Jersey?"

"I left some papers here but I can still get back down in time for a later flight."

I can hear Lenny's laboured breathing as he climbs the stairs and then a flash of orange as his fake tanned head passes the door. I can't believe that he hasn't looked in. The speaker crackles into life again.

I hear Lenny's voice. "Silly mare's left the bleedin' phone off the hook." Followed by a click and then a dial tone. Lenny punches in a long number and after a few seconds is rewarded with a reply.

"Ja," says a curt guttural foreigner.

"Yuri?"

"Lenny it is I,Yuri. The shipment is ready to send, have you made all of the arrangements at that end?"

"Yeah, I can offload at least half of it straight into the schools and the rest I'll have no trouble shifting on the street pitches."

"That is good, I will set the wheels in motion and see you next week in the usual place."

"Nice one Yuri, Ciao."

So, Lenny is involved in drug smuggling and not only that but he's selling them in schools, possibly even my school. I'm so shocked I almost forget my immediate predicament. Suddenly all other thoughts are banished from my brain by the sight of Victoria walking past the door, carrying a drink but sans dressing gown, or anything else except high heels.

"Darling, are you sure I can't tempt you?"

"Only with the drink." Within a few seconds the orange blur flashes past again followed by a more leisurely and attractive one in flesh tones.

I hear more conversation taking place downstairs and about five minutes later. "Bye Vicky," followed by the slamming of a door.

I hear Victoria come back upstairs and she sensually slinks back into the room, dressing gown hooked over her shoulder and a smug smile on her face.

"There's no turn on quite like the excitement of almost being caught, is there?"

I can think of a thousand answers to this but settle for. "It depends where you're looking at it from."

"Oh yes, well, looking at it from here it's shrunk a bit since I left but I'm sure I can do something about that."

"Just set me free please, you could have got me murdered. Why didn't you shut the door?"

"The doors to all of the rooms are open when they're not in use. If this one had been closed he'd have wondered why and looked in. That's why I came on to him, I knew the one thing guaranteed to get him out of the house pronto would be to sexually harass him. I'm far too much for Lenny these days."

"It was still a big risk but it's all just a game to you isn't it?"

"I'm so sorry Darling, let me make it up to you," she says, climbing over me and despite my short-lived and feeble protestations, I have to admit that I forget all about being scared.

Chapter 18
Trouble – Coldplay

It starts like any other school day although I'm a little late arriving it's nothing drastic. Year nine for double English literature sets the wheels in motion. We fight a pitched battle with 'The Taming of the Shrew' and the Shrew wins a narrow points victory. I enjoy a stroll around the yard at break time, as it seems a waste to spend such a pleasant spring day indoors. The second part of my morning should have been free but instead I'm filling in for yet another of Miss Lewis's visits to the dentist, I can only presume she's run out of family cadavers to bury. I don't really mind, it's History with year eight and we enjoy a merry session reviewing the repeal of the Corn Laws. At a little after eleven o'clock our concentration is broken by Mr Jeavons.

"I'll take over here," he whispers to me. "You're to go to see Miss Francis in the staff room."

"Is she ill?" I ask, immediately concerned.

"I don't know," says Jeavons, indicating towards the kids with his eyebrows.

I quickly gather my things together and head for the staff room where I find Lyndsey sitting alone, face wreathed in a strange blankness.

"Lyndsey, what's the matter?"

She looks at me and eventually heaves a huge sigh.

"Everything. I got back to my classroom after the break and all hell had broken loose. There's been a row brewing for a long time between Darren

Johnson and Marcus Rose and it had finally erupted. By the time I broke my way into the circle, Marcus was on top of Darren and seemed to be throttling him. I shouted at him to let go but he seemed to be totally out of it. I panicked and hit him around the back of the head, more of a slap than anything. But Marcus fell sideways and hit his head on a desk. There was quite a lot of blood and they think he may be concussed. He's been taken to hospital as a precaution."

"Bloody hell."

"Mark Shadwell told me to come to his office at twelve o'clock and to bring someone with me. He said he wouldn't be surprised if I didn't at least lose my job over this and the best thing I can do is to admit to the misconduct charge and hope for leniency when the official hearing comes up. Would you come with me I couldn't think of anyone else, only I'm not in the Union. I always meant to join but never got around to it?"

"Of course I will but I'm not sure that you should be putting your hands up to anything yet. I wish I knew a bit more about this sort of thing."

At this point the door opens and Victoria enters the room. "Hello, what are you two plotting?"

Between us we repeat everything that Lyndsey has just told me.

"Bloody cheek," she says. "You stop the little shits from killing each other and this is how management thank you."

"Lyndsey's asked me to go in with her, how do you think we should handle it?"

"Would you like me to come in with you as well Lyndsey?" Victoria asks.

"Is that allowed?" asks Lyndsey. "He only said to bring one person."

"Would you like me to be there?" Victoria repeats.

"Yes."

"Then it's allowed."

∞

Lyndsey knocks on the headmaster's door and the three of us file in.

"I thought I said to bring one person," says Mark. "This is only a fairly unofficial preliminary meeting."

"It shouldn't be a problem then should it?" asks a belligerent Victoria.

"Very well," Mark sighs. "Can you explain exactly what happened again Miss Francis?"

Lyndsey recounts the events for a third time in short duration. I notice that Shara is sitting behind the desk quietly taking notes.

"Are you aware of what you did wrong Miss Francis?" Mark asks.

"Yes."

"Then can you explain why you took the course of action that you did, rather than for example pulling him away or calling for assistance?"

"No."

"Hold on a moment," says Victoria, butting in. "If this is a 'fairly unofficial preliminary meeting,'" she imitates Mark's voice. "Why the cross examination and why is the court stenographer sitting there taking contemporaneous notes?"

"I decide what the ground rules are in here," says Mark.

"Typical," Victoria says. "As my old Granny used to say, 'you can always tell a Yorkshireman, but you can't tell him much.'"

"Do we really need to lower ourselves to personal insults? I like people to be blunt and come to the point but..."

"But nothing," Victoria is working up a head of steam now. "If you really like people to be blunt then fine, is this blunt enough for you. You can stuff your rules and your questions and stuff your court stenographer as well if you want. You were expecting to persecute a young girl who's probably still in shock but you've got me instead and I don't scare easily so don't even dream of trying it with me."

"Very well no more questions but you do realise Miss Francis that your actions amount to common assault and I must therefore suspend you until the official hearing. Until that time you are barred from the school premises."

"May I say something here?" And it would be a very brave man that would attempt to stop Victoria Daniels in this mood. "On the subject of common assault am I correct in thinking that last term you enjoyed a difference of opinion with Mr Patar?"

"That incident has been dealt with to everyone's satisfaction," said Mark looking worried.

Alen Patar is one of our teachers and the incident in question happened after Alen, a heavy-duty smoker was indulging in a crafty drag in a cloakroom during a break time. On the day in question the inclement weather was obviously too great a risk to his health, so Alen passed on that responsibility to the Capstan full strength. Mark found Alen breaking the no-smoking rules and instead of using official procedures, lost his rag and physically threw Alen against a wall, threatening him into the bargain. This was all hushed up and to our surprise no more was said of it. Billy Singh another Asian teacher told me that Alen is low caste and is terrified of Shara, who in turn had bullied him into silence.

"Only because the Local Education Authority didn't get to hear about it but who knows what they might pick up if Miss Francis is suspended. They might even start looking into other things, such as headmasters who promote their 'favourites' to deputy head over the heads of better qualified people." Victoria made exclamation marks around favourites with her fingers, just in case anyone's in doubt about who it is she's referring to.

I expect a storm from Mark in return but the wind seems to have abandoned his sails. "Look, this is standard procedure in these cases. I have to suspend Lyndsey but I'll emphasise that it's totally without prejudice. I'll make sure that it's on full pay however long it takes and I'll write a glowing reference for the hearing."

Victoria looks at Lyndsey. "Is that okay with you love?"

Lyndsey nods.

"Very good," says Mark. "Just one other thing Lyndsey, you know Mrs Banks is your Union representative don't you? My advice is to go and see her. It won't do you any good at the hearing to threaten me, as I have no say in their findings whatever. You'll need to fight it on proper grounds."

"I'm not in the Union," Lyndsey says disconsolately.

"Go and see her anyway, throw yourself at her mercy. I know Julie Banks, she's a decent woman she'll not turn her back on you."

"Thanks Mr Shadwell."

"Any meetings you have with her will have to be held elsewhere though. As soon as you've collected your personal things you must not come back into the school. Mr Wilson, may I ask that you remain with Miss Francis until she leaves? See that she gets home and preferably that there's someone with her."

I nod my assent and as we troop out Lyndsey thanks Victoria.

"Think nothing of it," says Victoria. "It doesn't mean we're going to be bosom buddies or anything like that. I only did it because Mark Shadwell's a blown up pompous little bully and I'd never willingly miss an opportunity to piss on his parade.

155

Oh and never forget my favourite motto about dealing with the kids, 'if you can't beat 'em, what's the point of being a teacher,'" she adds with a smile.

I help Lyndsey carry her personal belongings to her car.

"Will you be alright on your own this afternoon? Shall I ring Violet and tell her what's happened?"

"Don't be daft I'll be fine, I'll look on it as a holiday. If you ring Violet she'll only get upset and come dashing home, I can tell her all about it tonight."

"I'll go and see Mrs Banks this afternoon and get some advice."

"If she is willing to help me then ask her to come round ours for a meal whenever it suits her. I'll get Violet to knock up something special."

Chapter 19
I Can Help – Billy Swann

During afternoon break-time I warily approach my quarry in the staff room.

"Mrs Banks, excuse me," I say.

I notice she's reading *Les Miserables* and that it's in French. She stops stirring her coffee and looks up with an enquiring smile. It's all I can do not to turn tail and run. This is the same effect that Victoria exerts on me, albeit in a different way. Where Victoria has always seemed sharp and prickly as well as supremely confident, Mrs Banks enjoys equal self-assurance but exudes an easy-going congeniality. I haven't experienced this charm at close quarters before today, mainly because being Head of Art and Design she inhabits a different departmental sphere to mine.

"It's Mr Wilson isn't it?" Mrs Banks asks pleasantly.

This throws me a little as I don't feel mature enough to be called 'Mr Wilson' by someone as grown up as Mrs Banks.

"Er, call me Gerry, please."

"Only if you call me Julie, Mrs Banks sounds so stuffy. I think I may know what you're going to ask me, is it about Lyndsey Francis?"

"Yes you've heard what happened then?"

"It would be impossible not to in this place, the rumours spread like wildfire."

"The thing is Lyndsey's not in the Union."

"I know but I'd never let that stop me from helping a colleague in trouble."

"She's been meaning to join for a long time but she's not the most organised of people."

"As I've said, I'd be only too glad to help her anyway but if she agrees to join now and pays a few back subs, I'll do her a membership that will testify that she joined weeks ago. It certainly won't hurt at the hearing to have the Union in her corner."

"That would be great," I said, pleased at how well it was going. "Lyndsey said that if you were willing to help then I'm to ask if you'd like to go round their flat for dinner one evening to talk things over. She's not allowed onto school premises at the moment."

"I'd like that and actually I'm free this evening, do you think that would be too short notice? I was just thinking that I can probably set her mind at rest a little and the sooner that happens, the better."

"Yeah that'll be great, she tries to hide it but I think she's quite frightened by the whole thing. Anyway, she said whenever suited you would be fine, shall I tell you how to get there?"

"Ah we may have a minor problem there, I don't drive."

"I could pick you up." I jump in without considering all of the pitfalls in this offer.

"Thank you, what time?"

"Would seven-thirty be alright?"

"Lovely, I'll jot down my address and some directions. Oh and my phone number in case you get lost."

I'm not really sure whether I should broach the subject but decide I really must. "You know that Lyndsey's er..."

"Gay," she whispers.

"Yes."

"I had guessed but thanks for being considerate enough to let me know, I'll see you later."

∞

Julie lives in a village called Blakedown that is situated on the A456 Birmingham to Kidderminster road. I remember Lyndsey once telling me as we drove through Blakedown that it was home to a Chinese Garage. Finding my blank look hilarious, she explained that it was the Blakedown Garage. Despite its diminutive size it boasts a railway station that somehow escaped Dr Beeching's cuts and makes it possible for commuters to live in such a lovely place while earning their living in a less lovely place. I've had sufficient time to tidy up my trusty steed as well as myself and the purchase of a new strawberry air freshener has achieved for the car what a spray of Kouros has done for me.

The directions are spot on and I drive straight there The 'there' in question is the front door of a chocolate box country cottage, that at the right time of year I feel sure must have roses growing

159

around this very same door that I currently find myself knocking.

"Come in," says Julie. "I'm sorry I'm not quite ready, I've been pulling bits and pieces together that might be useful and lost track of the time. Sit down, I won't offer you a drink as you're driving but would you like a coffee or a soft drink?"

I settle on a coke.

"I'm a bit early actually, I left plenty of time to find it but your directions were very clear."

"That's good because we didn't have much time to talk this afternoon did we? Well actually I don't like talking too much in the staff room, too many wagging ears. I wanted to apologise, I don't think I've ever made the effort to introduce myself to you at school."

"I think it's me that should be doing the apologising. I was the one that was already there when you arrived. It's just that I've never been very good at that sort of thing."

"Oh well let's call it quits and make a fresh start from here. The little that I know about you is straight from rumour control I'm afraid. I'm sure that most of it is probably fiction."

I recount the tale of my life so far and how I come to be here. I don't know if there are any rumours about my affair with Victoria doing the rounds at school but I judge it best not to mention it, after all it might even sound as though I'm boasting.

160

Since entering the cottage I've been feasting my eyes on the décor. In contrast to the traditional look of the outer shell, the inner sanctum could not be more different, not a horse brass to be seen. Not only that but everywhere you look there are things of interest, a frieze of ceramic tiles on the wall, some type of old farm implement adorned with silky scarves and numerous other disparate pieces, yet they all meld together beautifully. Seeing this place, along with my recent visits to the girls flat and Victoria's house hammers home to me that I live in a tip.

"Your house is really fantastic."

"I was able to afford it because James gave me a very generous divorce settlement," she says. "That's it, I think I've found everything now, let's get going and I'll fill you in on the way."

We set off and Julie continues. "As I was saying..."

"There's no need to tell me if you don't want to," I interrupt. "I'm sorry I wasn't prying."

"Don't worry, it's hardly a state secret and anyway I always think it can be so cathartic talking things over."

"Yeah, I tend to keep everything to myself."

"You've just told me about your divorce."

"I know, you're very easy to talk to."

"Thank you. Anyway, I married back in the dark days of nineteen-seventy, I bet you weren't even born were you?"

"I was just about to be."

She laughs and it makes my stomach flutter for no apparent reason.

"I was on the rebound and James, my husband was strong and decisive, he gave me a feeling of security, all the things that I hadn't been used to with my previous boyfriend. I stupidly became pregnant by accident and we ended up getting married much earlier than I'd ever intended. We had two kids and I suppose they kept us together. He was a good provider and we seemed to be the perfect happy little family."

"So what happened?"

"James is a barrister."

"I'll remember that if ever I get into any trouble," I interrupt with what I hope is a 'man of the world,' smile.

"It wouldn't help you much he's a corporate lawyer. Wouldn't dream of rubbing shoulders with the great unwashed, your annual salary might just secure his services for a few weeks."

"Wow, and he doesn't even need to mix with any criminals."

"Hold on now, I didn't say that. He works for the biggest criminals of all, the ones that rarely get caught and they rarely get caught because they employ James. Modesty was never his strong suit, something I liked when I first met him as his self-assurance seemed a breath of fresh air at the time."

"But it didn't last?"

"No, it took a long time for the penny to drop but when it did you could have heard the thud in Timbuktoo. James liked to boast to me about how deceitful his work required him to be. Do you know that hes even learnt how to hack into other people's computers? He taught me how to do it and it's surprisingly simple and untraceable if you know what you're doing. I did my dutiful wife and mother routine for a long time, like something from a nineteen sixties American sitcom. He started getting careless though and made some mistakes in his dalliances. He spent a lot of time away from home and I suppose he was easy prey to pretty, young, ambitious legal secretaries with pert breasts and firm bums."

"I'm sorry."

"It's alright," Julie smiled but the smile seemed tinged with sadness. "I don't believe in dwelling on things that are in the past. Anyway when the kids grew up and flew the nest James and I became increasingly distant, until we both arrived at the same conclusion and agreed on a divorce."

"Do you see your children?"

"Occasionally I do, they both stayed in Leeds, it's where we lived. They had their careers by then and James had his practice there. I'm always inviting them down but they're usually too busy."

"Why didn't you stay in Leeds?"

"Oh I don't know, I suppose I wanted a complete break. My mom still lives down here and she isn't getting any younger. I was at University when I became pregnant and back then pregnancy put a stop to education, career, everything. I'd wanted to be a graphic designer so when I suddenly found that I had time on my hands and enough money to live comfortably, I decided to retrain as an art teacher and here I am."

"Are you sorry that you married James?"

"I don't know, you never know for certain do you? There's a lot of truth in the saying, 'youth is wasted on the young,' but I like another saying, 'sometimes you get what you need, sometimes you get what you deserve, sometimes you get what you want, but mostly you get what you get.' I'll settle for that."

"You're a great one for the sayings."

"Sorry I'm a great one for the talking. I sometimes forget that conversation is a two way thing."

"It's alright, I'm a great one for the listening."

Julie picks up a CD that's on top of the dashboard rack. "Elmore James! Are you a fan?"

"Yes, I'm a bit old fashioned in some of my tastes although I do like a lot of modern music as well. My dad's always been a fan of the blues, I got it from him."

"We must be kindred spirits, my dad was a blues fanatic. Back then I could take it or leave it but as I've grown older I've picked up his enthusiasm. I wish now that I could have shared it with him more, he died a couple of years ago."

"I'm sorry."

"Thank you. Apart from music, art's my other love. You're not by any chance an art lover as well are you?"

"I'll hit you with a saying now, 'I may not know anything about art but I know what I like.' Which is true, I look at something and think, I like that although I've no idea why I like it."

"That doesn't matter," Julie says. "You can always learn that part of it. Perhaps I could give you some pointers sometime."

"That would be nice," I say, thinking, 'can we begin right away?' as we pull up outside the girls' flat.

∞

Before the meal Julie runs through some of the generalities of the case. She emphasises that they will be stressing three main strands. One, that Lyndsey believed that Darren Johnson's life was at risk and therefore immediate action was necessary and because of this fact drastic action wasn't out of place. Two, the injury resulted from Marcus hitting his head on a desk not from Lyndsey's slap. Three, all of this came about because of the boy's actions and it would be an injustice if Lyndsey were to be punished because of bad behaviour by the pupils.

Julie laughs when we mention Victoria's intervention.

"That's so Victoria. I'm not saying I like her but I do admire her at times," Julie says. "And it won't have done any harm to fire a shot across Mark's bows with the threat of revealing his little peccadillo's.

165

He won't dare give you anything but a glowing reference now."

Over dinner the case is put on a back burner as we engage in general chitchat. Violet and Lyndsey recall numerous embarrassing anecdotes concerning me, that I'd rather Julie didn't hear but the mood is convivial. After dinner Julie begins to bring out papers and books on employment law and tribunal procedure. I don't listen too much to the content, as it's enough to know that Lyndsey's in safe hands while I'm happy just listening to Julie's voice and observing the animation in her face as she gets to grips with her subject. I guess from what she'd told me earlier that she must be in her late forties at least, although she looks younger. She dresses well but in a different style to Victoria, more Bohemian, more flamboyant, yet as with Victoria still managing not to look like mutton dressed as lamb.

I'm in a comfortable torpor, warm, well fed and generally at peace with the world when a nudge in the ribs from Lyndsey interrupts my agreeable musings.

"Come on dozy, Julie needs a lift home and we've volunteered you."

"I'm so sorry to put you to this trouble Gerry," she says while looking genuinely sorry.

"No, it's you that's put yourself out to help us." I reply, knowing I've been looking forward to this moment all evening.

"Nonsense, I've had a lovely evening and I hope I've made three new friends."

I drive Julie home, disappointed with myself that I can't think of a plausible reason to prolong my assignation with this enchanting woman.

Chapter 20
Nobody Told Me (There'd Be Days Like These.) – John Lennon

It's a Friday and the day of the hearing has finally arrived. I've made the effort to get up early in order to see Lyndsey before school and wish her luck. I'd attempted to get the day off to go with her but as Lyndsey and Julie as well as Mark and Shara are all attending, the staffing levels simply won't allow it. Even if it had I wouldn't have been allowed into the hearing and I know she's in very good hands. As it's impossible to teach a group of children and concentrate on anything else at least I don't have much time to worry about what's happening elsewhere.

The main threat has already been neutralised. Marcus Rose's parents had been threatening to press assault charges against Lyndsey and to sue the school for lack of proper care. This situation lasted only until a combined deputation of Mark Shadwell and Julie Banks pointed out that involving the Crown Prosecution Service may lead to criminal charges against Marcus for serious assault on Darren. Not to mention a counter claim from Lyndsey for the stress suffered and the probability of Marcus being excluded from the school.

Lunchtime sees me racing to Lyndsey's flat to find out what's happened. I'd rung the LEA and they informed me that the hearing was no longer sitting but wouldn't tell me more. Surely if it had finished this early it could only be because the charges had been dropped.

Violet answers the door. "Come in Gerry," her face is fairly non-committal.

Lyndsey is on the settee, listlessly watching 'Home and Away.' I fear the worse.

"What happened?" I ask, matching Violet, lack of commitment for lack of commitment.

"The useless bastards have postponed it," explodes Lyndsey. "The Chair of the tribunal has been called away and they had no one to replace him, so I'm just supposed to kick my heels for another month."

"Well, at least you get another month off on full pay."

"I know but that's not what I want. It's not like being on holiday, I thought I'd enjoy it but I can't. It's really weird it's almost like being under house arrest. I just want to get back to work and get my life back on track."

"Sorry Lynds, if there's anything I can do just say the word."

"Thanks Gerry," she says and then her face suddenly brightens. "Hey hang on a minute, there is something... Remember your promise at Christmas?"

"You mean the baby one?"

"Yeah, at least it would give me something else to fixate on and take my mind off this. You know the world of motherhood and all that."

"I thought you might have forgotten about it by now and you know there are no guarantees that you'll get pregnant."

"I know that and if you've changed your mind and you really don't want to do it you don't have to. We know it's a lot to ask isn't it Vi?"

"Yes, if you have the slightest misgiving just say no, we won't be offended honest Gerry. We'd never make you do something you didn't want to."

"I said that I would and a Wilson's word is his bond," I said in mock serious tones and then. "But can we make it into a sort of party, you know have a smoke and a drink and a laugh. Then at least I can assuage my conscience with the fact that it's two salacious harlots taking advantage of me."

"This just gets better," says Lyndsey. "I've always wanted to be a harlot."

"I'll ring Joey at work," says Violet. "He always knows where to get the best shit around and what do you fancy to drink?"

"Definitely not beer, start with wine and then Bacardi and Coke. That should get me out of my tree but not quite incapable."

"We'll see you about eight thirty for nine then," said Violet. "Don't eat, I'll do a finger buffet 'ooh er missus.'"

"I'm looking forward to it already," I laugh, trying not to let my nerves show.

∞

Ten past two and my year elevens are half-heartedly participating in a question and answer session about 'Jude the Obscure,' when my mobile rings. I normally switch it off in class but in my current state of anxiety it's slipped my mind.

"Better answer that Mr Wilson, it might be important," chirps Claire Fletcher.

That settles it I switch the phone off without looking to see who's calling. I'd normally have made a joke of it but I'm too frazzled today. During the break I check my mobile and find a text from Victoria. 'Come O 2 house post school,' I translate this as 'come round to my house after school. Victoria has always refused to use text speak on the grounds that it's common, favouring instead a cryptic crossword type code. I feel a little ashamed of myself because although I can stand up to a bunch of sixteen year olds I still can't say no to Victoria Daniels. I'd thought she was teaching this afternoon but find her classroom deserted.

∞

The afternoon finally peters out with Jude retaining most of his obscurity. I get into my car, turn the key and after the engine struggles to turn over twice the battery dies on me. I've put off replacing it for weeks and it's finally given up the ghost. After arranging for the garage to collect it I call a cab that drops me at the Daniels homestead where Victoria opens the door.

171

"Come in quickly, Lenny's away on business but he's left one of his pet goons behind. I think it may be to keep an eye on me."

"Which one? Harry or Jermaine I mean, not which eye"

"Jermaine."

"Oh great, my favourite."

As we go through to the lounge I explain about the car.

"I've had a shit day too Gerry. On the way to school this morning some idiot slammed his brakes on in front of me and then refused to accept that the accident was his fault."

"Well technically speaking if you went into the back of him it wasn't his fault, you should leave sufficient space to stop."

"You're supposed to be here to support and comfort me, not to side with that imbecile."

"Sorry."

"Then I had a row with Mark. I ended up telling him that he could stick his job up his arse and walked out."

"Yeah but it's not official unless it's in writing is it? There should be no problem if you apologise."

"Me," she explodes. "Apologise! You don't even know what caused me to say it and yet you assume that I'm in the wrong."

"I'm sorry, what did he say?"

"It doesn't matter now, I don't know whether I want the poxy job anyway. I don't know what I want any more."

"You'll feel better tonight when you're out on the town with your friends. They'll cheer you up won't they?"

"They would if Jenna hadn't rung this afternoon to tell me that she and Serena had to cancel and the evening's off, that was the final nail in the coffin. Then I thought bollocks to the lot of them, I know who can cheer me up and that someone is you."

I attempt to intervene but get steamrollered.

"I'm going to run you a hot bath, lay out a big fluffy dressing gown, cook you a lovely meal and then fuck your brains out all night."

I feel sure that what I'm about to say is going to hurt me much more than it will Victoria but I plough on regardless.

"I'm sorry I can't, I've given Lyndsey a cast-iron promise that I'll go round and talk over what happened today, Violet's preparing a meal."

I almost feel obliged to invite her to join us but know that I can't possibly, even though I'm sure that Victoria would revel in the situation. The expected storm doesn't materialise as Victoria looks suddenly defeated, which actually turns out to be a hundred times worse than the anticipated rage.

"Make love to me," she says, almost pleading.

And I do, right then and there on the rug. For once it's gentle and all the more lovely for that. After a short time lying entwined in post coital slumber, Victoria stirs.

"That was bloody great, come on let's do it again."

173

"I can't, I told you, I have to go."

I start picking up my clothes and putting them on but Victoria grabs my trousers and runs behind the sofa.

"Come on then, if you want them you'll have to fight me for them."

I chase her around the sofa, I'm in my boxers and Victoria is totally naked. The thought crosses my mind. 'What must the neighbours think?' There are two large picture windows in here but I imagine those that inhabit the houses opposite and who are easily offended have long since developed the habit of averting their eyes. I make a lunge and we career into a six-foot tall and rather splendid, multi-faceted floor lamp. The lamp in turn comes toppling down in what seems slow motion, to crash through a glass topped table.

"Oh my God!" I shout.

"Don't worry, I never liked it anyway," said Victoria. "We've more important things to be getting on with."

"No, I've got to go but I'll help to clean up the mess first," I say, picking up some of the glass.

"Oh don't bother," says Victoria, angrily sweeping the glass from my hand. In doing this, a piece slices across the side of her forearm.

It looks a bad cut and the blood immediately runs freely onto the pristine white of the carpet and mingles into the sheepskin rug that we've just found Nirvana on.

174

"Have you got a first aid box?" I ask. "I can dress the cut and then I'll take you to the hospital."

"On the wall, in the kitchen."

I fetch it, and after cleaning the wound, make a rather neat job of applying the bandage.

"Come on, you still ought to go to hospital, it might need stitching."

"No, you go to your assignation I can get myself to A&E if I need to. You mustn't let your friends down." This is said in a voice drained of the anger that had been there until now.

"They'll understand that it's an emergency."

"No I'm fine, go to your friends now, you've made such a big thing of it I'll be angry if you don't go. I'm quite capable of getting myself to hospital"

"Can I use your phone to ring a cab?"

"Yes of course you can. No," she says, handing me her car keys. "Here take my car you can use it until you get your own back. It's booked in for repair on Monday but I'll let the garage know that you'll drop it in to them when you can."

"I can't do that, what will you do for transport?"

"Please, just take it, I want to be alone. I can get Diana to pick me up or take a cab."

"Are you sure?"

"Yes, and... Thank you Gerry."

"What for?"

"For everything, for being decent, for putting up with my moods, for making me think straight, now go. Please just go."

175

Chapter 21
Three Is A Magic Number – Blind Melon

I spend my drive to the girls flat trying to exile Victoria from my thoughts. Not an easy task as the car smells of her and seems determined to career along at the speed Victoria normally drives at. I knew that once she'd made her mind up about me leaving, I wouldn't be able to change it.

Lyndsey and Violet come to the door together and the tableau they portray immediately dispels all thoughts of Victoria as they've obviously had a lot of fun getting themselves ready. Lyndsey is the saloon girl, she's teamed red satin basque and fishnet stockings with a black bra that judging by the spillage is a little on the small side. A headband that boasts a scarlet ostrich plume sets off her ensemble. Violet has assumed the guise of a French Apache dancer in black beret and red neckerchief, wearing a skin-tight stripy jumper, black leather skirt split to the waist with black stockings and suspenders. Both sport long black eyelashes, 'all the better for fluttering at you with,' bright red lipstick and a plethora of beauty spots, both also appear considerably taller than usual due to tottering precariously on very high stiletto heels. "Hallo big boy, I'm Lady Marmalade," purrs Violet. "Looking for a good time? Charlotte the harlot is here to give you one," says Lyndsey huskily, before they both fall into a fit of the giggles. I don't need the logical powers of Sherlock Holmes or indeed the massive intellect of his brother Mycroft to deduce that they have already been sampling the grape rather freely.

"You two are tiddly," I state unnecessarily.

"Come in and start catching up," says Lyndsey. "Don't forget this is just as weird for us as it is for you, as well as being much, much, much more unnatural."

"Ah," I say, after taking a long swig from the proffered glass of Zinfandel. "But you two have safety in numbers."

"Let's forget all of that," says Violet. "We're all friends after all and if we're going to do it let's forget our inhibitions and do as you said, let's just party and enjoy ourselves."

"I'll drink to that," says Lyndsey.

"Me too," I concur, and that's just what we do. Drink long and hard, interspersed with eating, dancing, karaoke singing, air-guitar playing and some very silly party games. This carries on long enough to make me realise an important fact. I've been so wrapped up in my own misgivings over this venture that I've failed to realise that despite their bravado the girls are actually far more nervous even than I am.

Finally Violet, as usual the one to make the big decisions says. "Come on then. Gerry, bring three of the shots glasses and I'll get the peach vodka. Lynds fetch the cards, we'll go and play strip 'Stop The Bus,' on the bed."

The bed's a new one and it's the biggest futon I've ever seen. The girl's very chic boudoir is illuminated by lamps veiled with purple and red scarves and the candles that Violet is in the process of lighting.

"Have you ever played 'Stop the Bus,' Gerry?" Violet asks.

"Yes."

"Well this is just the same except that instead of losing a life, whoever calls it takes a shot of vodka and the other two take off an item of clothing, it makes it a lot more fun."

In God's great plan, being good at poker, pontoon or even bridge are all very useful skills at the right time. I've been blessed with none of these but have been gifted with what until this moment has been a questionable talent for Stop the Bus. In no time at all I'm sitting cross-legged, extremely drunk, but still wearing my shirt, tie and boxers, while playing cards with two exceedingly naked girls. I'm ashamed to say I comment that this state of undress suits them well and they should consider employing it more often. I don't remember saying this but I'm regaled with the fact the following afternoon, when I finally regain sufficient consciousness to open my eyes.

Opening my eyes is a big mistake on two counts. First it intensifies what must be the mother and father of all hangovers. Second I realise that not only am I naked on their futon but that Violet and Lyndsey are standing over me also totally naked.

It's like a bizarre version of, 'What Not To Wear,' in which the answer to the query is nothing and Trinny and Suzanna are your best friends, correction, your naked best friends. Their arms are folded and Lyndsey taps her foot as they start to recount all of the rude things I've allegedly said and done the night before. They decide that as I thought nudity suited them so well, that they're going to stay like this for the rest of the day to remind me of my misdemeanours. My senses are still dulled enough to make me believe that they're serious and that I have indeed overstepped the mark. Until that is, they give up the pretence and dissolve into laughter, falling on top of me on the bed. This could have been quite enjoyable but instead sets off a wave of nausea and my headlong rush for the toilet merely adds to their mirth.

We breakfast at three thirty in the afternoon. Violet has dosed me with what she assures me is her, very well tried and tested hangover cure and it does indeed seem to do the trick.

I'm concentrating intensely on my food, still not sure how embarrassed I should be, when out of the blue Violet asks. "Are you alright Gerry?"

"Yeah, I feel a lot better now, your 'cure all' worked wonders."

"Oh good but I didn't mean that. How are you about last night? I know you weren't totally sure about doing it."

"To be honest I can't say that I fully remember everything we did. There were a lot of blurred bits

179

and I'm not sure that we actually managed it. I think I remember but I'm not sure if I dreamt it now?"

"Did we ever manage it," giggles Lyndsey. "I can't say that it turned me on exactly but at least I know now why Lady Chatterley keeps you on the payroll."

"Last night I was too drunk to worry about what we were doing, I was more bothered about having to face you two this morning but I seem to have coped with that. My only real concern in the whole thing was that it might have a detrimental effect on our friendship and I was dreading that. Anyway I don't know what you two think but I feel that we're even closer now."

"In that case," says Lyndsey. "You might as well stay again tonight and have another go."

"Just sleep in the bed with us," says Violet. "But there'll be no pressure to perform, if anything happens it happens and if it doesn't fair enough. What do you say?"

"Yeah, that would be nice and I suppose it will improve your chances of you know..."

"Getting knocked up," shouts Lyndsey.

"I was going to put it a bit less crudely than that if I could have thought of the right words but that's what I was stumbling towards."

"Anyway Gerry, if ever the subject should come up so to speak," says Violet. "At least when you're old and grey you'll have something to boast to your mates about at the Sons of Rest."

"Yeah," added Lyndsey. "Your wild nights of passion with two red-hot, gorgeous, rampant lesbian strumpets."

"I could never tell anyone about it."

"It doesn't matter, they wouldn't believe you anyway. Would you in their place?"

"I don't suppose I would as it does all sound a bit unbelievable."

After what in the end proved to be a night that was more about love than about sex, I go home at around midday on Sunday. The girls had hatched a plan to pack a bag each and take the first available flight from Birmingham airport on Monday morning that took their fancy. I envy them their bond and decide that I definitely want a soul mate, as the Reverend Al would have put it, 'I'm so tired of being alone.'

∞

My flat, apart from seeming dingy by comparison now feels quite cold and very lonely. I need to get out of it for a while and a run over Kinver will provide the best tonic to raise my spirits. Kinver is an area of hills, woods and heathland that's tended by the National Trust and it's a place I love. The weather's not particularly cold but it's a day that's interspersed with showers that in turn have the pleasing effect of keeping the area clear of all but the most determined walkers. Running in the countryside never fails to improve

181

my mood and is always a guaranteed panacea, to whatever my latest imagined dilemma might be.

I return home and as I'm carefully locking Victoria's damaged Mercedes outside my flat, a police car draws up behind. My heart sinks as I can only think this is the long awaited revenge that Lenny has been dreaming up. No doubt some trumped up charge of criminal damage or theft of a car is about to be revealed. Two uniform police officers get out and approach me.

Chapter 22
Have You Heard? – John Mayall's Bluesbreakers

"Are you Gerald Wilson?" The first of the PC's asks.

"I'm sure Lenny Daniels has given you a good enough description."

"What's that supposed to mean?" he asks.

The older of the two policemen intervenes. "You are Gerald Wilson?"

"Yes."

"I think you'd better accompany us to the station before you say any more."

"Am I under arrest, do I have a choice?"

"You are not under arrest at the moment and therefore you do have a choice but if you refuse then you won't leave us with much option and it may look better for you in the long run to be seen to have co-operated."

"Can I have a shower first and get changed, I've been running."

"Better not keep the DI waiting sir. You can do all of that as soon as we've finished with you, we'll see that you get home again."

I get into the back of the police car. The young one puts his hand on my head as I get in and it makes me realise that I've seen this done with real criminals on the television news. The thought excites me for a second before a little chill runs through me. I'm expecting to go to the local station in Stourbridge but instead I'm informed that I'm being taken to Kidderminster. On questioning this, I'm reassured that it will all be made clear by the DI.

I'm guided along some corridors and through a door that proclaims itself to be Interview Room Three. A young uniformed officer appears to have taken over responsibility for me and asks if I'd like a drink. I plump for tea with milk and no sugar. Within minutes I'm presented with my plastic cup of black coffee.

"Sorry chief. It's all that's in the machine."

Two men, in much sharper suits than my old friend DS Cartwright enter the room and seat themselves across the table from me. They don't speak but the younger one breaks the seal on a cassette tape and loads it into the machine while the elder flicks through some papers. The tape recorder lets out a beep and the older of the two looks up at me for the first time.

"I'm DI Jenkins and this is DS Witherspoon. This interview is being recorded in accordance with the rules of the Police and Criminal Evidence Act. I must warn you that it may be regarded as evidence at any future criminal proceedings. Can you confirm that you are Gerald Lewis Wilson of Flat Five, Tennyson House, Lye, Dudley, West Midlands?"

"That's right."

"I must also inform you that you are entitled to have a solicitor present."

"Why would I need a solicitor? I've done nothing."

"As you will sir," said DI Jenkins.

"May I ask a question?" I enquired.

"Of course Mr Wilson, we appreciate your co-operation in volunteering to come to the station, please fire away."

"Well, no one has actually told me why I'm here yet."

"That's quite an interesting question," interrupts DS Witherspoon. "You agree to come to a police station without asking why."

Suddenly I'm racking my brain, had I actually asked why?

Before I can formulate a coherent reply, Jenkins re-joins the fray. "Apparently when PCs Howard and Knight first approached you, your words were," he stops here to carefully scrutinise his papers. "'I suppose Lenny Daniels has given you a good enough description.' What made you say that?"

"It's a long story."

"I'm a good listener and my shift still has another three and a half hours to go."

I run through a severely edited version of the last few months. Jenkins is as good as his word, only giving an encouraging nod here and an, 'I see,' there.

When I've finished my potted history, Witherspoon comes to life again.

"Did you see Mrs Victoria Daniels on Friday?"

"No,' I lie. "She left school early."

"So you weren't at Mrs Daniel's house at any time between the hours of fourteen hundred and eighteen hundred?"

A sickening feeling hits the pit of my stomach. They know something, but surely Victoria wouldn't tell them anything about it and she's the only one who knew I was there. My mind runs riot as all sorts of thoughts vie for supremacy. The damage to the car, could she have been involved in a hit and run and was this a cunning plan to throw the blame onto me? Surely not, but I don't know what to do and decide to stick to my guns. After all, whatever it is it'll be my word against hers. "No, I wasn't," I state confidently.

"We've checked the mobile phone company's records. It seems that Mrs Daniels sent you a text message at fourteen thirteen hours on Friday, is that correct?"

"Yes."

"And what did the message say?"

I'm not sure whether the phone company could tell them what the message actually said but decide that it's better to be safe and to tell the truth.

"It asked me to call at her house."

"And did you go?"

"Yes."

"So why did you tell us you hadn't seen her?" Witherspoon asked.

"She's married and I didn't want to cause trouble with her husband."

"And what happened when you arrived at her house?"

"We talked."

186

"Is that all?"

"Yes."

"Did you and Mrs Daniels engage in sexual intercourse?"

"No," I reply with what little confidence I can still muster.

I almost thought Jenkins had nodded off, when he looks up.

"A Mrs Hamilton registered a complaint, logged at seventeen twenty two hours on the day in question. Mrs Hamilton is a member of the local neighbourhood watch and believe me she does a lot of watching. It appears that Mrs Hamilton was walking her dog past Mrs Daniel's house when her eyes were assailed, her words not mine, by the sight of a naked man chasing what she recognised to be a naked Mrs Daniels around the sofa in front of the picture windows. In fact she was so shocked that she stopped to stare for several minutes. Mrs Hamilton gave us a very detailed description of someone who very much resembles you. Now would you like to rethink your last answer?"

I let out a long involuntary sigh and realise what a wise man Rabbie Burns was or Walter Scott or whichever Jock wrote, 'ae what a tangled web we weave when first we practice to deceive,' must have been.

"I did go to her house and we made love."

"And why did you feel the need to lie to us about it?"

"Well, it's not exactly something I'm proud of."

"Why not? Attractive older woman, most men your age would be boasting to their mates about it."

"I'm not like that, I wasn't brought up to be like that. My parents would be ashamed of me if they knew and anyway what's all this about? As you say adultery's not a crime is it?"

"Gerald Wilson I am arresting you for the suspected murder of Victoria Daniels. You do not have to say anything but what you do say, may be used in evidence. We'll resume our questioning tomorrow morning. I think it would be a good idea to reconsider your option of having a solicitor present to represent you."

"Victoria's dead?" I ask, unsure if this is some massive practical joke but knowing it isn't.

"Interview terminated at nineteen twenty six hours."

"Can I go home now?"

"You are joking aren't you sunshine," laughs Witherspoon.

"We can hold you in custody for seventy two hours, after which we must put you before a Magistrate or release you but your solicitor will explain all of that tomorrow," says Jenkins.

"I haven't got a solicitor."

"We'll call the duty solicitor tomorrow," says Jenkins. "I'll get you taken to the cells now, Sergeant George is on duty, he'll see that you're fed and watered."

The young constable returns and escorts me through a locked gate to the cells. I stand at a desk while an older sergeant, who looks too kindly to be a policeman, asks me interminable questions while filling in endless forms. Eventually he takes my photograph and fingerprints.

"Sorry son but the DI wants your clothes sent to forensics. Can you get a white suit Joe?"

The PC brings a white all in one nylon suit, the sort that the men from the council wear when they spray the weeds. He holds open a large plastic bag.

"Stick all of your gear in here," he says.

"What everything?"

"Don't worry, I'll avert my eyes. Not that it'll worry you all that much if you run around starkers in front of a picture window."

I hadn't noticed that he was in the room during the interview but then in a lightning flash of lucidity I realise that a juicy story like this would spread like wildfire, probably courtesy of Witherspoon. Anyway I'm past caring now and stick everything in the bag before slipping into my smart paper suit which finishes only six inches from the black slip-on plimsolls that have been supplied, I can't help noticing they're just like the ones we wore for PE in the infants school. I go into the cell and flop down on the plastic covered mattress that has only slightly more give in it than the concrete block it rests on.

I attempt to gather my thoughts. The shock of what's happening to me has prevented me until now from dwelling on the fact that Victoria must obviously be dead. I can't believe it. What's also dawning on me slowly is that I'm potentially in deep trouble and there's no one to help me out of it, I have to sort this out for myself. I know that I've done nothing wrong, yet I can see why it would look very different from a stranger's point of view but if I haven't done it then who has? They always say that the prime suspect in this type of case is the husband. What had Victoria said? 'Lenny's away.' I can't remember if she'd said where. Then I remember her words, 'he's left one of his goons behind.' Jermaine, could Lenny have planned this? Had Lenny persuaded Jermaine to do it? No, surely not. Another memory enters my confused train of thought. Victoria told me that after her affair with Jermaine, he wasn't overly pleased at being dumped. I could easily imagine Victoria being none too gentle with his brittle ego. Had Jermaine simmered away for all this time before exacting his revenge, knowing that Lenny and I would be the prime suspects rather than him? My mangled thought process is interrupted when the trap in the door flies open.

"Sorry about the delay son, the canteen's closed and I've had to cook this myself. Hope it's alright it's only heat and hope stuff in the micro-wave but it'll fill you up."

"Thanks."

"Are you okay?"

"I haven't done anything," I say miserably. "Do you think I've done it?"

"I've been at this lark for a long time now and in that time I've been surprised at a lot of things that people have done that I wouldn't have judged them capable of, but no, my gut feeling tells me that you're no murderer. Not that my opinion carries much weight around here. Anyway get that down you, it's not all that great hot but it'll be worse when it's cold. I'll come and get the tray later."

I start eating with little enthusiasm but soon realise that I'm ravenous and clear the tray

The Sergeant returns and asks. "Feel better now?"

"Not much."

"Well that's understandable I suppose."

"Will I have to share the cell?" I've noticed there are another two beds in here.

"Not tonight you won't, you might have done last night. Are you alright on your own?"

"Yes, I've a lot of thinking to do."

"I've put you a couple of extra blankets there and I'll look in every so often to see that you're okay."

"Thanks sergeant."

"Goodnight."

My thoughts return to Lenny and Jermaine or could it have been someone else, a break-in gone wrong? She'd had other lovers in the past and Lenny had his Russian connections. I'm sure bumping off a recalcitrant wife as a favour to a friend wouldn't cause the Russian Mafia to bat an eyelid. I must have eventually drifted into sleep. A sleep filled with death, violence, nightmarish

191

figures and even someone being hung, although thankfully I don't think I'm the one in the noose. The snapping open of the door flap wakes me.

"Morning son, it's nearly six and that's me done for the night. Now listen," he says conspiratorially. "The fella on the next shift, well he's not a bad bloke but he's not blessed with great patience if you get my meaning, so don't try it too much okay? Look after yourself and I'll see you tonight if you don't get released that is."

"Bye, and thank you sergeant."

Chapter 23
There Are More Questions Than Answers – Johnny Nash

The replacement 'dungeon master' wastes no time in announcing his presence.

"My name is Sergeant Todd," he barks in tones of Glaswegian. "You have a bell there but it's not for room service it's an emergency bell and as such is only to be used if you're dying and then you should think twice. I'll have some breakfast sent along shortly, in the meantime fold up those blankets and don't lie on the bed. Any questions?"

"No" I reply.

In what seems like a couple of hours I'm taken to an interview room. A man dressed in a slightly shabby sports jacket and flannel trousers is already seated at the table. Sartorially, he could have disappeared into the St Winston's staff room as easily as a chameleon in a green salad.

"Good morning, I'm Graham French, duty solicitor. I assume that you will be using my services and not employing your own solicitor."

"Yes."

"Good. Sign here, here and here and then we can get down to brass tacks."

I do as I'm told by appending my signature to a number of long and complicated forms. I could be confessing to the Brinks Matt job for all I know.

"Good. Now, I've been listening to the interview tapes and I think that we should have excellent grounds for appeal when we come to it. They weren't nearly transparent enough about your right to a solicitor and they didn't make it at all clear what you were being questioned about."

"Appeal," I said, appalled. "I haven't been found guilty of anything yet."

"No, no of course not," he muttered. "Perhaps I'm getting a little in front of myself but in my experience it's always useful to have a safety net."

I really don't like the sound of this.

"You haven't asked me whether I've done anything yet," I say.

"Not really my concern old boy. As your legal representative my job is to get you off."

"Even if I'm guilty."

He gives me a look that suggests that he's dealing with a three year old.

"Of course."

A knock on the door signals the arrival of Jenkins and Witherspoon, looking much fresher than I feel.

"Morning Mr French, Gerry," says Jenkins. I hadn't realised we were on such informal terms but let it go. Witherspoon gives me a curt nod.

"Right Gerry, the DS and I will continue with our questioning where we left off last night. If there's anything Mr French isn't happy with he'll let us know."

The ritual switching on of the tape recorder takes place and Mr French is added to the pleasantries.

"Right," says Witherspoon. "We'd reached the point where after first denying seeing Victoria

Daniels last Friday you then admitted going to her house. Then after denying that you had engaged in sexual intercourse with Mrs Daniels you later admitted that you had. On both occasions it was only when confronted with further evidence that you changed your story. Is that correct?"

"Yes."

"And according to your story you left the house later that afternoon?"

"Yes, I'm not sure exactly what time," I say. "It was late afternoon or early evening."

"And when you left the house, Mrs Daniels was in good health?"

"Yes, she was fine."

"Can you explain to us why, when Mrs Brimble the Daniel's cleaning lady let herself in on Saturday morning, she found traces of blood on the living room carpet and more blood on a rug that had been stuffed into a dust bin along with some broken glass. Before you answer I can tell you that the blood and possible semen samples have been sent for DNA testing."

"It's alright I can explain that, the semen is mine from when we made love. After we'd finished, I said that I had to leave but Victoria didn't want me to go..."

"So you quarrelled about it?" Witherspoon asked.

"Yes, well no. It wasn't like that."

"Like what Gerry?" Jenkins asked.

"We didn't argue as such. I had to go somewhere and Victoria wanted me to stay with her but she just sort of went a bit stroppy."

"And that made you angry?" Witherspoon again.

"No," I shout. "It wasn't like that either, it turned into a joke. She stole my trousers and ran around the settee waving them, that was when the dog woman must have seen us and I wasn't naked I had my boxers on."

"Oh that's alright then," said Witherspoon. "Let's pack up and go home."

"Is that meant to be humorous sergeant?" Mr French asks. "I hardly think that this is the time or place for levity."

"No, I apologise. You were saying Mr Wilson."

"I made a lunge for my trousers and knocked over a tall lamp and that in turn smashed a glass topped coffee table."

"And?"

"I started to pick up the pieces of glass but Victoria told me to leave them. She had a flash of temper and tried to knock them out of my hand but caught her arm on the glass. That's where all the blood came from because it was quite a nasty cut."

"So you're telling me that the DNA tests will show the blood to be Mrs Daniels'?" says Jenkins.

"That's handy," says Witherspoon, earning himself an old fashioned look from Mr French.

"I bandaged the wound up and offered to drive her to hospital but she told me I should go to

Lyndsey's. She said that she could make her own way to A&E if she needed to."

"So she was angry when she told you to leave?" Witherspoon asks.

"Sort of; I mean she had been angry that I wouldn't stay but when she told me to go she just seemed sad, and then she thanked me. I think she said it was for being decent or something like that."

"And did you leave at this point?" Jenkins asks.

"Yes."

"And to be clear, Mrs Daniels was in good health at this point?"

"Yes, apart from her arm but that wasn't too serious."

"So tell me, where was this important appointment that you had to keep?"

"It wasn't an appointment as such."

"I'm sorry," said Jenkins. "I got the impression that you'd told Mrs Daniels that you had an unassailable assignation. Did I get that wrong?"

"No not exactly, it was important."

"Oh good, would you care to tell us about it."

"I'd promised to go and see some friends."

"I see, special occasion, birthday, wedding anniversary?"

I can't tell him the real reason because I can't bear the thought of some leering policemen interrogating Lyndsey and Violet about that night, let alone the possibility of a cross examination in court with the Press ready to splash it all over the front page. I must admit my story is beginning to have more holes than a mouse damaged Emmentaler but they're sitting waiting and I have to tell them something. "No, just to play records and talk."

"And who are these friends? I assume they will corroborate your story?"

He seems to emphasise the word 'story.' I provide the girl's names and address.

"Is this where we can find them?"

"Well it would be but they've gone abroad for a break."

"Where to and for how long?"

"Er, I don't know."

"What do you mean?"

"Well Lyndsey is suspended from school for a month and they'd not decided where to go or for how long."

"How very convenient, still I don't suppose you'll be using them as character references," says Witherspoon, making the sneer less obvious this time.

"When you were picked up yesterday Gerry," says Jenkins. "You were driving Mrs Daniels car, would you like to tell us why?"

"Yes, my own car broke down on my way over there and when I told Victoria, she insisted I borrow hers."

"Even though she was angry with you for not staying with her?"

"I know it sounds funny but she was in a strange mood. She was all over the place."

"I'm not sure that I fully understand your meaning."

"May we take a short break there?" Mr French asks. "I need to relieve myself."

"Good idea," says Jenkins. "See if you can rustle up some tea Sergeant."

Mr French hurries out of the room. As he opens the door there's a noisy commotion going on outside. These rooms must have remarkably efficient soundproofing as the closing door shuts out the noise again.

Witherspoon picks up the phone. "Send us four cups of..." He's cut off by the deafening sound of a bell ringing.

"Come on some poor bugger's in trouble," says Jenkins to Witherspoon, then to me. "You stay here." With that they bustle out of the door.

I sit staring at the handle, I'm certain they haven't stopped to lock it. Can I get anywhere if I walk out? Would I dare? What would I do if I did get out? The one thing I'm sure of is that this window of opportunity is a limited one and is unlikely to be repeated. The instinct to panic is intensified by the fact that if I were a juror I wouldn't believe a word of my own story so far.

I take the plunge and with my heart beating like a steam hammer, go to the door. My whole body shaking, I try the handle and as it turns the door opens. Down the corridor mayhem has broken out as police do battle with unseen miscreants. In my mind I try to picture the layout of the building by retracing the way I was brought in. Geography has never been my strong suit but as the other direction is no go due to the battle, I head west. To my amazement the rest of the station is deserted. I could steal the tickets to the policemen's ball and no one would be any the wiser. At the main doors I edge outside where the road is quite busy and I realise I'll stand out like a snowflake in the Sahara if I try to walk around in my white paper 'all-in-one.'

A large removal type van is parked a little further along the road with its back doors open and ramp down. Two men come out of the building and go into the back of the van then return shortly carrying a desk.

"This is the last one," shouts the one at the back. "I'll get the paperwork signed up while you lock the back up and have a look at the A to Z for the next drop."

"Yeah, it's somewhere over Brierley Hill way I think."

I recognise my cue because if this opportunity isn't heaven sent then I'm no judge of a harbinger. I approach the back of the van as nonchalantly as I can manage in the circumstances. Passers-by seem too wrapped up in their own affairs to take much notice of me. Once inside, abstract shapes of office furnishings shrouded in dustsheets and roped to the sides loom out of the gloom. Making my way to the far end of the van I find an untidy pile of blankets and diving underneath spend the next few minutes trying to stop my arms and legs from trembling, I'm shivering like an aspen that knows it's living on the San Andreas fault. The roller shutter crashes down and a quick peep from under my comfort blankets reveals that the fibreglass roof allows enough light for me to see reasonably well. I'm trying to gauge how long it's been since I left the interview room, it seems an age but is probably no more than a couple of minutes.

The engine roars into life, causing me to jump and the whole van to shudder. With a few jerks we pull away and I venture out of my hiding place. My main problem apart from getting out of the van unseen, remains that dressed like this I'll stand out like a sore thumb in a forest of healthy hands. A quick search of the van, while being thrown from pillar to post reveals a donkey jacket and two tan coloured cow gowns hanging in a corner. As I'm now beginning to live the part of the fugitive on the run from justice, I harbour little of the guilt that I would have done twenty-four hours earlier in appropriating the donkey jacket.

By the time the van stops again and the engine has shuddered into silence I've resumed my cloak of invisibility under the blankets. The roller-shutter goes up and I hear voices.

"I hope it's a bit quieter here, it makes me nervous when the coppers are running all over the place like that."

"I know Jim, I've never trusted the buggers, I always think that they don't need a lot of persuasion to draw their truncheons and hit you with them."

"What do you think was going on?"

"Looked to me like they'd lost somebody."

"Good luck to the poor bastard, come on let's get these cabinets in."

Chapter 24
Bad And Ruin – The Faces

One of the men is already in the back untying the cabinets, soon followed by the other. I feel the thrown weight of a blanket add to my pile of camouflage as they begin to manoeuvre the first item off the van.

"It's only on the second floor but they're bloody narrow stairs with banisters, I hate these old buildings," says one voice.

I count off the seconds in elephants to estimate how much grace I'll have to get clear of the van but in reality I know I'm doing it to give myself more time to pluck up the courage to leave my cosy den behind. They take two hundred and ninety four elephants or almost five minutes, I could be half a mile away in that time. The van bounces as they step off the back with the second item. I allow them thirty elephants to enter the building before emerging from my cover, grabbing the donkey jacket and putting it on as I go. Standing on the back of the van I survey the scene while trying to assess my exact whereabouts. I'm sure that I'm on Brierley Hill High Street, an area where a workman's donkey jacket won't look out of place.

I'm about to set off while attempting a jaunty confidence when the younger of the men reappears. He stares at me as though I'm Lord Lucan, before finding his voice.

"What are you doing?"

I don't really have an answer to this and take to my heels, heading for the nearest side street.

"Bill, somebody's pinched your donkey jacket," he shouts. This is a major tactical error on his part. If he'd given chase immediately he may have had an outside chance of catching me but with a lead and the fear of God in me, I'm fast becoming a demonstration of diminishing perspective on his distant horizon. He's game but after a distance and with no sign of Bill reinforcing him, I look over my shoulder to see that he's given up the chase. Slowing to a fast walk I fight to regain control of my breathing as well as my equanimity. Despite a few strange looks no one challenges me. I have no idea which direction I've run in but it looks the sort of area that even the married couples walk around in pairs. I keep moving in the hope that I'll soon get my bearings.

The scream of a siren fills the air. While it may well be just a fire engine or ambulance, or for that matter even a police car going about its own lawful business, my nerves aren't up to close scrutiny. Across the road is what looks to be the side entrance to a park. It's a narrow drive of about twenty yards, leading to some gates, flanked by the sides of houses and lined with shrubs and bushes. I cross over trying not to look suspicious, although there appears to be no one about.

As the siren gets nearer I hide behind one of the bushes. Peering out I see a squad car shoot past and at almost the same moment feel a touch on my shoulder. I've never been a fighter and quite frankly haven't the heart to run again. I turn around only to be to be confronted by a dog. Not thankfully a police dog but a scruffy type of indiscriminate make and model.

"Didn't know you had a dog Sir."

Coming out of the park is Melanie Bateman along with her constant companion Sonia Jameson. They were both in my form until they left school at the earliest opportunity last year. Melanie has always been physically well developed and sexually precocious, at least if you gave credence to her reputation. Although she can be a little threatening and overpowering, I've always liked Melanie. Despite the cheekiness that Melanie exuded in buckets, I'd always judged her heart to be in the right place. Due to her physical attributes the other kids, and indeed a few of the teachers called her Mel double D, the sixth Spice Girl. The two girls make a good team, Sonia's quiet almost to the point of mute and not a little sullen. She's dedicated to Mel and in turn Mel looks out for Sonia.

"Going clubbing then sir?" Mel asks, looking at my clothes, Sonia almost manages to stifle a snigger.

"I'm…" I flounder around for a story that might explain my strange attire.

"You weren't hiding from that police car, were you sir?"

"No, of course I wasn't"

"It's okay we don't mind, even if you've been flashing in the park. You get a lot of that and I mean nobody really gets hurt do they. We won't tell the police, we don't like the police do we Son?"

"Nah."

"Of course I haven't been flashing."

"Are you sure? We won't tell honestly," chides Melanie.

I suddenly feel very tired and quite frankly can't be bothered making up stories for a seventeen year old.

"Look, the police think that I've murdered Mrs Daniels."

"What old Dogger Daniels?"

"It's Mrs Daniels, show some respect Melanie."

"Why, she's never showed me any?"

"You earn respect."

"She's never earned any."

"I'm talking about you now Melanie, not Mrs Daniels. If you go through life disrespecting everyone and everything then no one will ever show you any."

"I show respect to you sir, 'cause you always showed it to us and anyway I like you."

"That's not the point and we seem to have drifted a long way from the point, which is that I'm in a lot of trouble and you two shouldn't be with me."

"Even if you have murdered her, well that's probably not even as bad as flashing is it Son, bit of a public service if you ask me?"

"But I didn't kill her, I wouldn't do anything like that."

"No, come to think of it you wouldn't would you. Oh well never mind."

"Anyway you two had better get on your way, you can't be seen with me."

"You're joking, this is the most exciting thing to happen to us since Sonia thought she had AIDS. Turned out to be tonsillitis didn't it Son? We can help you get away sir."

"No you mustn't."

"Yeah we will, you'll soon get caught on your own. Look at that back garden over there," said Melanie indicating one of the adjoining gardens with her head

"What about it?"

"Clothes line with men's clothes on, you won't last two minutes dressed like that. Sonia, grab anything that looks like it might fit."

"No," I say but Sonia is over the fence with an agility and aptitude that was never apparent during PE sessions at school. She quickly returns, carrying her booty of assorted garments. I sort out a shirt and a pair of jeans that hopefully won't look too out of place on a man of my age. After persuading the girls to look the other way, I try them on. They'd fit someone a foot shorter than me like a glove. Fortunately there's also a hooded top, tracksuit bottoms and a T-shirt that obviously belong to a teenager addicted to growth hormones. I slip these on.

207

"Wow sir, cool. I could quite fancy you now."

"That's all I need, molesting a minor."

"I'm not a minor any more, I'm nearly eighteen."

"Melanie, I very much need to get away from here."

"Yeah, course you do, is there anything you need out of that?"

It hasn't occurred to me to go through the pockets. I make a quick search of the donkey jacket removing a penknife, a box of matches and a woolly hat, before throwing it down. Melanie picks up all of the discarded items and hides them behind a bush.

"Watch out," hisses Sonia, as a police car pulls up at the end of the drive.

Melanie grabs me, throwing her arms around my neck and pressing her ample charms into my chest we engage in a prolonged and what shouldn't have been but was, very arousing kiss. When the danger has passed she comes up for air.

"Ooh sir, is that a gun in your pocket?" Melanie asks.

Sonia giggles as I blush profusely.

Melanie looking totally unabashed merely takes my arm and starts walking.

"Good job those jogging bottoms are nice and baggy innit sir."

I think she's enjoying the discomfort I'm experiencing. No doubt revenge for some long forgotten slight on my part.

"I don't think you need to call me sir, now that you're no longer at school."

"Okay Gerry."

"Perhaps Mr Wilson would be more appropriate."

"You call us by our first names, aren't we equal now that we've left school?"

"Yes I suppose we are. Anyway thank you for what you've done but you'd better leave me now, I don't want to drag you into the mess I'm in."

"You need us to stay with you sir." Sonia takes me totally unawares with one of her rare forays into verbal communication. "People see what they expect to see and the police are looking for a lone man in a donkey jacket not three teenagers."

She's right of course.

"Thank you Sonia, that's a very astute observation."

"She's not the thicko everybody thinks she is are you Son? She's the brains and I'm the gob, it's the perfect combination. We'll get you out of this Gerry, it's a good laugh as well innit Son?"

"We'll compromise, I'd be eternally grateful if you'd stay with me until I'm clear of the police search area."

"You can come and hide in my bedroom for a few days if you like Gerry, like I said I'm legal now."

"I don't think that would be a very good idea would it?"

"Do you want to come as well Son? We could have a threesome, ever had a threesome sir?"

"No of course not," I'm still juvenile enough to cross my fingers behind my back, as I give voice to the lie.

The perfect depiction of distaste crosses Sonia's face, confirming that even if I was willing, this definitely isn't going to be my second experience.

"Well Gerry, the offers there. Might be the last chance you have of getting banged up before you get banged up." As her ex-English teacher I'm very proud of Melanie's imaginative verbal dexterity. Only the implication ruins my momentary satisfaction.

We proceed with Melanie hanging off my arm and Sonia at our side, looking embarrassed by the whole thing. I notice that the dog has chosen to follow as well.

Several more police cars whiz past but as Sonia observed, company has made me invisible. None of them are looking for three teenagers dawdling along. Eventually we reach Lye. There's been no sign of police activity for a while now and I decide the time has come for me to part company with my deliverers.

"Thanks, you've been lifesavers for me."

"It's the least we could do for the best teacher in the school," said Melanie. "Any of the kids would have done the same."

"That makes me very proud. Although I'm not saying that I approve of you obstructing justice."

"Where you going sir?" asks Melanie, relapsing into the formality that seems more normal.

"I'm not sure yet and it's probably better that you don't know"

"We wouldn't tell anybody sir."

"No, I didn't for a minute think that you would. I just meant that if you know nothing then you can't get into any trouble over it."

"Have you got any money?"

This was something that hadn't even occurred to me.

"No, I'll manage."

"How much have you got Son?" Melanie asks.

After searching through their purses, "twelve pounds thirty three," says Melanie, handing it to me.

"I can't possibly take it."

"Don't be daft, you won't get far with no money will you? In fact you won't get all that far with twelve pounds thirty three. Pay us back when they find out you didn't do it."

"Thanks again girls, I'll never forget this."

"We won't neither," says Melanie.

Am I being over-zealous in worrying about her syntax at a time like this?

"No," says Sonia, ever the verbal economist.

Chapter 25
Run For Home - Lindisfarne

The only plan I can concoct at such short notice is to go to my flat for a change of clothes and to get some more money. Melanie was right that twelve pounds thirty three won't get me far. Yet I know the real reason for doing this and one much more important than the financial consideration, is that the nightmare I find myself in makes the thought of my own flat, my own clothes and my own possessions suddenly seem tremendously important. I feel like Mr Mole in 'Wind in the Willows,' perhaps if I can climb into bed and go to sleep then when I wake it will all have been a bad dream.

I'm only about twenty minutes from home and set off at a brisk walk. The dog trots along uninvited but nonetheless seems quite happy at my side. The building that houses my humble abode is set slightly further back than those either side of it. As I reach it I find a uniformed PC standing outside the front door, I hadn't seen him until now. The dog approaches him, tail wagging and has the effect of distracting his attention from me for the moment. That moment is enough to gather my wits and hide my confusion.

"Hallo boy," he says, patting the dog's head. "What's his name?"

I'm totally nonplussed, I have no idea what his name is or if indeed he's ever aspired to one and at this moment my brain magically evacuates every dog's name I've ever heard in my life. I look at the next house along and inscribed on a stone over the door is 'Vernon Villa 1904.'

"It's Vernon," I say in my finest attempt at a Black Country accent, at the same time thinking, 'who calls a dog Vernon?'

The PC has the same thought. "That's an unusual name for a dog."

"Ar, we named 'im after mi great uncle," I say. "Cum on Vernon let's ger ourselves 'um fer ower dinner." In my woolly hat I must have looked and sounded like the brother that 'Benny from Crossroads' feels sorry for.

"He really should be on a lead sir."

"I'm sorry officer, I had 'im off the lead in the park and it must have fell out of mi pocket. I only live round the corner though."

"Keep an eye on him then, he could cause an accident."

I hurry away, all the time expecting to hear, 'hey you,' as the penny must surely drop that he's just been talking to 'Stourbridge's most wanted.' The shout doesn't materialise and my mind reluctantly addresses the next problem, 'where to now?' I consider my options. Lyndsey and Violet are out of the equation, will Shaun be under surveillance or even Julie come to that? This consideration raises another spectre. I've automatically assumed until now that my friends will all take my innocence for

213

granted but will they? Will my friends still want to know me after this?

As I carry on walking, the tumble dryer that has been standing in for my brain for the last couple of days now, registers the fact that I've passed through Pedmore without even noticing. I'm now heading toward the countryside of the Clent Hills and make an instant decision. I decide to spend the night in the open while considering my options. It's late spring, and although the summer heat has yet to arrive, I'm confident that it won't be too cold. The sight of a small sub post office and general store reminds my stomach that I've eaten nothing since the very early morning breakfast at the Police Station. Giving Vernon his orders to wait outside the door, I venture inside. After a quick appraisal of the stock, I purchase a bottle of water, crisps, biscuits, a Danish pastry and a packet of some sort of dried dog food. The elderly woman behind the till is looking at me suspiciously. I can't discern if this is because of my cod Black Country accent, my strangely youthful attire, my nervous fumbling with the money or possibly just my growing paranoia?

I reach Clent and head up onto Adams Hill, one of the popular range of Clent Hills. It's an area that a man with a dog, no matter how he's dressed will arouse little suspicion. The police still have my watch and it surprises me to register that I've totally lost track of time. I suddenly feel completely exhausted and after trudging up Adams

Hill, I find a patch of springy turf just off the main path near the summit and collapse onto it. Vernon lies at my side panting and I realise that like me, nothing has passed his lips since our coming together. I have a drink of the water and realising I don't have a bowl I pour a little into my cupped hand. Vernon laps it up eagerly and I do this a number of times until he seems to have had his fill. After struggling with the easy opening on his packet of food, I tip it onto a patch of clean grass.

Vernon looks at the food,

Vernon sniffs the food,

Vernon looks at the food again,

Vernon reluctantly picks up a morsel and half-heartedly moves it around his mouth,

Vernon spits it out and sitting back on his haunches stares at me expectantly.

We share about half of the supplies that I've purchased for myself and I pack the remainder to keep for the morning.

The sun is beginning to surrender its warmth to the chill of the evening air. I've decided on my refuge for the night and while I don't want to reach it too early and look suspicious by hanging about, I realise that if I leave it too late I run the risk of not finding the spot in the dark. As dusk approaches I head for a conifer tree that's slightly off the beaten track. I'd spotted the tree while out on one of my runs, it has foliage that is so dense the ground beneath its branches is covered in a thick carpet of dried needles and never seems to get wet, even after heavy rain. Whenever I've run past, I'd always thought how cosy it looked, never imagining that one day I might be putting my theory to the test.

I look around in what I imagine to be a nonchalant manner and after satisfying myself that I'm totally alone I crawl underneath. Some of the lower branches I rip off with the help of the penknife, to give me a little headroom and utilise them as primitive draught proofing. It smells dry and earthy but not unpleasant. Vernon follows me in and taking his cue from me settles down, I can't help feeling sorry for him. He seems to have adopted me as his saviour, something akin to a stranded mariner being picked up by the Titanic. What will happen to Vernon when I'm back behind bars, as I feel is inevitable? I'll have to try to shoo him away or if I don't he may be rounded up and put to sleep. At least he can revert to his life as a dog with his eye on the main chance albeit one that lacks any real judgement.

My earlier calculation that it won't be too cold out of doors proves to be as far off the mark as everything else in my life at the moment and I start regretting the loss of the donkey jacket. I know from Uncle Barney's bequest that you're never cold in a donkey jacket. I move over and snuggle up to Vernon, who emits what sounds a contented groan. This unreasonably brings back memories of Matt and Mark. I'd met these two while working at a mail order depot during the School's summer holidays, was it last summer? No it was the one before. They were discussing women whom they insultingly referred to as 'dogs' that they had slept with. The cause of their debate was Sue the depot supervisor. Matt said that she was a dog, Mark agreed but thought she had the potential to be quite respectable if she did something with her hair, her make-up, her clothes and her manner. I'd deliberately kept out of the debate on two counts. One was that I thought it disrespectful to call women dogs anyway but more importantly was the fact that I liked Sue. I had started to spend my meal breaks talking to her, nothing too racy, art, music, films etc. I'd even been to her house once when she'd bought some flat pack furniture from IKEA that had proved to be too voluminous for her Vauxhall Tigra and my trusty Volvo came to the rescue. After we'd unloaded Sue asked me to stay for dinner but I'd clumsily managed to decline even though I really wanted to accept.

Then it hit me like the proverbial bolt from the blue. Could I go and throw myself on Sue's mercy? Of course I couldn't, it would be too much of an imposition as I'd never kept in touch since leaving that job. Not through impoliteness but because I can never believe that people will want to see me again, especially after the clumsy way I'd handled our one near romantic encounter. It's at this point that sleep consumes me.

I wake with a start that makes Vernon jump and this in turn causes me to leap out of my skin until I remember where I am. Knowing where I am, is hardly a step forward, as where I am seems to be in an unfathomable mess. It's still dark but the beginnings of daylight seem to be forcing their way into the reckoning. I can't believe that it can be this cold at this time of year and I'm physically shaking. I still have the box of matches but dare I light a fire? How seriously will the police be treating my escape? In my mind's eye they have spotter planes and a line of hundreds of policemen combing the land, like the old black and white version of 'The Thirty Nine Steps.' In reality the more I think about it, apart from the embarrassment of my escaping their custody I'm sure I'm relatively small fry and anyway I'm too cold to care.

After collecting a pile of old and fairly dry wood I scoop together a pile of the needles, and at third attempt kindle enough of a flame to add some branches. Most of the smoke dissipates upward through the foliage and although some remains, the heat is worth the discomfort of stinging eyes. We wolf down what's left of our food, reminiscent of the stone-age hunter and his semi tame wolf. Although Vernon is actually quite friendly he still fits the bill of primitive survivor better than me. He's a fairly large and stocky Heinz 57 of a dog but at least he looks the part of fierce hunter. We share the remainder of the water and I can't help thinking, I'd sell my birth-right as well as a mess of pottage for a nice cup of tea.

Breakfast done and dusted I set my mind to the business in hand. In my heart of hearts I know that I've already decided that Sue is my only real option. If she turns me away or if she turns me over to the police, well that's just karma. Perhaps I'll think of a plan B en-route, after all Sue came out of the blue didn't she? Sue lives out in the middle of nowhere, an area suitably named Far Forest that is past Kidderminster and then Bewdley, somewhere in the region of twenty or thirty miles from my current location. I have no idea how long it will take me to walk there but one thing I'm not short of is time. I set off and Vernon trots alongside. We pass landmarks that I've only whizzed by previously in the car. Hunger informs me that it's lunchtime and a small local convenience store provides the means. The elderly proprietor is talkative and I inform him that I'm embarked on hiking across England glad that he can't see my black plimsolls. I tell him that my rucksack containing all of my provisions was stolen yesterday. He's very sympathetic and I make a point of dropping into the conversation that I'm heading in the opposite direction to my actual course. I bid farewell and set off into the unknown, feeling anything but confident.

Chapter 26
Delta Dawn – Bette Midler

The morning rush hour is in full swing and I've skirted around the outer limits of Kidderminster before following the road that goes through the centre of Bewdley. There are only two places to cross the river and the paucity of bipeds on the bypass would leave me very conspicuous to any sharp eyed policemen. I'm exhausted by the time I arrive at Sue's isolated cottage in the early evening. The approach is a rough drive over fifty yards long that leads off a quiet country lane. How she can live out here alone amazes me, I'd be freaked out during the hours of darkness. I'm suddenly struck by a devastating thought that could shoot my plans down in flames. Why had it not occurred to me before? What if Sue's married or even just living with someone? What if she's moved? What kind of stupid pillock am I? How could I think that just because my life's stood still then everyone else's has done the same?

I resolve that having come this far I'll at least go to the door. If a man answers I'll ask if he's interested in double-glazing and should he say yes, I'll run like the clappers. There's one vehicle outside, an MG sports surely not a man's car. The clicking of the engine cooling down tells me that it's recently arrived. My knock on the door is answered so quickly that it takes me aback a little. Sue is standing there, more or less exactly as I remember her. Hair scraped back severely, into a no-nonsense ponytail, dark framed glasses and a plain shapeless top and trousers. It could be my startled look or perhaps she doesn't recognise me, then again it's more likely to be the fear of an unexpected stranger but whatever it is she looks totally nonplussed, when suddenly a smile of recognition spreads over her face.

"Gerry! What a surprise, come in."

I follow her in. The room is more or less as I remember it although at that time Sue hadn't lived here very long. Now it's the finished article and very tasteful into the bargain, in a sort of Swedish minimalist style.

"It's looking great," I say, as if this is a totally normal situation and I've been invited for dinner. "Those must be the units that we brought over."

"Yes and the table, I'm really pleased with them."

"Are you still working at GMF?"

"Yes, how boring am I?" Sue laughs. "Are you still teaching?"

She's too polite to ask the question that must be foremost in her mind. 'What the bloody hell are you doing here when I haven't heard a dickie bird from you for almost two years?' I know the onus is on me to tell her and despite all of the stories I've considered on the way here I know that only the truth will do.

"Sue," I bluster. "Erm Susan." Somehow the seriousness of what I'm about to tell her seems to require the gravity of the full name.

"Actually it's Suzanne," she says. "But I never use it, Suzanne always seems much too glamorous for someone like me."

I want to say that it doesn't but she's right, she's not a Suzanne.

"I'm sorry, Suzanne" I correct myself. "Anyway I think it's only fair that I tell you why I'm here."

"There's no need if you don't want to."

"There is, it's only right that you should know. The police think that I've murdered a woman, in fact that's putting it mildly it's even worse than that, they arrested me for it and I've escaped. I'm on the run and if I'm found here it could put you in a lot of trouble, so perhaps it's better if I go now. I'm sorry I bothered you, I should never have come."

I move towards the door.

"Hold on, have you finished?" Sue asks.

"Yes."

"Good," she says. "The reason I said you don't need to explain is because I already know everything you've just told me."

"Then why did you let me in? I could be a murderer."

"Oh Gerry, you could no more murder anyone than I could become a lap dancer."

I'm surprised that Sue even knows about lap dancers.

"What do you mean?" I ask.

"I remember the time you wouldn't let me swat a wasp once, you caught it in a cup and put it outside," she laughed. "Hardly Boston Strangler material."

"What about the Birdman of Alcatraz, he loved birds didn't he?"

"Ah! Robert Franklin Stroud, guilty of two murders but hardly the saintly figure he was painted in the movie. Sorry, I'm sadder than you think, criminology is a hobby of mine."

"That still doesn't prove my innocence."

"I like to think I'm a good judge of people and you're on the soft side of gentle."

"How do you know about what I'm supposed to have done, has it been on the news?"

"I'm sure it has but that's not how I know. I didn't tell you before, there was no reason why I should but my father is an Assistant Chief Constable and when your escape details came up on the computer, he noticed that you'd worked at GMF and came to grill me for info on you."

"I'll go now then if that's alright, I'm sorry I've put you in this position," I say. "I'm sorry to have to ask but will you tell the police I've been here, I won't blame you if you do?"

"Why did you come here Gerry?"

"I suppose I panicked. I didn't know if they'd watch my friend's houses and I remembered you. It was a liberty I know, I'm so sorry. I had no idea about your father being a policeman, it was a bad idea I really don't know what I was thinking about."

"I'm glad you came here," Sue says, taking me totally by surprise. "And if you'll let me I'd like to help you."

"But why?" I ask. "The more that I think of it now, the more I realise what a bloody cheek I've got. You don't hear from me for ages and then as soon as I'm in trouble I turn up like a bad penny."

"That's okay, I didn't expect you to keep in touch, I knew that at the time you were still getting over your divorce. Anyway that's enough recriminations let's talk about your current situation, a little excitement in my life wouldn't go amiss at the moment."

Sue makes me a sandwich and a cup of tea, while I recount the events of the last year. All of the time I'm talking and eating, she asks pertinent questions and raises points that haven't occurred to me. Perhaps it's being a policeman's daughter that gives her this analytical quality or perhaps it's as I'd always thought during our meal break confabs at work, she's just much more intelligent than me.

When I've finished she sits there thinking for a few minutes before asking. "And what do you think?"

"I think I'm in a real mess and I can't see a way out of it."

"Yes but I didn't mean that, what do you think about the murder, who do you think may have done it?"

"Well, I know that I didn't do it. My first thought was Lenny, he knew about me and Victoria and I immediately assumed he was using me as the perfect scapegoat and getting his revenge on both of us into the bargain."

"But you're not sure?"

"Victoria always insisted that Lenny would never touch her. She said she'd had numerous affairs that Lenny probably knew about and as long as she didn't make them too obvious he wasn't bothered. He doesn't exactly live like a monk himself and he could easily have had me knocked off."

"So if you don't think it was Lenny, who else?"

"Jermaine's the other one that springs to mind, he was one of Victoria's previous dalliances that Lenny definitely didn't know about. When she finished with him he didn't take it well. And Victoria wasn't averse to threatening Jermaine that she'd tell Lenny about them and Jermaine's terrified of Harry Brown. The night they beat me up on the car park roof I was convinced that Jermaine would have thrown me off if Lenny hadn't stopped him. On the day it must have happened, Victoria told me that Jermaine hadn't travelled with Lenny and Harry that day, so he could well have gone to the house after I left, knowing the evidence would point to me. Victoria wouldn't have been frightened to let him in. Jermaine would also know that he'd removed the threat once and for all that Victoria would tell Lenny about them."

"I've picked up some facts about the case from the things my father asked me about. Would you just reiterate the reasons that the police are so sure that you did it again and why the police think it would stand up in court without the body being found."

"Well to start with there's the fact that I was having an affair with Victoria. I suppose a crime of passion is the oldest reason in the world."

"Yes, that's fair enough but that in itself isn't reason enough to be so sure it's you. Just stick to anything that could be used as evidence in a court room."

"Right I'll start at the beginning. All the teachers and their wives at the Christmas 'do,' saw us together as well as the taxi driver. That was the first dealing I had with Victoria, she'd asked me to go with her as a dance partner but I had no idea what it was going to turn into. Then there was the New Year fancy dress party, the headmaster and deputy head were there and the hotel records will prove we stayed the night. One day we were at Victoria's house in the Jacuzzi when her best friend Jenna turned up. They were devoted to each other and I'm not sure how Jenna would testify, she had no illusions about Lenny. Victoria and I spent another night at the Hummingbird Hotel. Jenna was there as well and was one of three other couples there and they all knew about us. I got on well with Jenna but if she thought that I'd murdered Victoria I think she'd happily kill me with her own hands. Oh and I left my video membership card by the pool that day and Lenny found it but Victoria covered for me. That was what led to the car park incident, he was suspicious about us but wasn't sure.

"Tell me more about what happened after the car park."

"The hospital called the police and a DI came to interview me. I explained to him what had happened but he laughed at me and told me that earlier in the evening, Lenny had lodged a complaint about me, saying that I'd been drinking all night at his club. It was St Patrick's Day and he said I'd instigated a fight with some lads and he had loads of witnesses. According to Lenny it was only his bouncers that prevented me from getting a real beating. I owe that man so much."

"Come on stick to the facts."

"Sorry. According to the police I also said to the bouncers, 'I'll drop Lenny Daniels in it,' as I was leaving. It would look to a jury as if that was just what I was trying to do, first murder Victoria and then blame Lenny for it. I know it was a stupid thing to do but this policeman seemed so biased that I said 'I might as well take the law into my own hands.' It was just a bit of bravado but in light of what happened later, it looks even worse."

"What happened later?"

"I'm not sure I should tell you this, with your Dad being a policeman. I wouldn't want to drop anyone in it."

"You have my word, I wouldn't do that."

"Well, I was still laid up from the beating when Shaun came to see me. He told me that a few of the Irish lads were unhappy at what had happened to me. They'd gone and exacted a little revenge on Lenny and his boys. They were dressed up like the IRA and I think Lenny thought that they were the real thing because he told Victoria it was a scuffle at the club and he didn't inform the police at all but if he were to bring it up at a trial it would be another nail in my coffin."

"Is there anything else that I don't know about?"

"No that's it more or less, until the day that it all happened."

"Go on, just run through that again."

"There's a bit that you don't know, nobody does. I couldn't tell the police but I need to tell you because it will help you to understand more, although I don't know what you'll think of me after."

I explain about Lyndsey and Violet wanting a baby. My promise to go round that night, as they were going away next day and how important it seemed, as Lyndsey was really down.

"It's certainly a bolt from the blue," said Sue, unable to totally hide her look of shock. "But I think anyone would see that you were doing it for the right reasons. Even if they didn't approve of what you were doing."

"While I was taking a lesson in the afternoon my mobile rang. I switched it off but when I checked during break time there was a text from Victoria, asking me to go to see her after school. I went to explain that I couldn't stay because of my promise to Lyndsey, although obviously I couldn't tell her why it was so important."

"Was she angry?"

"Yes, Victoria usually gets... Sorry I suppose that should be usually got her own way and I think she tended to treat me as her lap dog. Anyway for once I didn't capitulate and after the usual fit of pique she sort of went limp. This wasn't Victoria at all, she just... Well she just gave up and begged me to make love to her."

"And you did?"

"Yeah I did, I was a bit scared actually, not of her but for her, it was so out of character. I'd been expecting her to attack me and if she had it wouldn't have worried me as much but I made it clear that I still couldn't stay. After we'd made love I said that I was going and Victoria seemed to have gotten some of her old zip back by then."

"It must be your hidden talent," this shocks me as it's not the sort of thing that Sue would normally say, but more than that it's delivered with the hint of a mocking smile that I've never seen in her before.

I push on to hide my growing discomfort.

"Anyway, she picked up my trousers and started waving them, saying that I'd have to catch her if I wanted them back. It was while we were doing this that the lady with the dog must have seen us. We were both laughing but through a window I suppose it could have looked like we were fighting. I made a lunge for Victoria and we knocked over a tall lamp, I think it's called an up-lighter, anyway it toppled over and landed on a glass coffee table shattering them both.   There was glass everywhere."

"Did that make her angry?"

"No she just laughed, saying it would give her the chance to buy new ones. It was when I said that I had to go and started picking up the pieces of glass that she became angry. She told me to leave it and it was when she went to knock the glass out of my hand that she cut her arm. It was a nasty cut, nothing life threatening, but it was on the bone so the blood was running out like a tap. I said I'd drive her to the hospital but she refused, saying in a sarcastic way that I mustn't miss my important appointment. I put my first aid training to good use and bandaged her arm. I made a good job of it but it really needed stitches and she insisted that she'd go herself later if she needed to. Oh and she told me to borrow her car, because mine had broken down earlier but of course no one can confirm that now."

"And that was when you left?"

"Yes, but before I did there was one final little strange episode. Victoria went sort of, well all soft and lovey-dovey, not like her at all, that's why I didn't try to explain it to the police. She said, 'thank you.' I asked her 'what for?' and she said, I think I can remember it almost word for word. 'For being decent, for putting up with my moods, for helping me to see things straight.' Like I said, it was totally out of character."

"You don't think it could have been a verbal suicide note?"

"I suppose it could but it didn't seem like that. She seemed serene, almost positive, as if a weight had been lifted from her shoulders and anyway if it was suicide, where's the body? As far as I know they haven't found one yet."

"Sometimes people who are going to end their lives can react in the way that you describe, they're serene because they've made their decision and they're at peace with it. Sometimes people who throw themselves off Beachy Head aren't found for weeks or months if at all but from what you've told me of her, Victoria doesn't sound like the typical suicide. Much more like a murder victim or at least someone who could drive a person to murder, anyway go on what happened next?"

"Sunday evening the Police turned up and asked me to go to the station. I agreed without asking what it was about. I just assumed that it was Lenny playing another of his games. I actually said to the police officers, 'I suppose Lenny Daniels gave you a good description of me.' Which looks bad in retrospect because it would seem that I knew why I was being picked up, on top of the fact that I was driving Victoria's car. They asked me if I'd seen Victoria on the day in question and I said no, I just thought it would be easier. I didn't know she was dead at that time and assumed that Victoria would deny seeing me. First I said she hadn't been at school that day and then I denied going to her house. They knew about the text call and when they told me about it I had to admit going to the house but I still thought it was about some minor misdemeanour at that point. The Police asked if we'd made love and I realised afterwards how stupid it was but I denied that as well. They then told me about their eye witness, who had given a good description of me and was certain that she could pick me out of an ID parade, even though she didn't really want to set eyes on me again. I had to admit we'd made love. The officer asked me if we'd quarrelled. I said not seriously and without thinking, told him that she was in good health when I left. It was then that he asked me about the blood on the carpet. They'd found all of the glass in a dustbin, with the rug stuffed on top of it and an attempt had been made to clean the bloodstains out of the carpet. I explained what happened but I just got a load of dubious looks. I have to admit that in their shoes I wouldn't have believed a word of my story either."

"No," said Sue. "It doesn't sound too good does it?"

"Then there's the fact that the only people who could corroborate any part of my story have gone abroad for an unspecified length of time, to God knows where?"

"And the fact that you've escaped from lawful custody."

"I know. It was a stupid thing to do but I only had a second to decide and I was scared out of my wits."

"It definitely makes you look even more guilty."

"I know and I'm sorry to bring it to your door."

"Let me tell you something now. Despite the evidence against you, my father is far from happy with your case. My views about your not being capable of doing something like this merely added to his suspicion that it's all been pushed through far too quickly. The fact that Mrs Daniels had only been missing for two days when you were picked up and then charged, despite the lack of a body is most irregular. He's listened to your interview tapes, which were a little unorthodox in procedure and quite hostile. At the same time Lenny Daniel's interviews seem extremely congenial almost as if he was being led."

A memory resurfaces. "I remember once when I was going out with Victoria. I'd commented that she shouldn't be driving after the amount she'd had to drink and she said. 'No problem, Lenny will square it with the Chief Constable, they're in the same lodge.'"

"That's interesting, daddy was moved here from another force. He's always been straight down the line, believing that the police should be above any suspicion of corruption and definitely shouldn't belong to any organisations like the Masons. He says he'd rather lock up a bent copper than a dozen villains because of the damage they do to the rest of the force. He's not too popular with some of the other top brass but he thinks that some of them are a little too cosy with certain unsavoury characters."

"Could he help me do you think?"

"Only indirectly, it's a difficult situation. If he knew that I had any contact with you it would compromise him and he'd have to have you arrested and me as well come to that, if he knew I'd helped you. I might be able to find some things out but I can only do it in a roundabout way."

"That's something anyway Sue, when I arrived here I felt as if the world had turned against me."

"I told you, I want to help you as much as I can. You can stay here while we try to sort things out, no one ever comes out here by acci ..." Sue is cut short by the door slowly swinging open. My heart plummets through my boots and keeps going. She hadn't mentioned anyone else being here. Then a big furry head pushes around the door.

"Vernon!" I say, trying to keep the relief from my voice. "How did you get in?"

"Vernon," says Sue. "You have a dog called Vernon?"

I explain our meeting.

"He seems to have adopted me and actually he helped my escape from the police. I don't know how he got into the house?"

"He must have pushed the door open I never bother locking it, no need to out here. I've always thought about getting a dog but never seemed to get around to it."

"I don't suppose you have a shed or outbuilding that he could sleep in have you. It's just that I've grown to like him, in fact we spent last night snuggled together under a tree."

"That accounts for It, I didn't like to mention, but you do have an interesting aroma."

"Sorry, I haven't had a shower since Sunday morning. The police picked me up Sunday afternoon after I'd just come back from a run. Add to that the fact that I've been wearing these clothes for a day and a half solid and well..."

"He can stay in the house but he needs a bath first. Then you can have one while I get you some decent clothes."

"Where from?" I ask.

"It'll have to be the supermarket in Kiddy, it'll take me about an hour. Give Vernon a bath, there are some old towels in the utility room, you can use the hairdryer to dry him properly. By the time you've had your bath I should be back."

I do as I'm told. Vernon takes to bathing like a duck to water, considering that this may well be his first experience. I'm luxuriating in a hot bath and last night's cold is draining from my bones like a very bad dream as I start to doze. A tap on the door breaks in on my reverie.

"Are you decent?"

"I'm in the bath but you can come in, I've overdosed with your bubbles I'm afraid."

Sue enters rather tentatively but when she can see that I'm not exaggerating about the foam, relaxes a little.

"These are the best I could do," she says, showing me a pair of jeans, a shirt, a jumper and a pair of trainers that all look very acceptable. Women always seem to be much better at dressing men than men do themselves. "There are some socks and er underwear in the bag."

"I don't know what to say. I've come here Sue and ruined whatever you had planned for the evening. How can I ever thank you for everything you're doing."

"Actually that's the whole point. I had nothing planned for the evening except cooking myself a meal and listening to Classic FM. I've allowed myself to get into a rut and this is the most interesting thing to happen to me in ages, so don't keep apologising. In a strange way you're doing me a favour. Anyway your bubbles are beginning to dissipate so I'll leave you to get dressed. By the way Vernon's come up lovely, hasn't he, he looks as good as new?"

Chapter 27
Susanna – Art Company

I spend the next few days pottering about Sue's cottage while trying to relax. It's so remote that there's no real need to stay indoors, the peace and quiet of the countryside means that a vehicle could be heard approaching long before it actually appeared and for the same reason pedestrians are as rare as rocking horse poo. I make myself useful cleaning the windows, chopping firewood, by doing a bit of gardening or anything else I can think of to show my appreciation. I become an avid watcher of the local news on television and pick up a couple of mentions but with no sightings of me, interest seems to have waned. When I do allow myself time to think, my head's a whirl as I unsuccessfully attempt to formulate a plan to prove my innocence.

I prepare our meal each evening and Sue seems to appreciate this but my limited repertoire must be starting to pall, when on Saturday she says she'll cook us something special. I've noticed as the week has worn on that Sue's mode of dress for work has become more feminine and it suits her. The dresses and blouses that have replaced the trousers and sweaters reveal that she is in fact slimmer than I had always believed. Sue had good legs that as far as I could remember hadn't seen the light of day previously in my presence. I wonder if I should comment on this change of mien but decide it might embarrass her or even seem that I'm being cheeky and therefore I don't. It also crosses my mind that flattery might appear that I'm taking a liberty and coming on to her.

I'm beginning to like Sue more and more as the week goes by but she still takes life a little too seriously and I know from my time with Alison, that I need someone to jolly me along a bit. I'm far too introspective in my own right to hook up again with a kindred spirit and perhaps its right that opposites should attract. While I'm musing on this, the sick realisation hits home again that my actual prospects aren't going to be sharing my remaining years with a personable woman, more likely an eighteen stone, tattooed cat burglar named Wayne, from Walsall.

Sue's Saturday morning has been spent shopping and she arrives home laden with carrier bags. There's a mixture of M&S food hall and clothes shop bags. Apart from the groceries and the clothes that she's bought for herself, some contain more clothes for me. I'm taken aback, as I have no means or even any prospects of means to pay her back and I tell her this.

"Don't worry," she says. "I told you on the first night that this is doing me a big favour, I'm enjoying having company. It's gotten me out of a rut by forcing me to make an effort with my clothes and forcing me into doing things, like this meal. Even just making conversation or watching TV together is nice. Before you turned up on Tuesday

I was in the middle of another week of treading water. I don't know where I am now but wherever it is, it's a whole lot more bloody exciting."

"Well done," I say. "That's a great attempt at assuaging my guilt even if it's not true. Can I do anything to help with tonight's meal?"

"No you've cooked all week. Why don't you go and have a bath and get changed, try those new clothes on. I'll prep the meal and then I'll tell you what wants doing while I get ready. It'll be nice getting dolled up a bit for a change, even if it's only for a meal at home."

I do as I'm told and come back down to listen to my instructions. I lay the table, light the candles, simmer the soup, put out the bread rolls and then wait for Sue. The wait proves a worthwhile surprise as she makes her entrance with an endearing combination of confidence and uncertainty. The confidence is fully justified, her hair is down on her shoulders, I've only ever seen it in its utilitarian working guise previously. She's wearing proper make-up rather than her normal 'just a hint' amount, another first in my experience and the glasses are gone.

"Do I look ridiculous?"

"Sorry was I staring? I haven't seen you without your glasses before, you look fantastic."

"I've got my lenses in, I don't use them much. It seems too much like vanity and a little pointless into the bargain."

"Vanity suits you, you really do look great, the clothes, the hair, everything. You look a million dollars."

"Well, maybe a million lira."

"Don't be so negative, you're worse than me."

"I'm sorry but I'm not good at accepting compliments, especially from men. I'm way out of practice."

"Is that dress new?" I ask as she stands at the cooker. It's black, classically simple and teaming it with high heels is another first for me as she's always worn flats at work.

"Yes, what do you think?"

"It's really lovely it suits your figure, you wouldn't look out of place on 'Footballer's Wives'."

"What's 'Footballer's Wives?'" Sue asks and I realise she really does have no idea.

I explain the finer points of this trashily enjoyable programme as I'd forgotten just how little Sue follows popular culture.

"Another compliment, thank you sir, you're spoiling me."

"It's fully deserved and I'm genuinely honoured that you'd go to this much trouble for me."

"It's for me as well," she says looking slightly embarrassed.

"Can I ask you a personal question?"

"After some of the things I've asked you and that you've answered so candidly... Well it would be churlish of me to say no but you're not going to make me blush are you?"

"I hope not," I reply, meaning it. "It's just that I couldn't help wondering why there isn't a bloke in your life. I won't be offended if you tell me to bugger off and mind my own business."

"Is that all?" Sue lets out a relieved giggle. "Well, there was someone, his name was Malcolm and I was with him from the age of seventeen. He was older than me, seven years older and I was impressed and more than a little in awe of his self-assurance. He treated me like a helpless little girl and I suppose I played up to it. Mother idolised Malcolm and he worked the oracle with her and by saying and doing all the right things and although Daddy never criticised, I sensed that he didn't think much of Malcolm. At the time I just put it down to jealous father syndrome. Anyway we finally broke up a couple of years ago, just before you came to GMF. I was getting over the break up, that's why I was still settling into this place at the time. After the split I found out that he'd been seeing other women throughout our time together. Friends had warned me but I wouldn't believe them, I suppose I didn't want to. I should have known better with Daddy, he didn't know what Malcolm was up to but as usual his copper's nose had sniffed out a bad lot."

"Has there been anyone else?"

"No, I don't know why but I just seemed to lose confidence in myself, I think I lost my confidence in men too. I more or less became a recluse, friends came round but I wasn't very receptive. I'm afraid that I was probably a fairly horrible person to know."

"Trauma can affect people in different ways," I said, remembering my break-up with Allison and thanking my lucky stars for Lyndsey, Violet and Shaun.

"Luckily I have some good friends," Sue continued. "And they didn't give up on me, for which I'll be eternally grateful. The only problem was that they kept trying to act as unpaid matchmakers and I'll never allow myself to be that much of a charity case."

I'm enjoying the meal because apart from being much better than my own efforts, it brings back the cosiness and security of times spent with Lyndsey and Violet. I must have been musing on this when Sue says. "Penny for them."

"Sorry, I was somewhere else," I say and explain where. "It's just that everything seemed so safe then, life was fairly boring but at least I wasn't scared all the time."

"Finish your wine and I'll open a new bottle," says Sue. "Alcohol can be a great aid to temporary memory loss and short term euphoria."

"You sound like an authority," I say.

"I am," Sue replies and after a pause. "Malcolm would never let me drink more than the odd glass of wine, he was a bit of a control freak but I didn't mind at the time. The girls would try to take me on nights out and while he didn't physically stop me, he made his feelings clear and like a good little girl I obeyed and making my excuses to the girls I'd stay home even though he wouldn't be there with me. I suppose I was to blame in a way, I liked the feeling of security and the thought that someone cared about me enough to do that. In the aftermath of the break-up I'd wear a happy face at work, and that was the public me that I showed to you and the others at GMF but at home I often fell into deep despairs. Ernst and Julio Gallo became my new best friends, mainly at weekends because I was far too sensible to let it affect my job. I became a weekend alcoholic, what a sad little person I am."

"You're anything but that," I say, as she refills our glasses. "Er, is it okay for you to…"

"Don't worry," she says, realising where I'm going, while trying to avoid getting there.

"I've been back in control now for a few months. I made the decision that I would never drink alone again. In fact this is the first drink I've had since then apart from the odd one with friends after work. I'm afraid I'm back to being sad little in control me again but that's the way I prefer it."

Having finished our meal we take our drinks to the sofa where the subject has changed to the less sensitive one of politics. This suits me as the drink and the heat of the room have the effect of dulling my perceptions. I've started imagining that Sue is encouraging me to make advances, this is a fairly common side effect that drink has on me, imagined irresistibility syndrome. This in turn throws up a number of thoughts, could I grow to love Sue? I'd mulled this over earlier in the week and came to the conclusion that while on the one hand we are far too alike, on the other I've grown to appreciate her more as the days have passed. Do I find her sexually attractive? Again I know that with my PC head on this should be immaterial but in reality that will never be the case. The answer to this would have brought a snort of derision previously but tonight I know that if I saw her on the arm of another man I'd be jealous as hell. Is she just being friendly and I've misread the signs? It certainly wouldn't be the first time but being a coward I never act on these instincts and therefore never embarrass myself which is just how I intend to play it this time. In the words of some great thinker, 'I'd rather keep my mouth shut and have everyone think me a fool, rather than open it and confirm their suspicions.'

"Am I boring you?" Sue asks out of the blue.

"Pardon?"

"My views on New Labour seem to have sent you into a trance."

"I'm sorry, I think with all that I've got on my mind as well as the drink I might be drifting." What I'm actually thinking about has caused me to temporarily forget my real problems. This makes me giggle at myself, the fact that I'm considering a relationship with Sue when there's a strong possibility that I could be starting a life sentence any time now.

"What are you laughing at?" Sue asks.

"I'm laughing at me, at the situation I'm in. I'm sitting here and because I can't hold my drink the thing that's got me more frightened than being locked up for twenty years is whether I should make a pass at you or not."

"There's only one sure way to find the answer to that."

I think that I gulp audibly like Scooby Doo does when he and Shaggy think they've seen a ghost. While mulling it over as an abstract concept I'd been able to be cool and objective. Now that action is required I become every bit as immature as I felt when seventeen year old Melanie teased me. Stripped of the kryptonite that my schoolteacher visage provides, I'm very much the gauche little boy. I resort to the old first date ruse of stifling a yawn and slipping my arm behind Sue's neck. She actually laughs out loud.

"I can't believe you just did that," she giggles.

Have I made a terrible *faux pas*. "I'm sorry, I'm not ..."

"Don't apologise," she interrupts. "It's made me feel better, I'm usually the shy one," and before I can answer, we're kissing.

Sue comes up for breath. "Come on let's go to bed. I'd had enough of Tony Blair & Co anyway."

"What about clearing up?"

"This is so unlike me but it'll still be there in the morning."

She takes my hand and leads me upstairs. I haven't been into Sue's bedroom before because when I first arrived and she'd shown me around, the bedroom was pointed out but in our awkwardness we didn't go in. It's a lovely room, in a beguiling half grown woman, half young girl sort of way. Classy touches interspersed with giveaway hints of cuteness, fluffy animals and the like. It's immaculately clean and tidy, everything in its place. While this could be for my benefit I have the feeling that this is most likely its normal state.

Without a word being spoken we subside onto the bed. Sue gets up and unhooks her dress at the back before lowering the zip and stepping out of it. I guess that the underwear is brand new, it gives the impression of being expensive and the bra has that stiff, exciting, straight out of the box look. Encouraged by the effect that the disrobing is having on me, Sue carries on. She's trying to take off her bra slowly and seductively but either nerves or excitement intervene as the catch has other ideas. I lend a hand and somehow all of those years practicing on Alison bear fruit. The sadness of my life laid bare by the sense of satisfaction I get from this small, insignificant triumph, but in my defence I am after all, quite drunk.

I take this as my cue to take control and ease Sue onto her back, while venturing a quick nuzzle on the way. I start to undress, in fact I complete the task without making myself look too much like Frank Spencer, at least Sue doesn't laugh. She leans across and switches off the bedside lamp, leaving us almost in darkness, the only light being the slight glow from the landing. Sue isn't wearing tights, I ease her panties down as gently as I can manage and lie beside her. As I kiss her I realise that she's sniffling.

"I'm sorry," I say. "I didn't mean to upset you."

"Don't be silly you haven't, it's not you. You couldn't have been nicer, it's me."

"Do you want me to leave?"

"Not unless you really want to but I don't think I can carry on."

"That's okay but I hope you don't think I was trying to force myself on you."

"No of course you weren't but would you mind if we just lie together and I'll try to explain what this mad woman has been trying to do."

We get under the bedclothes and Sue puts her head on my shoulder.

"I told you before that my friends have been trying to fix me up. One or two of them have been really nice blokes but as soon as it started to get serious, you know towards the rumpy-pumpy stage, I've chickened out. I just couldn't handle it. I'd given up on men for a while now and my friends had given up on providing them. Then you came along. When you told me about what you did with your friends, trying to help them to get pregnant it set me thinking. I know it was very unfair of me, you know to use you as a guinea pig but I thought that with someone I trusted and was beginning to like a lot, that I might break my mental block. It didn't work and if anything I feel even more wretched. I've made a fool of myself and I've embarrassed you into the bargain."

"You haven't done either, I'm no more embarrassed than I usually am with women and you've certainly not made a fool of yourself. Can I tell you something?"

"Go on."

"I'm glad that we didn't go through with it. Don't get me wrong I'm a bloke and I wanted to make love to you and I'd have done it and enjoyed it. I'm not a freak or anything."

"What then?"

"Well it's that, 'When Harry Met Sally,' thing."

She gives a blank look. "What's 'When Harry Met Sally'?"

"You really don't get out much do you?" I asked and got a laugh for it. "It's a film from the nineties or was it the eighties, anyway it doesn't matter which. The premise is that Harry and Sally are best friends but fall in love as well. They're fighting the urge to make love because no friendship can survive all of the problems of jealousy etcetera that it brings with it. Over the last week I've begun to appreciate you more and more as a friend but if we'd become lovers and then broken up, I'm sure that the friendship would have gone up in smoke as well. I'm sure that you've done me a favour because I know that I'd never have had the moral fibre to have said no to you."

"Even if it's not true, you're very sweet to make such a complicated excuse for my silly, fickle behaviour."

"It is true and besides, I'll need you to visit me when they put me away."

"Don't say that, even as a joke. Tomorrow we're going to get down to some serious thinking. 'The Great Escape' starts here. There you are you see, I have seen a film."

Chapter 28
Plan B – Dexy's Midnight Runners

The sound of cups and saucers clinking retrieves my consciousness and I suffer the now all too familiar disorientation at waking in a strange bed. Sue has put a cup of tea on my bedside table and is climbing back into bed. She's wearing an oversized rugby shirt, a garment that looks so much better on a woman than a man and Sue's certainly no exception to this rule. It's a relief when she keeps it on as we went to sleep *au naturel* last night and close proximity to a naked friend is very weird, as I know only too well. As I sip my tea I notice last nights discarded clothes are no longer on the floor. Sue's are gone and mine are neatly folded on an armchair.

Putting her cup down, Sue sits up.

"I'm sorry," she says.

"What?" I ask, wondering what someone that's taken me in when I'm at rock bottom and fed and clothed me could have to be sorry about.

"About last night, I'm still mixed up about my attitude towards men and I was wrong to put you in that position but I really don't want it to affect our friendship."

"It won't affect it for me," I say. "It's not every day you discover a real friend and I'd definitely hate to lose you again."

"Oh good, that's out of the way then let's get down to your problems. We need a strategy, what can we do?"

"Apart from me doing a runner to Spain or South America, I haven't a clue."

"I was thinking more in terms of proving your innocence."

"I've been thinking of nothing else but I can't come up with anything. I think we're talking 'Mission Impossible?'"

"I've heard of that one, it's a TV show isn't it? Anyway I know it won't be easy but I've had an idea. I may have read too many Mallory Towers books as a girl but I keep thinking that there must be some sort of clue in Victoria's house, if only we could find a way to get in there. I don't suppose you know any cat burglars do you?"

"No and I've never read Mallory Towers but at the risk of sounding like spunky Harriet saving the day, I think I can do better than that. I know where there's a key to the front door."

"How come?"

"You wouldn't believe me if I told you."

"Try me."

"It was one of Victoria's mad games. I'd pretend be an intruder in the house and when she came home all unsuspecting, I'd jump out on her and have my evil way. Anyway she found it such a turn on the first time we did it that she put the key under a loose flagstone to the right of the front door so that she could have evil intruders on tap. I know the code for the alarm as well unless Lenny has changed it."

"This is too good an opportunity to miss. It's worth the risk of setting the alarm off, after all if it does I can dash back to the car and it will just look like an electrical fault."

"You said I," I say, hoping Sue doesn't mean what I think she means. "But you can't go alone it's too risky, I'll come with you."

"Now that would really be too risky. If you were to be caught everything would be lost and they'd throw away the key. I'll be fine, like I said if the alarm goes off I'm out of there."

"It's not just that though is it? Don't forget Victoria was probably killed in that house."

"I hadn't thought of that," says Sue, for the first time looking a little less gung ho. "But it's the only lead we have at the moment so it's got to be done."

"I think Shaun would go with you if I asked him."

"Shaun the pretend IRA man?"

"Yes, he's been a good friend to me. He's a really great bloke, unless he believes I'm guilty of course."

"If he knows you at all then I'm sure he won't think that. Give me his number and I'll ring him from a call box while I'm out. Does Lenny have a PC at home?"

"Yeah he has an office. I think it's where he does a lot of his dodgy deals from."

"Great, I'll have a look at it when we go in. I don't suppose Shaun happens to be a hacker does he?"

"I don't think Shaun would know how to switch a computer on."

"That's a shame, people tend to put all sorts of things on computers that they shouldn't but I would imagine that anything worth finding will be well buried."

A dim light clicks on in my memory. "I know someone who knows about hacking."

"No, really, who?"

"She's a teacher at the school, Mrs Banks. She helped Lyndsey with her disciplinary hearing. We got on well but I couldn't possibly ask her to get involved in something like this, I don't really know her well enough."

"You don't need to ask her, I will. You can't afford to be fussy in your position, after all, she can only say no."

"And tell the Police."

"Do you think she might?"

"No, in fact I'm sure she wouldn't."

"Right, do you know her phone number?"

"No, I had it once but I can't remember it."

"Never mind, give me her details and I can get it from the net on Yellow Pages. I'm going to visit daddy this morning and I can pump him for the latest info about your case. Then I'll ring Shaun and Mrs Banks who will probably both think I'm some mad woman but never mind."

"Even if they do agree to take part, you still can't be sure that Lenny won't come back while you're there."

"I've put a lot of thought into this, I'm not just a pretty face you know." The manner in which this little quip is delivered suggests that Sue's spirits and self-confidence have lifted considerably. "You said that Lenny spends a lot of time away on business trips, I'll ring his secretary. I'll be Miss Lennox, PA to Mr Hudson at Euro Holdings needing to know Mr Daniels availability during the next couple of weeks in order to arrange a meeting. If you sound confident and high handed enough people will tell you anything."

"Could you really carry that off? I'd be tongue tied and confess what I was up to."

"I have no idea if I can, you don't think I've ever done anything like this before do you? But there's only one way to find out. Anyway, all this waffling isn't getting the baby bathed is it? I need to get going." And with this, she disappears into the bathroom.

For all Sue's self-assured enthusiasm, as soon as she leaves the room my own confidence evaporates. The more I dwell on my predicament the more I feel it's only a matter of time before I end up back in custody. When Sue comes out of the bathroom I make the supreme effort and get out of bed. She's on her way out by the time I go downstairs. I'd planned that I would tidy up last night's mess but everywhere is already spotless.

Instead I embark on a job that I've had my eye on all week, cleaning out the guttering. I need something to occupy my time in order to keep my mind off my problems and I'm fast running out of odd jobs that are within my capabilities. It's a dirtier task than I'd thought, and I'm coming out of the shower when Sue returns.

"Any luck?" I ask.

"It couldn't have gone much better," she said. "Shaun's all for it, he's right behind you, he was worried what had happened to you. He invited me back to his flat to ring Julie, we're on first name terms now by the way. Julie asked if Shaun and I would like to go for a drink to talk things over and so we did, we went to a pub in her village. I've never known so many people who don't drive by the way. Anyway I took Shaun and we picked her up, we all got on like a house on fire."

"I don't want to seem like a wet blanket but I've been thinking and I can't possibly let any of you go through with this. You could all three end up in court and lose your jobs and all sorts of other bad things. I mean, what would your dad say if you got caught."

"Well first of all, it's actually the four of us. In my excitement I forgot to tell you that when I got to Shaun's flat one of his friends had arrived, Aiden, a strange little person."

"He's that alright."

"Shaun had to tell Aiden who I was and why I was there. Aiden insisted that he wanted to help and

255

volunteered to act as lookout and getaway driver. He said that he regretted that he'd always been a little unfairly hostile towards you and wanted to make amends."

"He's never been that bad."

"Don't look a gift horse in the mouth, if he wants to do it I think we should let him. Shaun said that in their younger days they'd both been inside for short sentences for fighting, as well as drunk and disorderly, he said prison holds no fears for them. Julie was even more enthusiastic, she told me that when she was younger she'd always wanted to be more involved in political causes that also held the risk imprisonment but because of her husband's profession and the children she couldn't. Now because of her divorce settlement she's financially independent and she can always get work as a private tutor anyway."

"That still leaves you."

"Yes it does and I didn't tell you this but when I first met Malcolm I was set on joining the Force, you know following in daddy's footsteps. Although he's never said anything, I know he always wanted a son who could have picked up the baton. Malcolm talked me out of joining, I realised afterwards that being a police cadet would have taken me out of his control but at the time I was totally besotted and did whatever he asked. As for daddy, he's always had an innate sense of rightness. He'd want me to do what I thought was just and if I can see this through then one day I'll be able to tell him all about it. It will show him that I might have made a good detective after all. Anyway, at the end of the day I'm still his little girl and he'd forgive me anything."

"Are you really sure?"

"Yes and there's one final reason. Apart from any of that, this is the most exciting thing to happen to me in years and I want to help you. I think that goes for the others as well."

"Jesus! I feel very humble," was all I could say. "Changing the subject, how did you get on with Shaun and Julie?"

"Julie and I got on like a house on fire, she's so easy to talk to. I wish she'd been around when I was going through my dark period."

"I thought the same when I first met her, it felt as if we'd been friends for years. I won't ask what you made of Aiden but what about Shaun?"

"Like you said, he seems very nice," I sense a change in her tone of voice when she says this, she seems a little guarded. Perhaps she doesn't think Shaun's such a great bloke as I do, I suppose women look at these things from a different perspective. "I can't wait to get started now," Sue continues. "I'm going to ring Lenny's office first thing tomorrow morning."

"Did you see your dad? I was just wondering if it might make him suspicious, mentioning me."

"Oh yes, I almost forgot in all of this excitement, I did see him and we had a good chat. He didn't seem at all suspicious when I asked about you, in fact I think he'd have found it strange if I hadn't been curious as I used to work with you."

"I hadn't thought of it like that."

"Interestingly daddy said that when he spoke to DI Jenkins, it seemed almost as if he was pleased that you'd escaped, daddy thought it might be because the case had so many holes in it. He got the impression that Jenkins had been pushed into charging you but he couldn't get him to admit it or let on who'd done the pushing or why. Daddy has a lot of respect for Tom Jenkins; he's known him for years. He told me that they're not actively looking for you in this area any more. It seems they've convinced themselves that you'd head for Ireland and they've alerted the ports and airports. There have been a couple of sightings over there already and they have the Garda searching for you."

"I don't know whether I should be reassured by the inefficiency of the police or really worried by it."

"Not all of the police are bad you know, daddy grilled me about anything I could tell him about you. I had to be careful not to let slip anything that I shouldn't know while telling him everything that might help you."

"Why's he so interested in me?"

"As I told you before, he thinks the whole case stinks and the more he finds out about it the more suspicious he's becoming."

"Oh well, I suppose it's a little reassuring to know that at least one person in authority is on my side, however tenuously."

We spend the remainder of the evening cooking a meal together and watching an old black and white melodrama called 'Flamingo Road'. I'm enjoying a sense of security that I want to wallow in forever but feel sure this feeling of comfort can only be fleeting at best.

Chapter 29
Tonight's The Night – Rod Stewart

The days that Sue is at work begin to drag, the odd jobs that need doing around the house are rapidly diminishing as I work my way through them, we must have the cleanest windows in the Western Europe. Sue keeps me supplied with books and magazines, anything to keep my mind occupied and in normal circumstances I enjoy nothing better than lazing around doing very little. It's not just that the 'Sword of Damocles' is poised over me in such a precarious manner, as the fact that I can't see a way out of my predicament despite Sue's well-meaning optimism. Physical work acts as my opium but as each day passes I look forward to Sue's homecoming with increasing desperation. My pleasure at Sue's return is reflected in her delight at the novelty of not coming home to an empty house.

Sue is bouncing as she arrives home today.

"It's on for tonight," she says. "I spoke to Lenny's PA this morning and he's abroad until Wednesday."

"Will the others be able to make it?"

"Julie was easy, I rang her at school and she sounded as excited as me. Eventually I managed to get Shaun to answer his mobile."

"That's quite an achievement in itself, he hates using the phone."

"Anyway the result of my day's work is that it's all systems go. Zero hour is eight o'clockish."

"I'm scared," I say truthfully.

"Me too but excited at the same time and a bit of adrenalin's no bad thing in the right circumstances."

The time flies until Sue is ready to leave and my last minute pleas for her to call it off fall on deaf ears. I think my hand wringing is beginning to get on her nerves and when the time comes she's glad to get away. I try to watch TV and then to read and to listen to the radio but eventually find pacing the room is the only panacea to my nerves. It's almost ten thirty when a car draws up outside. I'm only expecting Sue but the four of them burst in.

"We did it!" shouts Shaun throwing his big arms around me.

Sue organises drinks for everyone, I suppose I should have thought of that but my head's a shed at the moment.

"No problems?" I gasp using what little breath I've managed to retain post bear hug.

"Like a dream," Shaun continues. "But these two are the real heroes. Suzanne organised it like 'Ocean's Eleven' and Julie working that computer was like... like... Well I can't think like what exactly but they were both just brilliant. Aiden and me were like a couple of jumpy schoolboys while these two were as cool as cucumbers."

"Nonsense, it was a team effort and we all played our part," says Julie.

"What did we find by the way, I was concentrating too much on driving the car to listen?" Aiden asks while still pumping my hand like a long lost friend.

"Well," says Sue. "Julie managed to get into Lenny's business accounts and we've run off copies of them to go through at our leisure. I found a load of dodgy looking invoices and cargo certificates from Cyprus. But here's the best, we've found the tapes from the security cameras for St Patrick's Night at the club, the night that the cameras weren't supposed to be working."

Aiden lets go of my hand and as Shaun also lets go of me I notice that his aftershave is far more in evidence than normal. Looking him up and down I realise that rather than dressing down for a burglary he's wearing some of the new clothes our visit to Merry Hill had harvested. My brain's been obsessed with my own complications of late but suddenly it bursts into cohesive action and concludes that Shaun is out to impress. But who is the quarry? Obviously not Sue as there definitely seems to be a distance between them therefore it must be Julie and for some reason this depresses me more than my other troubles. I suppose it has brought home to me the folly of even dreaming of a future involving Julie given my distinct lack of prospects. When I think about it Shaun is closer to her age than me and I shouldn't confuse her natural warmth in conversation with any real feelings for me. I know that I should be pleased for them, especially as they're both going way beyond the bounds of mere friendship in their efforts to help me out of a massive hole.

"That sounds great, better than we could have hoped for," I say, putting on my best happy face.

"It's a start," says Sue.

"But will the tape be acceptable as evidence, given the way we've, er, obtained it?" Shaun asks.

"There are always methods of doing things," says Julie. "We may need to post it anonymously to Gerry's legal team. When he has one that is."

"When will that be?" I query, thinking that I ought to show a little more interest and enthusiasm than I feel.

"You must have the final say on that Gerry but I should think it's some time off yet," says Sue. "Once we have enough evidence to put a good case together you can hand yourself in on your own terms."

"Yes, surrendering yourself will look much better for you," adds Julie. "And along the same lines, it struck me yesterday that if we encounter any problem with Gerry being here we don't have a plan B, an escape clause."

"Another bolt hole you mean?" Shaun says. "He could come to my place or Aiden or Brendan's."

"Wouldn't that be the first place the police would look, you know with you being friends?" Julie asks. "What about my house?"

"There's still the teacher connection," says Sue.

"I don't think so," I intervene, I suppose in some desperate attempt to maintain a contact with Julie.

"Even if they asked at school no-one would associate me too closely with Julie. They'd think of Dave Stack first, I sometimes went for a drink with him or Kim Sheffield, we were an item for a while."

"You went out with Kim?" Julie asks, stifling a laugh.

"Well I don't suppose we were exactly an item."

"Sorry to laugh, it's just that you're so chalk and cheese."

"We really are, Kim's a PE teacher and she's a bodybuilder as well," I explain to the others. "We went out for a drink a few times when I first split with Alison, Dave fixed us up. Kim persuaded me against my better judgement to go to the gym with her. I think the idea was to make me less likely to get sand kicked in my face, anyway we drifted apart, I think she thought I was a bit effeminate."

"Compared to her you probably are," says Julie. "We were showering together in the school gym the other day and she does have a fantastic physique but I'm not sure I'd want to look like it."

"Yeah," I said. "I was a bit of a disappointment I think but the parting of ways was very amicable. We carried on going for drinks and to the cinema as friends. It came as a bit of a relief really, even though I liked her a lot. She's very bubbly and good company but a bit full on for me."

"I'm sorry to break up the party," says Julie. "But I need to be getting home, I think we're all at work tomorrow and I desperately need my beauty sleep."

"Nonsense," says Shaun. "You've been overdosing on it by the looks of you."

"You're a terrible man you're so full of the blarney," giggles Julie as she punches his arm while colouring a little.

A jealous pang shoots through me and I wish I'd said that? Not that I could get away with that sort of cheeky quip the way Shaun does with such aplomb. It would have come out stilted and probably embarrassed everyone. That together with the fact that I'm growing more certain that Julie wants to hear it from Shaun rather than me. Sue drives them all home leaving me to my personal, invidious hell. How can I be so grudging of two people who are going out on a limb to help me? I feel even more disgusted with myself and the little green-eyed monster gnawing away at my insides is being no help at all.

Chapter 30
Fox On The Run – Manfred Mann

I get up next morning still feeling more than a little unsettled. I've spent the night in a fitful state, more awake than asleep. I still can't purge myself of the guilt I'm suffering over my feelings about Shaun and Julie but can't rid myself of my resentment either. I'm behaving like a spoilt child being unreasonably jealous of the new baby and decide to fall back on hard work as a panacea. I've noticed that the bushes bordering the drive are encroaching and set about cutting them back. Starting at the top end of the drive I'm steadily working my way down and by late afternoon I'm nearing the bottom and find the cure is working. The only things on my mind are scratched hands, an aching back and a sense of satisfaction at a job almost completed. It's at this point that my cosy little world is invaded as I experience the eerie feeling of eyes boring into my back.

I turn around to find myself being evaluated by a stranger. The man is in his fifties and stocky with a ruddy complexion. He's dressed like a farm worker in a bucolic ensemble that is topped off with a flat cap
"Can I help you?" I ask.
The sudden shock lends no real conviction to my adopted Black Country drawl.

He carries on staring for some time, showing no sense of urgency to frame his reply then suddenly shocks me by speaking, just as I'd given up hope.

"Is Miss Taylor at home?"

"You must mean Miss Wilder," I laugh.

Another long pause while he sucks ruminatively on his pipe. "That's right," offering no explanation of his mistake.

"She's out," I reply, equally non-committal.

"And who might you be?"

I toy with an indignant, 'mind your own business,' but can't afford to raise suspicion. "She's paid me to do a few odd jobs."

"Where's your van?"

"It's up behind the cottage."

Without another word he turns and saunters down the lane. After finishing off the job I put the tools away and return to the house. Sue will be home soon and I put the cups out ready for tea before heading for the shower. I'm about to take off my T-shirt when the ringing of the mobile stops me in my tracks.

Before I can speak, Sue's voice bursts in. "Gerry, get out of the house right now, a Police car has just passed me with the blue light going and it's headed your way. Don't worry about Vernon I'll look after him, just take off. Keep the mobile with you and I'll ring you when the coast is clear."

"I'm gone," I said.

I pocket the phone and picking up the rucksack that's been kept permanently packed since the formulation of plan B, I head out through the back door and start up the hill. The siren sounds very loud and the reason becomes obvious as a police car shoots into the drive. It pulls up by the house and glancing over my shoulder I see two PCs jump out. One of them spots me and sets off in pursuit. As I climb I hear the car start up and reverse down the drive.

I anticipate the distance between me and my pursuer is probably closer to one hundred metres than fifty but I'm carrying the rucksack and that will undoubtedly slow me down. I make a decision and after rounding a clump of undergrowth, toss the bag in to it as far as I can manage. Leaping a gate into a field I can see that my follower has narrowed the gap considerably. He's in shirt sleeves and hatless, giving every appearance of being young and fit but looking as though he's wearing a deep sea divers belt around his waist, hung with various accoutrements. I'm surprised it allows him to run at all.

We're heading downhill now and as long as I don't lose my footing my long strides are having no trouble keeping me in front and possibly even increasing the gap. I notice a road at the bottom of the hill that snakes across about three fields further down from my current position. I'm just feeling confident about reaching the road with my lead intact when the police car re-enters the equation as it moves along anticipating our crossing point. I've no option but to keep running and the sudden panic seems to give me a second wind despite my lungs feeling on the point of bursting. For the first time I'm forced to consider failure.

Out of nowhere an unlikely saviour appears in the shape of a milk tanker. The tanker is trundling along towards the police car and as the distance diminishes it becomes obvious that this is a single-track country lane. I alter course for a point well up the lane from the milk vehicle. The driver jumps out of the police car and I can see his quandary, as he tries to decide whether he should risk abandoning his car to chase me on foot. He's obviously a cavalryman at heart and getting back in the car starts reversing madly up the lane. This is a bad error of judgement, as on foot he couldn't have failed to intercept me.

I reach the gate from the field and my pursuer shows no sign of giving up. The lane leading away from the tanker is uphill and looks to be going nowhere. Unexpectedly the familiar sound of an old fashioned train whistle pierces the quiet of the countryside. The Severn Valley Railway operates a rail service around this area that is run by steam enthusiasts. I can hear the puffing of the engine now as well as seeing some smoke despite having no sighting of the train itself. I keep running and at last I can see the engine struggling toward the same summit that I'm labouring to reach. Our paths are diverging and it's a toss-up which of us is puffing the most. Further up the lane the gates of a level crossing block my way forward.

I push my reluctant legs even harder but I seem to be re-enacting the slow motion sequence from 'Chariots of Fire.' The gates are still fifty metres away and the engine of the train has already passed them, how many coaches does it have? I keep going and the coaches keep trundling past. Almost there but as I reach the gates so does the guards van and I launch myself over the gate realising as I do that one slip will see me mangled under the heavy merciless wheels. I grab onto the buffer or whatever the big round things on the back are called and hang on for dear life. The track has now started its downward journey and the train picks up speed. I feel almost sorry for my adversary as he slumps against the gate, beaten not by me but by the Industrial Revolution.

I'm wondering how far I might need to hang here until the next stop when a head appears above me. It belongs to a white haired man who appears to be decked out as a nineteen fifties railway official.

"What the hell do you think you're doing?" demands a posh voice.

In my present position any sensible explanation proves a bridge too far.

"Is this the eight ten to Paddington?" I enquire.

"You cheeky young hooligan, get off, this minute."

"I can't."

"We'll see about that," he disappears.

A sudden screech and the train slows down in a series of sickening lurches, I decide that now might be the ideal time to disembark. Relieved to let go of my buffer I bounce down the gravel of the embankment as the train eventually stops another fifty metres down the track. I set off at right angles to the line, towards what looks like civilisation. Out here in open country I feel extremely exposed and despite trying to hurry, it seems to take forever. Eventually I reach what I recognise as the outskirts of Bewdley.

It's almost déjà vu being here again, still on the run. The difference this time is that I have money in my pocket and somewhere to go. I have mixed feelings about going to Julie's. On the one hand I still enjoy a warm feeling at the mere thought of being in her presence but on the other, seeing her and knowing she's in love with another man will be torture. On the third hand if I had one, I'm the beggar who definitely can't afford to be a chooser. Bewdley is not, as I'd been half expecting the hub of a major manhunt. Instead it's going about its own business in its normal lazy manner with not a uniform in sight. The cab rank on the High Street yields not one but two taxis. I get into the first and the driver, a softly spoken middle-aged man asks me, 'where to sir?'

"Blakedown Railway Station please. I'm meeting a friend there to get a train into Birmingham." I add, in case he wonders why I don't want to go to Kidderminster to get it.

"You've just missed all the excitement," he says. Two police cars shot through the town centre as if they had all the hounds of hell on their tails."

"Going which way?" I ask trying not to sound too interested.

"They went over the bridge, could have been going towards Stourport or Kiddy. Perhaps a lion's escaped from the safari park," he chuckles.

We reach Blakedown without seeing any police cars or indeed any marauding lions. I pay the driver and wait by the station until he's pulled clear. Then I set off for Julie's house and when I reach it the road outside is as quiet as I hoped and expected it would be, it's that sort of road. There's a Transit van outside the house next door and a couple of other cars parked further down the road. Although I've got the key that Julie gave me when plan B was hatched, I expect her to be home at this time in the evening and knock the door. The door opens and there stands a grinning DS Witherspoon.

Chapter 31
Karma Police – Radiohead

"Hello Gerry," he smirks.

I glance over my shoulder, if only to confirm what I know will be there. My pursuer from earlier in the day has three colleagues in tow and they're issuing forth from the back of the erstwhile dormant Transit van. Turning back to DS Witherspoon I can now see Julie and Shaun further back in the room behind another policeman.

"Guess what? You're nicked sunshine," sneers Witherspoon.

"You'll never take me alive copper."

Although I felt lower than ever I've always wanted to say that and as he was stealing from 'The Sweeny' I felt no compunction in being just as corny.

"You what?" Witherspoon said.

"Never mind I'll come quietly, it's a fair cop Guvnor."

While I'm being handcuffed a squad car magically materialises and I'm efficiently ushered into the back seat between two of the PCs. I'm given no opportunity to speak to either Julie or Shaun. We whiz along, sirens blaring, at a somewhat inappropriate speed ending up at Kidderminster Police Station. Once again I'm processed but this time I'm allowed to keep my clothes, minus belt and shoelaces. This despite the fact I've told them that as a coward the only way

I'd consider ending it all is by carbon monoxide poisoning. My little joke elicits no hint of a smile or indeed any other recognition that humour is intended. The failed witticism takes me back to my weak joke about 'Albanian peasant caps,' when Victoria first asked me out. Apart from the obvious thought that if I'd stayed in character and declined her offer I wouldn't be in this mess, it suddenly hits me again that someone I'd grown close to and in a strange way very fond of, is dead. I think that somehow until now it's all been a bit like a TV drama and the actress playing Victoria would turn up in a different series next week. I feel a strange mixture of sick, alone, depressed and frightened and if I had a car and a length of hose in the cell at this moment I might seriously consider using them.

My morbid thoughts are interrupted as I'm taken for questioning, which at least distracts me from dwelling on my problems. I know that I must concentrate now and not give away the friends who have risked so much to help me. DI Jenkins has arrived and with his trusted Indian companion Tonto Witherspoon in tow, the interrogation resumes. We start by regurgitating my memories of the day Victoria disappeared and nothing new comes to light, except to emphasise that my escape merely adds credence to the case against me. Was it really the action of an innocent man? The happy reunion party is completed by my old friend Mr French the solicitor. I'm almost glad to be reacquainted with him and his sports jacket. After all, now that I'm all but certain to be convicted his expertise in appeal procedure may prove invaluable.

"Now then, can you tell me where you've been since your escape?" Jenkins asks me.

"I've been stopping in bed and breakfasts all over the place."

"But when you escaped you had no money, did you steal some?"

"No I went back to my flat, I had some hidden there."

"Your flat was being watched."

"Not very well."

After my experiences with the police I had no qualms about dropping any of them in the doggy do's and I knew this story couldn't be disproved.

"And yesterday you were stopping at the house of a Miss Wilder, that's where you were reported by a member of the public, a Mr Kevin Edwards earlier today. He became suspicious and reported you to the local police, thinking that you were a traveller and up to no good."

"His name was Kevin Edwards? He looked more like Walter Gabriel. Anyway I haven't been stopping at that house I was just doing a job there for cash, cutting back the bushes on the drive. She seemed a nice lady and paid me for the work before I'd done it, even left the house unlocked so that I could wash and use the toilet. You don't meet people that trusting every day."

"Was Mrs Daniels one of those trusting people?" Witherspoon jumps in.

By this time I've stopped denying anything out of sheer boredom and let the comment sail over my head.

"And why did you turn up at Mrs Banks' house today?" Jenkins continues.

"She helped a friend of mine once, Lyndsey Francis. I suppose it was a last chuck of the dice to throw myself on her mercy. I couldn't think of anyone else."

"Ah," says Witherspoon, looking very pleased with himself. "That reminds me, your other two female friends still haven't surfaced. Should we be looking for three bodies rather than one?"

"Is that a serious accusation Mr Witherspoon?" Mr French asks, in the process reminding all of us that he's still there.

"I think that may be a good place to leave it," says DI Jenkins. "We'll be in front of the magistrates tomorrow and I think it goes without saying that we will oppose bail. I'm sure you have things that you wish to discuss with your client Mr French."

We talk and it appears that we will merely go through the motions at the court tomorrow. We'll ask for bail and due to my escape it will be refused and I'll be remanded in custody to a prison not of my choice.

The following day goes pretty much to plan as I'm first delivered to the court then remanded in custody and subsequently delivered into the tender care of the private escort service. These people seem to do the job in a fairly unmotivated but nonetheless reasonably efficient manner. For some reason although I finish in court at ten thirty in the morning, I finally arrive at Winson Green Prison at seven thirty in the evening. If I thought that police custody was a mystifying array of pointless paperwork then nothing could have prepared me for this outbreak of rampant red-tape that would have left even Ionesco speechless. The positive effect of all of the form filling and question answering is that it prevents me from worrying about the ordeal of prison. I've been brooding over it in my cell at court all day but have been kept by myself so far and wonder if this is normal but hadn't dared to ask anyone before now. As I'm being moved from reception to the wing I venture to ask the question of my escorting officer.

"You're an 'E' man now 'cos you escaped from the police, that's why you're dressed in that suit with the yellow patches. It'll all be explained to you later."

And indeed it is. After putting my bedding pack into my cell, I'm taken to a screened off area where a young female officer tells me to sit down. There are four screened off desks and it's like a sausage factory as prisoners are processed. The officer looks tired and bored as she goes through what sounds like a well-practiced preamble. We decide that I'm probably not suicidal and I resist the temptation to reprise my carbon monoxide quip, not difficult given its earlier reception. I learn that my escape from the police entitles me to special treatment. Mostly this involves extra security precautions but the real bonus is that I won't be sharing a cell. Finally she asks me if I want to apply for the rule.

"What rule?" I ask innocently.

"You're in for murdering a woman. Do you think you'll be in danger of assault from other inmates?"

"I didn't do it though, I haven't been found guilty of anything yet."

"That won't cut a lot of ice in here. You can never tell with cons though but the thing is not to look like a victim, act confidently."

"I don't feel very confident."

"Give it a try on normal location. If you get any threats and you think you can't hack it, ask a member of staff for the rule, they'll know what you mean."

"I really haven't killed anyone."

"Believe it or not that's what they all say."

Chapter 32
Inside – Stiltskin

I'm taken to a cell and told to change into a set of blue pyjamas I've been given as all of my other clothes and plastic cutlery will be removed for the night as a security measure. It's a surprise to find a colour television in the cell but my mind is buzzing to such an extent that I can't concentrate on anything. I switch off the light and despite the combination of a rock hard mattress, a pillow that's barely softer, someone checking my door at regular intervals and a head that's buzzing like an empty fruit tin full of wasps, my certainty that I won't possibly get any sleep dissolves into almost immediate somnolence.

I'm woken by the sound of a door bolt being rattled and the brightness of the fluorescent light flickering into life. After my fairly regular waking disorientation at not being able to think where I am, it all floods back. I decide I'd better get up, not wanting to get into trouble on my first day. My cell boasts a sink and a toilet behind a screen. Neither of these is in a particularly hygienic state but to be honest are better than I'd expected after the horror stories you hear. Following my ablutions and while waiting for something to happen, I remember that I was given a breakfast pack last night. This cheers me considerably as I realise I'm ravenous, only that is until I recall that I've no utensils to eat any of it with. Oh well, patience is a virtue.

After what seems an age, a key turns as a precursor to the door opening. The box that I'd put my clothes into the night before is kicked in through the door.

"You alright son?" enquires an officer, who looks ten years younger than me.

"Yes thanks."

"Do you need anything?"

"I'd like something to clean the sink and toilet with and something to read."

"You can clean your cell out later and this wing goes to the library on Monday."

"Er, what day is it?"

"Thursday."

"Thanks Officer."

"Listen, I'd call the staff Boss or Guv or Mr whatever their name is. If you say Sir or Officer, you'll get the piss ripped out of you by the other cons."

"Thanks Boss."

∞

I can't imagine that there could be any more forms to fill in or questions to answer but I'm wrong again there are plenty, including an interview with an African nurse who brightens the surroundings with a wonderful bray of a laugh. Not only am I given a health check but also advice on smoking, drugs, drink and safe sex. It's only when I primly say that I've no intention of partaking of any of them while in prison that the nurse tells me that the last three are meant to be for my eventual release. I thank her, suggesting that this service should be offered to people outside that haven't done anything wrong. The repeat of her raucous laugh confirms the absurdity of such a suggestion.

Eleven thirty brings my first experience of prison food. As an 'E' man I'm escorted down to the servery by my landing officer. I'm getting used to being stared at by other prisoners although I'm still not sure what the looks signify. Some seem hostile, some curious, others merely indifferent. I have a choice of main meal and opt for something that's wrapped in pastry. Other prisoners serve up the food and these inmates are dressed in kitchen whites. The vegetables are sloshed on whether I want them or not along with an orange and some bread and butter. The food isn't as bad as I'd expected, something of a curate's egg, 'good in parts.'

During the afternoon my door is unlocked and the same Officer that unlocked me this morning, Mr Richards, asks me if I want to go out on exercise. I tell him that I'm happy enough in the cell.

"Take my advice and go out, you don't need to go out every day if you don't want to but if you stay in the cell today the other cons will think you're scared."

"I am scared."

"The secret's not to let them know that, it's all about front in here. If you show weakness the jackals will come out of the woodwork and pick you off."

"I'll go out then."

"Good and remember play it cool, don't seem too eager to be friendly."

"Thanks Mr Richards."

The yard turns out to be a tarmac area at the side of the wing. It's about the size of two five-a-side football pitches and is surrounded by a high mesh fence. I don't think I've ever felt so vulnerable, it's like being at the zoo but I'm inside the cage with the lions. There are about seventy of us out here, some huddle in groups around the edge, others walk around in twos, threes and fours. I orbit like a lone satellite trying to appear bold and confident while shrinking into my shirt. A short stocky individual his hair mousy with a hint of ginger joins me.

"What's your name?" he asks.

I look at him trying not to seem over eager but in reality I'm so relieved that someone has spoken to me that I could almost have kissed him.

"Gerry."

"Not your first name, you only use your mates first names in here and you ain't got any."

"Wilson."

"I'm Blakeway, got any burn?"

"What."

"Got any burn?" he persists as if talking to a moron.

"What's burn?"

"Fuck me, are you thick or what, got any tobacco, fags?"

"No I don't smoke."

"What have you got?"

"Nothing."

"You must have something, you got your reception pack today."

"Oh yeah, I got a phone card and some sweets."

"I ain't interested in sweeties, I'll have the phone card though."

"I don't have it on me."

"I'll have it..."

"Fuck off Blakeway," interrupts a rasping voice behind me.

"This ain't none of your business McCall."

"I just made it my business, now fuck off you ugly little troll before I improve your looks without the aid of plastic surgery."

Blakeway does as he's told, muttering obscenities as he goes. I look at my saviour, wondering if he's about to become the fire to Blakeway's frying pan. He's as tall as me and about three times as broad but none of it is spare fat. McCall looks as if he could take Harry Brown's phone card off him if he were here.

"Thanks," I say. "I'd better keep out of his way for a bit."

"Don't worry about him, as long as he thinks I'm looking out for you he won't dare to bother you."

"Can I ask why you looked out for me?"

"I've no love of little shitehawks like him. Let's say that seeing him stymied is reward enough, is this your first time inside?"

"Yeah, I've never even had a parking ticket before now."'

"And now you're in for the big one."

"I've not killed anyone though, I swear to you."

"Everybody's got a story in here son, we all think we've been stitched up by the Old Bill. If I was you I wouldn't keep telling people you're innocent, nobody wants to hear it. You've got plenty of friends in here for escaping from the filth and making them look like arseholes into the bargain. If you keep saying you didn't do it, well it wears a bit thin."

"I thought people might hate me because of the offence."

"Anybody who fucks the police up can't be all bad."

"What about the officers, the ones I've met so far have been alright."

"Screws are screws, most of them ain't too bad, some are right bastards but mostly if you play the game they're okay. Just remember one thing, if you don't trust anybody in here you won't go far wrong."

And with that it seems that my brush with the great McCall is over, except for the effect that it has on my street cred that is, or I suppose I should say, yard cred. Suddenly it's as if the green light has been given for others to talk to me. I'm told that McCall is a contract killer and everyone is scared and respectful of him. I learn most of the things that I need to survive, how to fill in my canteen sheet, how to get a pair of jeans that fit, how not to upset the screws and most important, how to make phone calls and book visits. I'm reluctant to contact anyone for fear of getting them into trouble over helping me during my time at large.

The dilemma is solved when I receive a letter from Shaun. It says that he and Aiden would like to visit me and Julie will come with them if that's okay. I put the three of them onto my visitors list and call Shaun. Speaking to him gives me an unbelievable feeling. It's a sort of warmth from knowing that my friends are out there, still getting on with their lives but not having forgotten about me. I'd known that this would be the case but somehow hadn't been able to convince myself. I don't say too much on the phone in case they're bugged and then feel slightly ridiculous for thinking this.

The evening of the visit arrives and after a day of nervous trepidation, I'm taken into the visits room. I don't know what I'd expected but it's a large room and there are four rows of low tables with three seats one side and one on the other, everything firmly fixed to the floor. As soon as I enter I spot my three visitors and as I approach the table I can sense they're almost as nervous as I feel. Shaun pumps my hand while Aiden shakes hands lightly and I sense that he's very emotional, a fact that surprises me. Julie leans over the table and kisses me on the cheek, creating a chemical reaction of emotions in my head, stomach and legs. The only outward sign of this fortunately, is a slight reddening of my cheeks.

"How are you bearing up boy?" Shaun asks.

"I'm fine," I reply, giving them a rundown of 'life inside,' leaving out the more sordid aspects and hopefully allaying some of their worries.

"Sue wanted to come," says Julie. "But with you being at her house when you were spotted, we managed to talk her out of it. We said we'd sound out your opinion."

"You were right I'm sure, it could get her into a lot of trouble as well as causing problems for her dad. Tell her I think it best that I don't contact her directly and I can let her know everything when I write to the rest of you. After I've been found guilty and all of the fuss has blown over we can take a rain check."

"Don't say it like that," says Shaun. "We're still working on finding proof that you're innocent."

"Thanks for that but I need to be realistic and it's not looking too good."

"There's still Lyndsey and Violet to come back and give their evidence."

"I know and don't think I haven't thought long and hard about that as well but all they can do is to confirm that I was with them at a certain time. I could have killed Victoria before I went to their flat and had plenty of time after I left them to go and get rid of the body."

"Are you talking like this because you're depressed or are you just being realistic?" Julie asks. "Only there's a big difference. You know that a lot can still happen between now and the trial so you shouldn't give up hope. But if you're looking at it as a worst case scenario and then anything else is a bonus, well I suppose that's quite a sensible outlook."

"I'm trying to be a realist," I say. "It's not easy but I heard a poem on the radio the other day by a lady poet. While I can't remember it word for word, the gist of it was that she saw a bedraggled swallow flying in over the coast at the end of its migration from Africa and if it can undergo a journey like that then how can I ever say again that anything is too much to face."

Aiden, who has been uncharacteristically quiet until now, suddenly bursts in.

"That's beautiful, you're so fucking brave. I'm sorry for my language Julie but he is."

"You're excused, in the circumstances," she smiles.

"It's not really bravery is it, I don't have much choice? I say. "The only alternative is to commit suicide and apparently that's against the rules. I don't know if it infringes my civil liberties but even if I had the bottle to do it, some poor screw would be hauled over the coals for not stopping me and I couldn't live with myself then could I?"

"See, he even jokes at a time like this," adds Aiden seemingly on the verge of tears.

"Seriously though, you're not thinking along those lines are you?" Julie asks, suddenly looking concerned.

"No of course not," I say trying to smile. "Please don't worry about me, I'll be fine."

The conversation continues along practical lines. Shaun reveals that he is now the proud owner of a car, which he used to bring them here tonight. He doesn't have a licence yet but is driving on a provisional one. The provision seems to be that he expects to pass a test at some future date and hopes not to get caught in the meantime. I suppose it makes sense as he and Julie can hardly rely on public transport to get to and fro between Lye and Blakedown. They insist that they'll send in regular financial contributions to keep my body and soul together, a bit like Billy Bunter's postal orders from the folks. Various people have promised to write, some of the names coming as a surprise. I suppose this is an unexpected bonus of being in prison, finding that I have unsuspected friends.

The bellow of, 'finish your visits off please,' signals that the time has passed remarkably quickly. Another surprise is that on saying our farewells, I seem to be the only one without tears welling up. We get through it and I return to my cell, feeling more positive although I can't put my finger on the reason why.

∞

Weeks pass and I devise my own method of getting through the time. First of all on a daily basis I look forward to the little things, like exercise or a TV programme. Then on a weekly one, canteen day and library are my goals. My long-term bonuses are the visits and letters.

The news that I've been waiting for finally comes through as Lyndsey and Violet have arrived home. By the time their security clearance has been granted on my visitors list, the re-arranged tribunal has already taken place. Lyndsey has been cleared of assault and a minor slap on the wrist has been administered in respect of her judgement. The visit is very emotional for all of us and I'm pleased about the tribunal result while obviously they're devastated about my predicament, saying it's removed any vestige of pleasure regarding Lyndsey's job. They tell me that the police have taken statements from them both about the night in question and also asked questions about their relationship with me, and indeed Victoria. They say they've told the police the truth about what we were doing that night as they were sure that I would have done the same and anyway it usually pays to be honest. After all, they point out, we've watched numerous crime dramas on TV and seen how much trouble deception can lead to. If only I'd

289

had them advising me before my police interview. The visit ends amid three gallant attempts at stiff upper lips and once again it has lifted my mood.

The next bombshell to be dropped comes down the phone line when Shaun announces that my parents have arrived in the country and want to visit me. A friendly Senior Officer on the wing manages to expedite the security clearance and the visit takes place. As soon as I see them in the visits room I know that this is by far the worst crime that I've committed by bringing two of the most decent, law-abiding people imaginable into a place like this. I have no idea how they will take my situation but I'm relieved when they both hug me at the same time before we eventually sit down.

"Your sister wanted to come up too but can't get the time off at the moment," says mother.

"I wish you hadn't come," I say. "I feel terrible dragging you to a place like this."

"And so you should but you're our son," says Dad. "Nothing would have stopped us."

"I didn't do it," I say.

"You think we don't know that," says my mother. "You were brought up properly."

"But I have to tell you that there are some other things that I was doing that you wouldn't approve of and if you knew about them you probably wouldn't have come."

"Try us," said my father.

"Well to start with I was having a relationship with the woman, and she was married, although she didn't get on with her husband."

"Is that it?"

"No it gets worse. There are two friends of mine who are a lesbian couple and they wanted a baby," I gabble out. "And I agreed to be the surrogate father." Deciding that discretion is the better part of valour, I don't go as far as revealing the method.

"Any more?"

I judge that I can probably get away with this for now.

"No, apart from escaping from the Police and that was because I panicked."

"Well that's understandable," says my dad.

"Don't think we condone it though," says my mother. "And as for those other things, well don't for a minute think we're excusing that sort of behaviour. We brought you up fairly strictly, knowing that England as well as changing values would be bound to corrupt you to a certain extent, but at least you would have a loftier peak to begin your fall from."

"We never expected you to be a mirror version of us," says my dad. "That would have been unrealistic."

"Both sets of your grandparents didn't attend our own wedding," my mother tells me. "Or even speak to us for months after it. That was because we married across the divide, in their eyes we were sinners."

"So you see we were every bit as bad as you, in our own way," add my dad. "What we're trying to say is that we're not the strict old fuddy-duddies that you think we are and we needed to see you, to tell you that we love and support you."

I don't know what to say, as this certainly isn't what I'd been expecting.

"I'm so grateful to you both. I know how hard this must be for you."

"Nonsense," says my mother. "We knew you couldn't have done a thing like that and we're going to stay here until the trial."

"I really appreciate that but there's no need. For one thing, apart from visiting me there's nothing you can do and I'd feel even worse than I do now, it would just be something else for me to worry about. When the trial comes up the press might hound you and I'd hate that. The biggest favour that you could do me would be to get on with your lives at home, keep writing to me and then come and see me when the trial is over."

I don't add that I'm sure that I will still be in prison and facing a long sentence.

"Are you sure son?" asks my father, his voice quivering a little now, while mother is fighting to hold back the tears.

"Yes. I love you both so much," I say, mustering all of the self-control I can manage. Dignity is the only thing that I seem to have left, and holding on to it seems to assume an all-consuming importance.

Chapter 33

Here Comes The Judge – Pigmeat Markham

Weeks turn into months and Mr French visits me a number of times. On one of these occasions he's accompanied by a younger, plummy voiced man who, it seems, is to act as my barrister at the trial. His name is Timothy Jordan and he's very business-like but in contrast to Mr French he gives the impression that he may even have considered the possibility that I might be innocent.

My friends continue to visit and do a grand job of keeping my spirits up even though there is no sign of any further evidence that might allude to my innocence turning up. My status as an 'E' man remains and one day when I'm chatting to one of the prison officers he vouchsafes to me that he's surprised that I'm still, 'on the book,' as they call it, after such a long period of time. He seems to consider this is an injustice, bearing in mind my behaviour. I tell him that I'm more than happy to remain in a single cell and laugh about the fact that I must have enemies in high places that think they're discomforting me. Although I pass this off as a joke it still worries me that if Lenny wields influence with the police and in here then it may be possible that he has some sway with the judiciary. I then realise how paranoid I've become, of course he has no influence with prison governors and judges. Or does he?

∞

The day of my trial arrives and although I'm full of foreboding, it's still a relief in a strange way. After all, even a life sentence can't be much worse than the current limbo I'm in. I've learnt to adapt to prison life and I'm planning how to deal with the boredom when I'm sentenced. I can improve my education, extend my reading range and acquire new skills. I can learn the guitar, speak another language or even make gypsy caravans from matchsticks. Forget the last one although maybe I'll be able to make an internal combustion engine out of matchsticks thereby keeping the carbon monoxide exit route open should I become that desperate.

Monday morning and I'm back in the hands of 'Artifice', the private escort service. Two of their operatives escort me to some steps that lead into the dock at the back of the courtroom. I'm told that we must wait here until the Judge has made his entrance as he will bow to the court but not the accused. When we go up the steps the people already in this large chamber are all smartly dressed, some of them sporting black gowns and grey wigs. The one thing they all have in common is that they're staring at me. The public gallery is inhabited by a smattering of people, varying in degrees of sartorial elegance. Julie is there with Aiden and Brendan, but Shaun, Lyndsey and Violet are possible witnesses and must remain outside.

Mr Jordan has been to see me earlier when he ran through what is likely to happen. First comes the laying down of the ground rules and any legal points that either side may wish to raise. A rather feisty looking lady barrister called Ms Callard leads the prosecution team. I realise I'm being ridiculous in feeling jealous she isn't my barrister, Mr Jordan seems very capable if a little relaxed and easy going. This is followed by the jury being sworn in, Mr Jordan has told me that we can object to any of the jurors but will only do so if I know any of them, I don't and it all goes smoothly. Seven women and five men, I reassure myself that women will be more sympathetic and probably more incisive and try to ignore the fact that they are more likely to see me as an abuser of women. Finally the time has come for the charges to be read and for me to plead.

"Are you Gerald Lewis Wilson?" intones the Clerk of the Court.

"Yes."

"Gerald Lewis Wilson, you are charged that at a time between the Nineteenth of April Two Thousand, and the Twentieth of April Two

Thousand that you murdered Victoria Daniels. Do you plead guilty or not guilty?"

"Not guilty."

"You are charged, that on the Twenty First of April Two Thousand, you escaped from lawful custody. Do you plead guilty or not guilty?"

"Guilty," I reply. Mr Jordan had explained that not only was it pointless pleading not guilty because I had escaped but doing so would alienate the judge.

"You are also charged that on Twenty First of April Two Thousand that you stole clothing and property to the value of one hundred and fifty seven pounds. Do you plead guilty or not guilty?"

"Guilty." Again I had done it and it would be counterproductive to deny it. In my defence, I think whoever put that valuation on the clothes should be in the dock with me.

We're ready to rock and roll. The judge gives the jury a pep talk, that they must not be influenced by anything that they may have seen in the media etc.

The prosecution call their first witness, the officer in charge of the case, DI Jenkins. The evidence is gone over with a regard for minutiae that would have put Perry Mason to shame. After Ms Callard has finished with him Mr Jordan sets to. Eventually DI Jenkins is allowed to stand down, and I find myself pleasantly surprised by his lack of bias. DS Witherspoon follows and no one could accuse him of not wearing his heart on his sleeve. His evidence displays all of the neutrality of a Premier

League referee in a game involving Manchester United.

The lunchtime adjournment closely follows DS Witherspoon and Mr Jordan comes down to see me. "That couldn't have gone much better," he says beaming.

"I thought Mr Jenkins was very fair."

"Not just that but the disparity between his and Witherspoon's accounts didn't look good and I don't think the jury missed the significance. Anyway I'll see you after lunch and we'll push on."

∞

A police scene of crimes officer is called after the luncheon adjournment and gives some specialist evidence. He's cross-examined and clarifies some points before being allowed to leave. All parties agree that some scientific lab reports may be read out as none of their contents are in dispute.

The next to be called is Lenny. He looks very much the broken man, slightly unkempt, head bowed, a listless shuffle as he enters the witness box. Lenny affirms his name and address in a cracked, unassuming voice that is nothing like his normal tone. He begins to answer Ms Callard's questions, speaking quietly, wringing what seems every ounce of sympathy from the jury. That is until he steps up a gear, suddenly breaking down and sobbing into his handkerchief. The judge intervenes to ask if Lenny needs a break. 'No,' weeps Lenny bravely controlling himself. 'If I could just have a glass of water, I'd prefer to get it over with.' I notice the looks of pity on the faces of the jury, especially the female members. The questions continue, covering even the tiniest detail. How my affair had broken his marriage and with it his heart, how he had immersed himself in his business hoping that the liaison would blow over and he could return to his former wedded bliss, even citing that I had sneered at him on the occasions that our paths crossed.

Eventually Ms Callard runs out of questions, coincidently just as Lenny's tears appear to be drying up. Mr Jordan picks up the baton but he's on a loser from the start. The jury have fallen for Lenny's 'Oscar' winning histrionics and the ladies, far from being sympathetic to me are casting glances of pure malice my way, while the men are enjoying strong feelings of empathy with Lenny. Mr Jordan does his best, questioning the strength of the marriage and Lenny's extramural bedroom activities, the latter at the risk of being lynched by the jury. Lenny doesn't blow up but denies it all in a quiet cracked voice, wiping a tear from his eye and saying that he understands that Mr Jordan is just doing his job by asking these questions.

The St Patrick's night incident follows and Lenny sticks to the company line, saying that I had been beaten up at the club after provoking the trouble myself. While being ejected from the club I had apparently shouted in front of witnesses that I would stitch him up over it. Lenny is asked about the security videos covering the night in question and of course he recites his tale that as he told the police, the system was down at that particular time. It's at this point that the metaphorical rabbit is produced from the hat as Mr Jordan lifts a brown envelope from the table.

"In this envelope is a video tape that was sent anonymously to my office. I have viewed the tape and the date is the Seventeenth of March Two Thousand. The location is clearly the interior of the Purple Flamingo Club. I invite the court to view it but I can assure your honour that neither my client nor any sign of an altercation appear on it."

Ms Callard stands. "Your honour, if it is of assistance to the court the prosecution feels that the truth or otherwise regarding this tape is very much peripheral to the case. Mr Daniels accepted the word of his employees that there were no tapes. It is quite possible that they may be clever forgeries and no doubt a lot of time and a lot of money could be wasted on having them tested. Therefore to expedite the matter, the prosecution is happy to accept Mr Jordan's word that the tapes are genuine and that nothing untoward appears on them."

"That would seem to be a satisfactory conclusion, don't you agree Mr Jordan?"

I judge that this is more in the style of a statement than a question. My counsel has been outmanoeuvred and is forced to agree.

"Thank you Your Honour, I bow to your judgement," although I feel sure that he doesn't he continues. "I hope members of the jury will take this piece of evidence into account and as it is uncontested will give due weight to it when the time comes to weigh up the evidence in this case," again as I look at the jury they seem to be looking at Mr Jordan with the same distaste they've reserved for me until now.

The judge decides that this will be a good time to bring the day's proceedings to an end in order to allow Lenny to recover from his ordeal. Mr Jordan comes to see me downstairs.

"Not so good," he says. "The morning was ours but the afternoon most definitely swung back their way and then some. Mr Daniels performance was of almost Shakespearian proportions and it hamstrung me. If I pushed him too far I risked totally antagonising the jury."

"He was very good," I said.

"Yes he was and I hope that you're going to be as good, because I'm going to have to call you to give evidence when the time comes. It's not always a good idea and I hadn't intended to call you but there are so many things that need explaining, that it can't really be avoided."

"I'll do my best."

"You'll need to do that. When the time comes tell the truth, don't try to be clever and don't say more than you need to. Don't anticipate questions, when the cross-examination starts you will find that Fran

Callard is a very smart operator and a very tough cookie. She hasn't come here to finish second."

"You make it sound like a race."

"Try war, she's ruthless. This is about her career and reputation and your guilt or otherwise is incidental. You are just collateral damage."

∞

Tuesday morning finds us all, unremarkably gathered in the same place at the same time. Proceedings resume with Harry Brown being called to give evidence. Harry's performance in the box is closely followed by Jermaine's and both are so word perfect that I feel sure they have received some fairly intensive coaching. Mrs Hamilton the neighbourhood watch lady comes next and gives a bravura performance describing what she saw. There are a couple of occasions when she unintentionally raises laughter in the court. These are smothered at birth by the judge, bearing in mind the gravity of the occasion. Ms Callard wrings out every last drop from Mrs Hamilton's evidence before passing her over. Mr Jordan can only pick up a couple of points to clarify while attempting to highlight Mrs Hamilton's extravagant view of the facts. Next is Mrs Brimble, Victoria's cleaning lady. This is the first time I've been able to put a face to the voice and it's hardly been worth the wait. Although she doesn't have a great deal of evidence to give as most of what she has to say has been covered in the forensic evidence, nevertheless she certainly makes the most of her moment in the spotlight. In a film it would have been described as a cameo performance. She even has to be reined in on a couple of occasions when she begins speculating on Victoria's liaisons and that she always knew they would lead to a sticky end.

There follows a cast of bit part players. The statements of the Doctor, the Nurse and the Police Constable who interviewed me at the hospital on St Patrick's night are all read out unchallenged. Then my old friend DS Cartwright takes the oath, wearing what looks very much like the same suit and it doesn't appear to have troubled Sketchlys in the intervening period, a sort of Columbo without the redeeming feature of intelligence. He is led through his interview with me, which is all on tape, including his assertion of my threat to stitch up Lenny. Mr Jordan intervenes here to say that this is hearsay and therefore inadmissible as evidence. The judge agrees and advises the jury to ignore the remark but again, the damage has been done and what has been heard cannot be unheard.

Kevin Edwards is called next. He's the taciturn bumpkin that 'grassed me up' to the police. He wastes no more words here than he had on the day, only venturing an opinion when pushed. It turns out that he'd had no idea who I was when he spotted me in Sue's driveway. He only phoned the police because he was suspicious of my motives and believed that I was trying to disguise my Irish accent and felt sure that I was a tinker and ergo must be up to no good. The PC who had chased me is the final prosecution witness. He gives a fair summation of the pursuit, even complimenting me on my efforts. It turns out that he is a club standard runner and in the witness box he oozes youthful vitality, looking every inch the athlete.

That's that for another day and I go back to prison to prepare for my big performance. Tomorrow is to be the day and I'll be centre stage. Just the sort of thing I've spent my whole life avoiding.

Chapter 34
Don't Look Back In Anger - Oasis

Wednesday morning and proceedings begin with Mr Jordan rising to his feet.

"I would like to open the case for the defence by calling the defendant."

The usher opens the gate to the dock and accompanied by a security guard, I make my way to the witness box. It's much less harrowing than I'd expected, owing to Mr Jordan leading me through my relationship with Victoria from its first dawning to its untimely demise. All of this takes a considerable time and the afternoon is well advanced when he decides that he has 'no further questions.' The judge takes pity on me and wraps up the day's proceedings. I expect a visit from Mr Jordan but I'm informed by Mr French that as I'm in the middle of giving evidence then neither of them can speak to me about the case until I've finished.

∞

Thursday and today is to be my ordeal by fire. I notice that Julie is absent from the public gallery which surprises me as she's been there every day without fail until today. Now that I'm in the witness box and within striking distance of Ms Callard, I can see that what I'd interpreted as feisty until now is actually quite scary at close quarters. I'm the tethered goat about to be devoured by the great 'She Tiger.' We go over the beginnings of the relationship and she suggests that I did more of the chasing than I've let on, which I deny. I'm being grilled about my time with Victoria when St Patrick's night comes up again. I'm asked about my alleged threat to stitch up Lenny after supposedly getting beaten up at his club and DS Cartwright's refusal to believe my story.

"Did this cause you to feel some resentment towards Mr Daniels?"

"Yes," I answer, giving little thought to where this is going. "Of course I resented being kidnapped, beaten up and then told by the police how lucky I was that Lenny Daniels wasn't going to prosecute me after spinning a pack of lies."

"And you mentioned to DS Cartwright that you would be better off taking the law into your own hands."

Too late I see the light.

"It wasn't meant as a serious suggestion, I was just upset and letting off steam. I think my words were, 'I can see why people take the law into their own hands'"

"You think your words were?" she asks, looking at me over the half-moon spectacles she wears for reading "The court may be interested to hear that a few days after this conversation, Mr Daniels, Mr Brown and Mr Etienne were the victims of a vicious assault. This was carried out by a group of men claiming to be members of the IRA and warning them that it would go badly for them if anything happened to Mr Wilson here."

"I don't know anything about that," I said.

Mr Jordan interrupts. "I would like to object to this line of questioning your honour. First of all it is hearsay. It is also most unfair to my client, as no previous mention has been made of it. I should also like to know if it has been subject to a police investigation."

"Your Honour," said Ms Callard. "Mr Daniels did not report it to the police at the time because he was in fear for his life but I have no wish to distract the jury's attention from the case in hand, and therefore if it will assist the court I will not pursue this line of questioning."

"Thank you Miss Callard that's very helpful. Members of the jury, you will disregard the last question and its subsequent answer."

Once again the seeds have been successfully sown that Gerry Wilson is a man of violence with unsavoury connections. Ms Callard again comes over as the good guy by not pushing it. We continue to go over my time with Victoria. This time around however, it's much less comfortable as Ms Callard picks up on every minor inconsistency, making me look less believable by the minute. Early afternoon and I feel like a punch-drunk boxer reeling on the ropes but without the option of throwing in the towel. It's at this juncture that Ms Callard reaches the point that she's obviously been building up to all day, the opportunity to deliver the coup de grace.

"Mr Wilson, would you describe yourself as a truthful person?"

"Yes," I reply automatically.

"I have in front of me the transcript of your first interview with the police. Let me remind you that you had been officially cautioned at this time. I ask you again Mr Wilson do you consider yourself to be a truthful person?"

"I wasn't on that occasion but there were good reasons for it."

"So you are saying you are truthful but only when it suits your purpose," I attempt to interrupt. "Don't worry Mr Wilson, you'll be given ample opportunity to explain your 'good reasons,'" she announces, almost licking her lips in anticipation.

We wade through the now so familiar police interview. My explanations of the inconsistencies sound no more convincing now than they had at the time.

"Finally Mr Wilson, when you were taken in for questioning by the Police you were driving around in Mrs Daniels car. Is that correct?"

"Yes, she insisted that I use it while mine was being repaired."

"This was on the Friday, the last time you saw her alive?"

"Yes."

"And this was after, by your own admission that you had aroused her great displeasure by your refusal to stay? Yet despite this she still insisted on loaning you her very expensive car."

"I know it sounds unbelievable but that's the way she is...was, a mass of contradictions. Anyone who knows her will tell you the same."

"In my experience things that sound unbelievable usually tend to be because they are unbelievable."

By late afternoon I'm still in the box and my head is pounding. Ms Callard finally decides that I've taken enough punishment and calls a halt. The judge asks Mr Jordan if there will be a re-examination and being told that there will, thankfully decides that it will take place tomorrow.

∞

Friday finds Mr Jordan doing his best to salvage something from the wreckage that is my credibility following Ms Callard's demolition job. I'm finally allowed to return to the safety of the dock, after my odyssey in the witness box. Lyndsey and Violet are called and manage to say some nice things about me but are unable to throw much in the way of new light onto the evidence. This is reflected by Ms Callard's scant cross-examination. Shaun isn't called and it doesn't take a genius to work out that after 'the IRA episode,' the damage that his accent and physical size would do to our cause could outweigh any plus points.

The rest of the day is taken up with both barristers delivering their summing up. I have to admit that I find Ms Callard's version of the truth much more convincing than Mr Jordan's, the fact that I know I haven't done it makes me realise that

I cannot possibly expect the jury to believe my account. The judge starts his own summing up before announcing that he will complete it on Monday morning when he will send the jury out.

Chapter 35
Hello How Are You – The Easybeats

The weekend passes as I try not to think about the trial. This proves almost impossible as every prisoner seems to have acquired even more legal expertise than usual and they all want to share it with me. It seems that everyone has been avidly following my case, both in the papers and on television. The upshot of this is that I receive some of the most spurious advice in the annals of legal history. The majority of this is on appeal procedure, which suggests that my fate has been decided.

∞

Monday morning and the judge is as good as his word, he takes thirty minutes to complete his summing up, then spends another fifteen minutes informing the jury of the importance of the case. Telling them that they are under no time restriction to come to a verdict and should the time come when a majority verdict can be considered, then he will inform them but he would prefer a unanimous one. The final warning is not to discuss the case with friends and family and to avoid any parts of the media where it may be mentioned. They are to disregard anything that they may know about the case that they have picked up outside the courtroom, as only evidence given under oath is admissible and on that subject, any expert evidence that has been read out unchallenged should be taken as fact, the rest is for them to unravel, using their life experience.

I sit in my cell downstairs, mulling over the trial. It hasn't gone well but had I ever expected it to? What are my chances? The only possibility I can foresee might be Victoria's body being found and even then I'm not sure if this could reveal any new evidence that would change anything. If Lenny's Russian contacts have played a part then I feel sure there's little chance of that happening anyway, I'm certain they're bound to be very professional in the disposal of bodies. I spend the rest of the day trying to make myself comfortable on the hard bench in the cell. The jury stays out and by the following morning I've laid my hands on a 'Flashman' from the prison library. This at least makes the waiting more bearable, even hopeful. After all Flashman escapes from far more desperate and death defying predicaments than my current one and he does it on a regular basis. Late Tuesday morning and as Flashy is about to face another fate worse than death, the door opens and a guard looks in.

"Come on Paddy something's happening, they want you up in court."

"What for?"

"I dunno, his Honour normally tells me everything first but he's been a bit remiss today, I'll have to give him a bollocking."

Everyone including the judge is in place although the jury box is empty. An excited but very muted hum of conversation fills the air. Mr Jordan bustles in, gown flying behind him like a legal Superman. As he reaches his position he gives me a conspiratorial wink. I suppose he's trying to keep my spirits up because after all, if the jury have come to a verdict he couldn't possibly know the result yet.

"Mr Jordan," says the judge. "I understand that you have asked for the court to re-convene without the jury present."

"That's true your honour and I am most grateful. There has been an important development which I should like to put before you."

"Carry on Mr Jordan."

Mr Jordan nods to one of his clerks, the woman has obviously been stationed by the main doors for this very reason. She opens the door and in walks Victoria Daniels, very much alive and looking more subdued than I've ever seen her.

Chapter 36
Friends – Bette Midler

"Your honour, may I explain?"

"Yes, I think that would be a good idea Mr Jordan."

"This is Mrs Victoria Daniels, the alleged deceased. As you can see, Mrs Daniels is very much alive. It seems that a Mrs Julie Banks, a teaching colleague of both Mr Wilson and Mrs Daniels at St Winston's School has been watching the progress of the trial from the public gallery. When the defendant was undergoing cross-examination he mentioned that Mrs Daniels talked of the love of her life being a man called Ben Roberts and that she always regretted losing him. Mrs Banks recalled a conversation between herself and Mrs Daniels in the school staff room some time earlier. During that conversation Mrs Daniels stated that it wouldn't take much for her to go looking for Mr Roberts, to find out if there was still a flicker of their former love. Mrs Banks did some research on the Internet and found that apparently Mr Roberts is an artist of some repute. After finding that Mr Roberts resides on a fairly remote island in the French Polynese, Mrs Banks set about finding him. She succeeded in doing this and after undergoing a long and complicated journey to get there Mrs Daniels immediately returned with Mrs Banks. May I add that Mrs Daniels was totally unaware of the furore her disappearance has caused."

"Has this lady been officially identified as the person in question, the alleged deceased?"

"Your Honour, the prosecution and the police both confirm that fact."

Ms Callard nods her agreement.

"Very well," said the Judge. "May I ask Mrs Daniels, why did you choose to go away without notifying anyone of your intentions?"

"Your Honour, I can only apologise and say that it was a spur of the moment decision. I suppose it was a misguided attempt to punish my husband and everyone else because I was feeling depressed and dissatisfied with my life. I wasn't exactly thinking lucidly at the time, it never occurred to me that anything of this magnitude could happen and I deeply regret my thoughtlessness and its consequences."

"I think that this may be a good moment to bring back the jury, in order to explain to them the turn of events."

The jury return and when they are settled His Honour sets about explaining to them the bizarre happenings of the last few minutes. Before telling them that as a consequence of this they are dismissed as a jury but should remain in the jury box to see the culmination of the case.

"Mrs Daniels, I do not believe that you have broken any laws, however I will leave that matter for the police and the CPS to decide. Notwithstanding this your actions have caused a great deal of trouble for a number of people, not least the defendant. Your words of contrition nevertheless, are to your credit. Mrs Banks, we all owe you a great deal, especially the defendant. You have prevented what could have been a grave miscarriage of justice. On behalf of the court, I offer sincere thanks and I will take steps to see that the expenses that you have incurred will be reimbursed from public funds along with an award of two hundred pounds. Now I will pass on to the part played by the Police and the Crown Prosecution Service in this sorry tale. From its outset I have not been totally at ease with this case, the manner of its investigation or the way that it has been pushed through. I am therefore going to recommend an inquiry be instated. Miss Callard is there anything that you would wish to add?"

"Your Honour, I would reiterate your thanks to Mrs Banks and add that I have pursued the case as it was presented to me by the CPS in good faith."

"Thank you Miss Callard. There was no criticism intended of the manner in which you have conducted the case. Finally Mr Wilson, it only remains to deal with you. On the charge of murder, I find no case to answer. On the two charges to which you have pleaded guilty, I sentence you to a length of imprisonment that shall allow your immediate release. You may leave the dock."

"All rise," says the Clerk and the Judge departs.

Although the Head Honcho has told me that I can leave the dock, the months of following orders have taken their toll.

"You know you can't stay for your tea with us, don't you?" asks the guard, opening the gate from the dock to the court.

I step down into well of the court, where I'm mobbed. The news of what's in the offing has obviously spread and as well as Julie, Victoria, Lyndsey, Violet and Shaun. Aiden and Brendan have arrived with Emmeline and Sue. Dave, Kim and Sienna from school have arrived as well as a lot of Shaun's Irish mates, having obviously sensed a celebration in the offing. Amid the hubbub I'm surprised to find that DI Jenkins has slipped through the throng.

"No hard feelings lad, I had no choice," he says quietly.

I shake his proffered hand but say nothing. I don't really know what to say although afterwards I feel quite touched that he'd had the strength of character to make this gesture. It would have been easier for him to just slip away.

I'm swept from the court by a crush of tearstained women and backslapping men and on into the pub over the road. The drinkers already in situ, part like the Red Sea to admit our roistering mass of humanity. We more or less take over the bar and a pint of Guinness is thrust into my hand. I manage about two gulps and at least as much spilt down the front of my shirt before it's taken away and replaced with a glass of champagne, as I'm being made the subject of a toast. When the toast is complete I have to shout to make myself heard.

"I'd like to propose a toast myself. I feel very humble in thanking Julie and all of the other people who've risked so much to help me, they know who they are but I can't mention them by name," I look at Sue as I say this. "Without them I'd be sitting in a cell now. Friends are the ones who stick with you when things go wrong. They're the ones who believe in you when you've stopped believing in yourself. Thank you all, I owe you so much."

After a loud cheer the Irish lads set about some serious singing and I manage to flop into a seat at a table in the corner. Sue, Julie, Lyndsey, Violet and Shaun sit around me.

"Did Victoria really tell you about Ben?" I ask Julie.

"No, I've never spoken more than a couple of words to her at school. I had to make that bit up for the court. It was when you mentioned him during your cross examination, a little bell rang in the murky depths of my brain. I recalled that when I was scanning through the PC memory at Victoria's house, there were lots of searches for Ben Roberts but the name meant nothing to me at the time. I just guessed that Lenny must have been thinking of investing his ill-gotten gains in art. Anyway I contacted Sue and we went back to the house again. We thought that the locks might have been changed or the computer taken away but luckily Lenny hadn't bothered. When I checked back I found that all of the searches were done between five thirty and six fifteen on the day that Victoria disappeared. All I did was run back through the results and they threw up all of the information that I needed."

"And you actually flew out there and found her?"

"You make it sound far too easy," Julie allowed herself to look a little smug as she said this. "I had to fly to Paris first to get a flight to Tahiti before taking a local flight to the nearest island that boasted an airstrip. Finally I chartered a fishing boat from there to take me to Ben's island. And would you believe it, when I landed, the first sign of human life was Victoria lying stark naked on a sun lounger?"

"I can't believe that you did all of that for me."

"It just happened to be me but any of the others would have done exactly the same."

I can't help thinking to myself, what a lucky bloke Shaun is to have this wonderful woman.

"Sue, how are things with you?" I ask quickly, in case my envious thoughts show in my face. "You risked so much for me and I couldn't stop worrying that I might have caused problems for you and your father."

"I've explained everything to dad now and he said that strictly off the record, he'd have been disappointed in me if I hadn't helped you, although officially he will have to condemn it if my part ever comes to light. By the way, Vernon sends his love, he's doing fine."

"Lyndsey, Vi, how are you? I haven't had a proper chance to say welcome home. You know, with a drink in our hands "

"I think it should be us saying welcome home to you," says Lyndsey. "We didn't tell you before because it didn't seem the right time but you failed in your duty. You're not a daddy."

"But don't worry," adds Violet. "Our enforced holiday took us to Mexico and we've made some contacts out there to import ethnic furniture and bric-a-brac. We're setting up a business with my brother, so the family planning will have to go on a back burner for a while."

"And Shaun what are your plans?" I ask and although I'm pretty sure what the answer is going to be, I'm determined to be as pleased as punch for them both when he tells me.

"Ah well," says Shaun. "I've an important announcement to make. I'm getting engaged..."

"Gerry!" He's interrupted by a familiar voice as I experience a feeling of déjà vu. Wasn't this how it had all started?

"Victoria!"

"Gerry, I can't begin to tell you how mortified I am. To think that I've been the cause of all this trouble for you and you've been on the run from the law, then rotting in a prison cell while I've been enjoying the greatest contentment I've ever known."

"You hardly planned for it to happen that way did you?" I say.

"No of course I didn't but that just makes it seem worse. It was because of you that I've found happiness and the only thing you got in return was months of misery. It's so typical of the old me but I'm a changed woman now. I found Ben on the island he owns; well he doesn't actually own it but has it on a thirty-year lease from the local government or whoever it is that owns it. Anyway he'd more or less become a recluse, the only people he sees are the natives who live on the island. It turns out that he'd never forgotten me, well who could? But he supposed that I was 'happily married,' and did nothing to pursue me."

"I'm really pleased for you, you seem so happy."

"I am, Ben's a multi-millionaire and you know me, I could shop for England yet despite that, the strangest part of it all is that I can't spend a penny of it on the island and yet I've never been happier. I've found out what life is really all about. Not only don't I buy clothes any more but I hardly ever bother wearing any either. Ben loves it, he says I've inspired him to start painting again."

"So does that mean you'll have to move from the island now?"

"Yes but only for a short time. There's to be an exhibition of his new work in London at a date next year and guess what? I'll be the subject of every picture. Ben calls me his muse and I'm naked in every one of them, not that you'd recognise me, they're not exactly flattering but all those arty types love them and the 'nouveau riche' wankers are queuing up to buy them as investments."

"So what do you do now? I mean I know you say you're enjoying doing nothing but I can't imagine you being able to carry on like that."

"Well I've been doing all the cooking and one of the women from the village helps with the cleaning but I'm getting more into organising the business side. Ben uses an agent in Sydney and a firm of accountants in Tahiti. They're both worse than useless but I'm whipping them into line. Apart from that we spend the rest of our time going at it like rabbits but that's enough about me, well for now anyway. Since leaving the court I've been on the phone to the manager of the Humming Bird Hotel, he's an old friend. I've booked the function room for Friday evening and you're to invite as many people as you like. There will be loads of food put on by a local restaurant and a free bar on me. Don't worry I can afford it."

"That's great, are you sure?"

"Of course I am and I know it doesn't begin to repay the trouble I've caused for you but at least it's a start. Well actually I'm going to start by buying you lunch tomorrow. I'll pick you up at one, where will you be?"

"I don't know, I'm not sure if I still have a flat."

"You have," says Lyndsey. "Shaun's been paying the rent."

"The lads have chipped in as well," says Shaun.

"Anyway you're coming home with us tonight," says Lyndsey. "You can't go home to a cold flat."

"I'll pick you up there then, by the way, would you two care to come along? You'd be very welcome."

"No thanks," says Lyndsey. "Now the court case is over we need to push on with the business. We've left everything to Vi's brother for too long already."

"I'm off then," says Victoria." I'll see you tomorrow and everyone else on Friday, ciao."

We say our goodbyes and I suddenly remember what Shaun was about to say when Victoria took the centre stage.

"Shaun, you were about to tell us you're getting engaged."

"I was but I might as well leave it until Friday now. Doing it then will save me the expense of throwing a party."

He receives the brickbats and the accusations of being a tight arse in his usual good humour. I have no desire to expedite the news that will prove so bitter sweet for me and so I don't push him to tell me now.

Chapter 37
Road To Nowhere – Talking Heads

As the evening wears on, I find myself drifting away from the revelry. The court case must have taken more out of me than I'd realised, as well as being more out of practice at drinking than usual. Somehow I stray from listening to Violet reciting an anecdote that involves Lyndsey, a donkey, a bottle of tequila and a party of nuns outside a church in Guadalajara, to finding myself waking up on the back seat of a taxi, wedged between the storyteller and the subject, minus her props.

"How did I get here?" I ask.

"Well," says Lyndsey. "After an unsuccessful attempt to drown yourself in a pint of Guinness, Shaun carried you out and put you in here. We're taking you home to bed, to make sure that you don't get yourself into any more trouble."

I'm fussed over by the girls and after showering, finally allowed to go to bed. They say, jokingly I think, that as I'm a newly released jailbird I might need a woman and if this is the case they'll be only too glad to oblige. After all they say, they've done it before and it wasn't quite as revolting as they'd imagined. I say 'no thanks,' and politely make my excuses before going to bed. Despite my exhaustion at the pub, and the fact that after the prison mattress the futon feels like the most comfortable, not to mention sweet smelling bed I've ever lain in, sleep doesn't come easily. I toss and turn, have a fight with the duvet, go to the toilet and count sheep but all to no avail. Only one subject fills my thoughts and I can see her face, hear her voice and smell her perfume, even her laughter seems to invade my ears. I feel like a little schoolboy with a crush on his teacher because in reality I hardly know her. We haven't been out together, haven't shared a kiss, haven't even held hands and yet here I am head over heels with a woman whose love radar I've managed to fly right under without detection. I have to face the fact that for the last few months Julie and Shaun have been getting to know each other, while I've been sitting in my little cell pondering my navel.

Despite the certainty that I know I haven't had a wink of sleep all night, I'm woken from a deep slumber by Violet, bearing a welcome cup of tea.

"You look as though you've gone ten rounds with Mike Tyson," she laughs.

"I know, I thought I'd sleep like a log, being away from the prison bunk and all that but I had a hell of a job getting to sleep."

"Did the warders bring you tea in bed?"

"Only when I ordered it."

"Bet none of them had legs like mine."

"You'd be surprised. Anyway I've just realised I've only got the clothes that I wore to court, are you two off out yet? Could you drop me at the flat when you go."

"We'll be going in about half an hour but there's no need. Lynds brought all your decent stuff round here when we first got back, for safekeeping. All of your clothes are in that wardrobe and the towels are in the usual place. Will you be safe by yourself with Victoria?"

"After my enforced celibacy you should be asking whether Victoria will be safe with me."

"In your dreams," Violet laughs as she leaves.

∞

Violet's comments cause me a certain amount of disquiet, might Victoria be feeling lascivious? No, surely not. The reverie I've fallen into is suddenly broken by the strident sound of the front door bell. Victoria is smiling and looks so gorgeous that I almost find myself hoping for all of the complications that a liaison would bring.

"You look fantastic."

"Thank you kind sir. After taking my leave yesterday afternoon, I somehow ended up in the Mailbox, I've so missed my shopping. Perhaps because of my enforced abstinence from retail therapy I got a little carried away, do you like it?"

The 'it' in question is a cream ensemble that leaves little to the imagination as she gives me a twirl.

"It's lovely," I say, I'm no good at gushing. "It really suits you."

This seems to suffice.

"It cost a mint. I've had to come out without knickers by the way, as you can see they would have spoilt the line. You don't mind do you?"

"No of course not, that's great." I say, reddening as I realise the implication.

"Calm down, I'm not going to jump on you" she says. "All of that's in the past or were you hoping that I would jump on you, I owe you one after all?"

"No!" I say, again a little too hurriedly as we step outside.

"I've told you, relax, you're supposed to be enjoying yourself. What do you think of it?" Victoria's eyes indicate a car parked on the double yellow lines.

This time, the 'it' in question is a shiny, dark blue Porsche convertible, with the top down.

"Where did you get it from?"

"I have it on a week's trial with a view to buying it. I'm not going to of course but the salesman is an old friend and he turned a blind eye to that fact.

Even her driving seems to have calmed down and we must barely average seventy as we reach 'The Gilded Lily' in Birmingham, a naff name for such a fashionable restaurant. I'm half expecting people to recognise me but as we take our seats no one seems to bat an eyelid. Actually to be more accurate the men bat plenty of eyelids but all in the direction of my companion, much to my relief.

"I don't know if I'll be able to cope with such rich food, I say."

"Don't worry, if you want a fry up I'll make them cook you one. Was it really that bad inside?"

"No, the food was reasonable, if you're not a fussy eater."

"I didn't just mean the food, how were you treated?"

"Not too bad really," I go on to explain about my 'E' man status. "The worst part of it all was not knowing how it was going to turn out, being in limbo. Like everyone else, I thought you must be dead and had no idea what was going on, I thought all sorts of things. I thought Lenny might have killed you or he'd had Jermaine do it, or even his Russian friends."

"Ah yes that reminds me, that's where I've been this morning. After you were released from the dock the police officer in charge of the case asked me to attend the police station today. Except that it was more an order than a request."

"What did they want?"

"Well, it was made clear to me that they'd be well within their rights to charge me with wasting police time. I don't think for a minute they'd have gone through with it, as the last thing they want at the moment is anything that would put their mishandling of your case back in the spotlight. It was your friend DI Jenkins that set things going but he explained that he was handing the interview over to an officer from a neighbouring force. This was at his request, although he's under no suspicion of malpractice he didn't want it tainted with any. I got the impression that he didn't trust his partner, I can't remember his name."

"DS Witherspoon."

"That's it. Anyway the police are looking into Lenny's business activities. It seems that whoever sent the video tapes to your solicitor, also sent a great deal of paperwork that Lenny would much rather have kept private. I was talking to your friend Sue when we were at the pub. She told me that, 'off the record,' her father believes that Lenny had somehow been behind your arrest being pushed through with such indecent haste."

"I thought of that but that was when I still believed that he was behind your murder. I thought he was doing it to cover his own tracks. Why would he bother doing it when he knew that he wasn't guilty?"

"Who knows, perhaps in his twisted little mind he believed that you had killed me. Perhaps he actually loved me. More likely he just bore a grudge because he thought you'd deprived him of one of his possessions. The thing is that the police were using the 'wasting police time' rap, to try to scare me into giving evidence against Lenny. Obviously he's no longer flavour of the month in the police canteen now that his cronies wouldn't go near him with a barge pole. The irony there is that I'd be only too glad to sing like a canary if I actually knew anything about his business interests. I was never interested in how he made his profits, as you know my only function was to spend them. I didn't realise at the time, or even care to be honest, how crooked most of his dealings were. Actually, do you remember telling me about hearing him on the phone, discussing drug deals?"

"Yeah, it shocked me when he said he'd sell some on the street pitches and put the rest straight into the schools."

"The Police are fairly sure he wasn't involved in drug smuggling but that he was shipping in cars that are stolen in Cyprus. He owns some used car lots and a driving school, that's what he was talking about. Although his contacts may well have been hiding drugs in the cars to smuggle in, they needed Lenny to provide the false paperwork. Anyway, because of that a lot of Lenny's assets will be seized by the authorities."

"Oh well, you don't need to worry about money any more, you've got your own Prince Charming now."

"On the contrary, my solicitor is hard at work screwing every last penny he can from the businesses and I've already filed for divorce. I don't know if there'll be anything left but if there is it will go into a Swiss bank account as my safety net."

"But Ben's mad about you isn't he?"

"He is at the moment but I'm too old and cynical to take anything for granted. Besides I don't think dependence is a particularly attractive trait in a woman and you know how much I value my allure."

"Yes I remember."

"Cheeky sod, anyway, how about your love life?"

"Well there was Basher Bloggs on B wing but apart from that there's nothing to talk about. I mean there was the thing with Lyndsey and Violet that I had to leave you for on that fateful night but that's not what you mean is it?"

"No but that was so sweet. I feel awful now about trying to bully you into staying with me that day and you were desperate to go but couldn't tell me why."

"That apart, there was only the time I spent with you and we never really loved each other did we."

"No, we just loved fucking each other's brains out didn't we?" This is dropped into the conversation just as the waiter is in the process of serving our dessert course. Designed I'm sure to embarrass either him, me or possibly both of us. It certainly works with me and in a way it's comforting to know that the old Victoria hasn't gone completely. As the waiter moves away from our table, she looks at me archly. "Not all of your time has been spent incarcerated, you were unlawfully at large for a while. Didn't you connect with any members of the female species in that time?"

"You've met Sue, she looked after me and although she needs a bloke, I'm not the one she's looking for. I think we're too much alike."

"And no one else has caught your eye?" Victoria asks, with that look women have when they can see into your mind, a trick that men don't seem to have developed.

"Well there is someone I like a lot but I can't tell you about it."

"Come on, surely after some of the things we've done together, not to mention the sordid details that you know about my love life. I give you my word I'll keep your secret and I'm a changed woman these days. My word is my bond."

"Do you mean that?"

"Of course I do, now come along you're starting to get me ang…" she pauses. "Sorry that was the old me rearing its ugly head. I do mean it though, most sincerely, it will remain our secret but you only need tell me if you want to."

"I'm sorry but you know how easily I get embarrassed."

"You don't need to get embarrassed with me do you? I'm on your side."

"There's more than one reason that I didn't want to tell you. Firstly it's because she's classy and way out of my league."

"Yes but that rules out most of the female race. Only joking, go on."

"She's quite a bit older than me as well."

"But obviously the age difference doesn't bother you or we wouldn't be having this conversation?"

"No but together with the first part, it just makes the gap between us seem more like a chasm."

"Is there anything else, while you're in full flow?"

"Yeah and it just happens to be the biggest obstacle of all, she's getting engaged to my best mate. Julie's going to marry Shaun, so you see how impossible it is?"

"Now that you've explained everything to me, I see only too clearly but don't forget what the Mamas and the Papas said."

"What, Monday Monday."

"No silly, 'the darkest hour is just before dawn.' So come on, I'll drop you off and see you tomorrow night. Don't forget, invite anyone that you want and save the first dance for me, for old time's sake."

Chapter 38
Get The Party Started - Pink

I arrive at the Humming Bird in a taxi with Violet and Lyndsey. None of us wanted to drive for obvious reasons and my mind is set on nothing less than the total oblivion that will numb recent events of the heart. Despite feeling down I'm dressed to impress as almost everyone I know is coming, I've invited all of the school staff as well as any other stray friends and acquaintances I could think of. We're a little late due to the doubts the three of us suffered over our ensembles and the numerous changes this had necessitated. Because of our tardy arrival the room is already fairly full and I manage to slip in without too much fuss.

I've just laid hands on a drink when Victoria makes good her promise.

"Come on they're playing our song," she says, dragging me onto the floor.

I hadn't realised Bon Jovi's 'Bad Medicine,' is our song but then I'd never have imagined that dancing to it could be quite such an erotic experience either. As benefactor of the free bar, Victoria has obviously felt obliged to make use of it with gusto. She informs me that she's wearing another new dress or perhaps 'almost wearing' covers it, which is more than the dress does. As the track reaches its conclusion a 'merry' Irishman relieves me of my drunken strumpet and I head for my abandoned drink, only to be headed off again, this time by Kim Sheffield.

"Come on Gerry, have a dance with me for old time's sake."

"Don't tell me, they're playing our song."

"What?"

"Never mind," I say, as 'Strong' by Robbie Williams, pumps out of the speakers and Kim takes me in a vice like grip. "Why the sudden urgency, did you realise while I was in prison that you'd made a mistake letting me go?"

"Don't be silly," irony had never been Kim's strong suit. "The hunk over there with the mop of dark wavy hair, is he a friend of yours?"

"Yeah I suppose he is," I reply, casting an envious glance at Brendan, who by the simple expedient of wearing a plain white linen shirt and jeans, is looking like the brother Colin Farrell is jealous of. The fact that I chose the shirt for him on our last shopping trip merely rubs salt into the wound.

"Is he spoken for?" Kim asks.

"No, I don't think so."

"Great, his luck's just changed and you can be the one to break the good news to him. Do you think you can manage that?"

"I suppose so but have you ever thought how much simpler life could be if you stopped beating around the bush and just came out and told people what you wanted?"

"Sarcasm is the lowest form of wit Gerry."

"Sorry, I'll do my best."

"I know you will," and after delivering what is by her standards an incongruously sloppy kiss, Kim returns to the two girls she'd been dancing with.

I approach my drink, which is in fortuitously close proximity to Brendan and thereby killing two birds with one stone.

"Brendan, hi how are you?"

"It's me should be asking you that. I'd planned to come and visit if you'd stayed in that place any longer."

"Sorry, I'd have asked for a longer sentence if I'd known."

"You wouldn't have had me restricting my lady chasing time would you? Don't forget I'm on my own now that Shaun and Aiden are both courting.

"No of course not, in fact I think I might be able to help you out. You see that girl over there, the one in the middle of those three, the one with the short dark hair and even shorter skirt?"

"Yeah, should I know her?"

"It's Miss Sheffield."

"Fuck me, the rest of the girls in Sheffield can't be up to much."

"No not like that, she's a teacher and her name is Miss Sheffield." I blunder on, as the smile breaking out on Brendan's face reveals that his perfect deadpan delivery has fooled me yet again. "Oh that was a joke wasn't it?" I say.

"Of course it was ya eejit," he laughs. "I thought the fact that she's actually quite tasty might have given the game away, even if she is a bit on the chunky side."

"Ah well! There's a reason for that."

"What, she likes her chocolate and chips too much?"

"*Au contraire mon ami.* She looks like that when she's dressed because of her shoulders. She's a body builder and when she's undressed she's got a tremendous figure."

"You mean to say you've shagged her too yer dirty little bleeder. Christ almighty and I've only just got used to the idea of Aiden having a woman, although she's still young enough to grow out of it, God help her."

"No, well yes I have been out with her a couple of times but I used to go to the gym with her as well and what she wears when she's training wouldn't hide the modesty of a fully grown hamster."

"Oh my God, that's fantastic! You know how some blokes have got a thing about women in uniform?"

"Yeah."

"Well strong athletic women have the same effect on me."

"Would you like me to introduce you to her?"

"I think I might just manage on me own," he says, stalking off with all the assurance of a Bengal tiger approaching a tethered goat.

∞

"Ladies and gentleman."

The music has died away and Shaun is on the stage in front of the DJ's decks. His voice would easily be loud enough without a microphone and the electronic equipment is howling in protest at being abused in this way.

"I have an important announcement to make," Shaun bellows. "Those who were at Wednesday's celebration will know that I was going to make it then but as luck would have it the lovely Victoria has been kind enough to throw this party for Gerry, which we all thank her for."

Pause for hearty cheers, especially from the Irish.

"Sometimes good can come from bad and that's what's happened here. Due to our friend Gerry being unjustly persecuted, I've been fortunate to meet the most wonderful woman in the world. The soul mate I've been looking for all my life without even realising I was looking. I've asked this very special woman to marry me and she's accepted, so you're all invited to the wedding in the summer," more rapturous cheering. "It's in Hong Kong. No I'm only joking, we might just hold it here. Anyway I've waffled on enough. I'd like to introduce you all to the future Mrs Reagan, Suzanne, come up onto the stage."

I stand gaping as Sue skips onto the stage, looking happier and more radiant than I've ever seen her. It's slowly sinking in that if Shaun is getting engaged to Sue, then he isn't getting engaged to Julie, unless he's a serial engager and he'd have to be a real bounder to do that, especially as Julie's here as well.

Chapter 39
Stars - Simply Red

I'm still reeling from the shock announcement. It's come as a bolt from the blue to me although obviously not to anyone else. I've joined a group standing by the bar, Julie's here as well but I'm too bemused by the events of the last few minutes to know what to say. Fortunately Julie breaks the ice.

"It's lovely news isn't it?"

"Yeah, totally unexpected, probably the best news I've had in ages."

"Well, since Wednesday at least," she smiled.

"Oh yeah, I hadn't thought that one through had I?"

"The rest of us knew about Shaun and Sue a long time ago," Julie explains. "I think I realised what was developing possibly before they did themselves. Anyway, they didn't want to tell you while the case was hanging over you, I think they felt guilty at being so happy, while you were miserable."

"I wish they had, I could have done with some good news while I was..."

As I'm floundering about and trying to keep the conversation going while plucking up courage to ask Julie out, Victoria interrupts my monologue.

"I'm glad to find the two of you together," she says, taking our hands. "Would you all excuse us?" Victoria asks everyone else.

The others voice their assent and Victoria leads us away without explanation. As we follow, Julie raises her eyebrows to me in a silent question that I have no answer to. We leave the bar traversing a corridor and then climbing some stairs that I know from my previous adventure here, lead to the bedrooms. The entire journey is completed in silence until we come to a stop outside one of the doors.

Victoria turns to face us.

"Gerry, I've been the cause of a great deal of distress to you which I've apologised for, and in your typically generous way you've not only forgiven but made me not hate myself over. Now I'm about to do something else that I will have to beg your forgiveness for. You told me yesterday that you were in love with Julie but swore me to secrecy because you thought she was about to get engaged to Shaun. I'm sorry to break my promise but it falls into the white lie envelope as it's in a good cause. Julie, while we were flying back from Tahiti you confided in me how you felt about Gerry. You said you were afraid that the age difference would put him off and you felt that you were too set in your ways to get involved with another man. If I've done the wrong thing then I apologise but I don't think I have. You two belong together and life's too short to go on living a lie, as I know only too well. So what do you say?"

It's probably the thing that if I had three wishes would have been all three. Yet I feel I've an enormous ball of superglue lodged in my throat, as I struggle to think of the right thing to say.

Julie rescues me

"You've put us on the spot Vicky but I think that it's a spot that I'm happy to be on. What about you Gerry?"

"It's the spot I've waited my whole life to be on," I say, with unaccustomed candour.

Victoria produces a key that she waves with a provocative smile.

"That's wonderful," she pronounces. "I couldn't be more pleased. I've taken another liberty and booked this room for you, it's the best room in the place but tell me to stop meddling and I'll leave you to go at your own pace if you'd rather."

Julie takes the key from her.

"You hit the nail on the head when you said, 'life's too short,' thanks Vicky. Is that okay with you Gerry?"

"Yes, thank you Victoria so much. What do they say, 'all's well that ends well,' it couldn't have ended any better for me."

"Go on then," Victoria laughs. "Your love life's had enough delays. By the way Lyndsey and Violet borrowed the key earlier and decorated the room. I don't know what they've done but they insisted, so if they've loosened the nuts on the bed I deny any responsibility for it. By the way, the old Victoria would never have believed that so much pleasure could be derived from being nice to

341

people, so thank you for helping me to become a better person as well."

We both hug Victoria before going in.

The room is very luxurious, and larger than the average hotel room. The lights are draped in what I recognise as Lyndsey and Violets trademark red and purple chiffon scarves.

"I don't believe it," says Julie, wiping a tear. "Everything's so lovely."

"Hang on, what's that?" I say.

A large cardboard arrow points down at the coffee table. We go over and find that the arrow highlights a hand written set of instructions from the girls. Julie laughs as she reads them out loud.

1. Light candles - matches provided. (Sorry Julie, we're used to leaving instructions for Gerry and they need to be simple.)

2. Champagne and orange juice is chilling in mini bar.

3. Chocolates and snacks on bedside table.

4. Something else to help you to relax on other bedside table, take the matches with you.

5. I pod ready to go, we've taken the liberty of choosing the music, just press play.

6. Get on with it, remembering the words of Woody Allen 'if sex doesn't feel dirty, you're not doing it right.'

Have fun, love L & V and all your friends.

"I'll light the candles," says Julie. "While you pour the drinks."

"Would you like a Bucks Fizz?"

"Ooh you are awful, go on then."

"This'll be down to Lyndsey, it's her favourite drink she always says Champagne is wasted without orange juice."

After pouring the drinks I press play on the I-pod. The unmistakeable sound of Peter Green's lush guitar ushers in 'Need Your Love So Bad.'

"How did they know that this is one of my favourite songs?" Julie asks.

"It's from my CD collection, I grew up listening to my Dad's music and he always loved Fleetwood Mac."

"That's a coincidence, I bought this when it first came out because my boyfriend had it and I loved it. I played it all the time and Dad used to say it was good but he preferred the original by Little Willie John. I've told you before that he was a fanatical collector haven't I? He had the original but whenever I hear this I can't help thinking of him, he'd have liked you a lot. Dad liked the original boyfriend after they got off to a bad start but never really took to my husband."

We sit on the bed with our drinks.

"I've got the nibbles on my side, fancy anything?" I ask.

"Keep them for later when we get the munchies," says Julie. "The real goodies are this side. They've left us half a dozen tailor made joints from the Jumping Frog Café in Amsterdam. God knows how the girls got them."

"That'll be Violet, she has contacts and can lay her hands on most things, legal or otherwise."

"When I had the two young children and James seemed to be away from home all of the time...' Julie begins.

"You'd have a joint to get through the day," I interrupt.

"No silly, I was going to say I'd lose myself in old black and white romantic weepies. Brief Encounter, Mrs Miniver, Casablanca but my favourite was always Now Voyager."

"I've never heard of it, did they smoke joints in it."

"No you'll see where I'm going in a minute. Bette Davis plays Charlotte, a put upon little mouse of a plain Jayne who spends her youth being dominated by a selfish, overbearing mother. Eventually Charlotte suffers a breakdown but after treatment from a sympathetic doctor at a sanatorium, she emerges with enough confidence to embark on a cruise. With the help of a friend the ugly bug emerges as a butterfly. During the cruise she meets handsome, debonair Paul Muni who plays Gerry, how's that for a coincidence."

"And they marry and live happily ever after?"

"Of course not, that would be much too easy. Gerry's already married, unhappily of course but he won't leave his wife because they have a daughter and he fears she'll use the girl as a weapon against him."

"I see."

"But you're still wondering why I'm telling you all of this aren't you? Julie said. "I hadn't meant to, it's just that my favourite scene is one where Gerry takes out two cigarettes and lights them at the same time and then hands one to Charlotte. Go on do it for me with two of these, it was so elegant when he did it and so romantic."

"Sounds simple enough," I said with my usual misplaced confidence.

Julie passes me two of the Jumping Frog's finest and the lighter. I put them in my mouth and keeping them together, take a long draw. It's not as easy as I'd thought, and feels as if someone has taken a flame-thrower to my throat, as the heat sears over my tonsils on the way to my lungs and my eyes seem to bulge out of my head.

"Are you alright?" Julie asks, striving not to laugh, as I proudly hand her one of the glowing reefers.

"Yes," I croak, tears running down my cheeks.

"I'm sorry, I didn't think it would be that bad, I'd better enjoy it now hadn't I?"

We lean back against the plush cream headboard, slowly drawing down the smoke and listening to 'World of Pain,' with an occasional interruption for a sip of Bucks Fizz.

"Are you happy?" I ask.

"I can't remember when I last felt this happy and relaxed. It's almost like being eighteen again."

"Me too, sex and drugs and rock and roll, and all of that, except that I never saw much in the way of sex and drugs when I was eighteen."

"Well, if we're communicating in song titles, how about Meatloaf, 'Two Out Of Three Ain't Bad,' why not be greedy and go for the hat trick, come on we've got the drugs and the rock and roll, get 'em off."

I start undressing without a second thought. The time I've spent doing Victoria's bidding has turned me from shrinking violet into what is by my previous standards, almost an exhibitionist. I'm down to my boxers before I suddenly wonder if she might have been joking.

"Sorry, did you mean that?"

"Yes of course," she laughs. "Except that now you're nearly naked I've suddenly realised that I'm actually a little frightened of taking my clothes off in front of you. You see since the end of my marriage, other than going out for the odd drink I haven't been with another man and I think that for the last twenty years of the marriage James had stopped looking at me anyway."

"We can turn the lights off if you'd feel better."

"No, let's start as we mean to go on. No secrets."

"If you're sure."

"It's funny you know, when I was young back in the sixties, before you were even born," Julie laughs. "I'd strip off at the drop of a hat. I remember on family holidays in the South of France, I used to laugh at mom because she wouldn't take her top off unless the beach was virtually deserted. Now I can see where she was coming from."

"Victoria always made a full scale production of taking her clothes off."

"If I had a body like hers I'd happily do the Full Monty for anyone that asked."

"Sorry, I wasn't trying to say that you should be like that."

"I'm being silly, it's just that I've got out of the habit of displaying my body to other people and it's a little daunting to start with someone young enough to be my son."

It's something that I hadn't really considered until now. Julie is Julie and I realise that I've almost become infatuated with her, even to the extent that I've not really considered what to expect a forty nine year old woman's body to look like. Julie had insisted on telling me her age in case it put me off. I know that whatever it's like I'm determined that I'm going to love it. As it turns out I needn't have worried as Julie lets her dress drop to the floor with a 'darrar' and her body turns out to require no major effort on my part to like it an awful lot.

"You can faint from the shock and horror of it all if you want to," she says.

"You're beautiful."

"Oh well to hell with it then, I must be on a roll," she laughs, and whips off her bra. "You see, they're like puppy dogs ears."

"You're a lot like me aren't you?"

"I don't think so, you don't have any man boobs."

"No, I mean you run yourself down as sort of defence mechanism. In case anyone else does, you get there first. Your breasts are lovely, you have a real woman's body not one that's been artificially rearranged. It defines you and you should be proud of it."

"Wow! I wish I hadn't put my big pants on now."

This proves my point, they're actually bikini briefs and not at all big.

We both finish undressing and it seems the most natural thing in the world to start making love. At first we're slow and careful, almost relaxed. This comes as no surprise because it's what I expected from a demure older woman. Then suddenly everything changes, it's as if someone has pulled the pin from a hand grenade as Julie explodes and it's like being back with Victoria on speed. I'm having difficulty keeping up until her breathing sounds on the point of bursting and with a scream she reaches her own Everest. Like the supportive Sherpa Tensing, I follow at a respectful distance. It ends up being every bit as intense as with Victoria but without the histrionics. It helps me no end not to feel under scrutiny as I always did with Victoria and to some extent even more so with Alison when I felt I was always being assessed but not always favourably. With Julie that pressure isn't there, it's simply pure enjoyment, perhaps because she's older but more likely I think, because I just love her so much.

"Oh God," she gasps, as we slump in a sweaty panting heap. "I've waited a long time for that, it's so different with someone you really love."

"Oh," I say, caught by surprise.

"I'm sorry," Julie says, suddenly serious. "I didn't mean to say that."

"Did you mean it?" I ask.

"I think I did but don't worry, I know you're much too young for me and I don't want to scare you off. I'd very much like to remain friends."

"I don't care about the age difference and I'd like to be more than just friends. Will you marry me?"

"Oh Gerry. We have the moon, why ask for the stars?"

"Pardon?"

"Sorry, I've drifted back into Now Voyager. At the end of the film Paul Muni asks Bette

"Is that a no then?"

"No, that was an old film and this is now and real. I let someone I loved slip through my fingers a long time ago and I won't make the same mistake again. The answer is yes... Yes, yes, yes, yes, yes."

Chapter 40
All Tied Up – Guns n Roses

I enjoy my best night's sleep in months. Partly inspired by contentment but I'm sure assisted greatly by exhaustion and also helped along by Julie waking me for another bout of energetic lovemaking at around three in the morning. My morning somnolence is breached by a knock on the door.

"Room service."

The clock tells me it's eight seventeen, Victoria must have taken it upon herself to organise our breakfast as well. Groaning, I throw on my shirt and boxers while crossing the room, still half asleep. The simple action of unlocking the door causes it to implode on me, as I'm knocked six feet backwards. Suddenly I'm very much awake and try jumping to my feet but find myself prevented by what turns out to be Harry Brown's size ten, planted firmly in the middle of my chest. I lie flat on the floor as the horrible orange moon of Lenny Daniels' face gravitates uninvited into my personal solar system.

"Where's my wife?" he hisses.

"Fuck off," I shout, with uncommon coarseness for me. In my defence the rudeness of this invasion of my own little heaven has proved something of a shock.

"Answer the question teacher boy," this polite request is reinforced by a kick in the ribs that I assume comes courtesy of an unseen Jermaine.

"Leave him alone!" I manage to lift my head enough to witness a totally naked Julie, launch herself at Jermaine.

Between the two of them Lenny and Jermaine restrain her and throw her back on the bed.

"Put some clothes on love and behave yourself if you don't want him to get hurt."

Julie looks subdued and starts getting dressed. I notice a trickle of blood running down the side of Jermaine's face, as he looks even nastier than he normally manages.

"Now then Paddy we're not playing games," says Lenny. "Unless you want to see your Granny here get hurt, you'd better tell me where Victoria is. According to the register this room is booked in her name," he takes a gun from his pocket. "Like I said, we're not messing about."

I'm no firearms expert and it looks too real to take liberties with and having just got together with Julie, I'm not about to risk a split that could prove extremely permanent. I quickly reveal to them that Victoria is located in the room next door. "You two go and get her, bring her back here."

Harry takes his foot off my chest and Lenny orders me to sit on the bed with Julie, while he sits in the armchair pointing the pistol at us. It reminds me of a scene from a film but I'm too agitated to remember which one.

"So, you've traded my missus in for an even older model," sneers Lenny. "I bet that pleased her."

"What do you want?" I ask.

"From you? Nothing, from Vicky's latest meal ticket, well, you tell me. How much do you think he can afford? One million, two million, more?"

"No wonder she was such a bitter person before she found Ben," says Julie. "Married to an obnoxious little bastard like you."

"Don't push your luck darling, unlike the court I know it was you and your little friends that somehow got hold of my accounts and grassed me up. If I didn't need you I wouldn't take a lot of persuading to pull this trigger."

"You wouldn't dare you little creep," although I admire Julie's spirit, I can't help wishing that she'd rein it in a little.

"What are you planning to do?" I ask, trying to take his mind off shooting people.

"If Roberts wants my lovely wife back alive, he's welcome to her but he'll pay for the privilege. She can act as go between," he says nodding at Julie. "It'll save all of that messy business of sending messages."

The sound of banging is followed by a stifled scream from next door and then it goes quiet.

"I should think sounds like that are nothing unusual in a knocking shop like this," says Lenny with a sneer and my experiences here make me tend to agree.

As the door opens, Victoria wearing a gag to compliment her very expensive looking negligee is hauled into the room by the Chuckle brothers.

"She started screaming the house down boss," says Harry.

"Vicky, are you going to behave if I take the gag off?" Lenny asks, pointing the gun at her temple.

A nod of acquiescence causes the removal of the offending article.

"There, that's much more civilised isn't it darling?"

"I'm not coming back to you, you can shoot me if you want but I'll never come back."

"Don't flatter yourself, you're used goods and I don't want you but we're going to see how much lover boy thinks you're worth. By the time the tax people and the fraud squad finish with me I'll have lost just about everything, thanks to you and your friends little games."

"Ben won't give you anything."

"Oh I think he will if he wants his little plaything back in working order. I think he'll give us two and a half million. That should buy us new identities and set us up in business somewhere with a little more sunshine. The Internet can be a very useful tool, you can find out just about anything. Did you know that your latest squeeze is worth around twenty-nine million? I'm sure you did, and now that I think of it I might as well round it up to three mill."

"Let these two go," says Victoria. "You don't need them. Ben will pay the money for me."

"I don't think so somehow, they might go to the police. Anyway it's much more difficult for two to escape than one and like I said, teacher lady can carry the message to the painter, he knows her. I'll take the teacher with me Harry and give her the instructions. You and Jermaine take these two to the place we agreed. Don't do anything else until you hear from me."

Lenny takes Julie by the arm and leads her out of the room. Without warning Harry turns round and punches me in the stomach. I hit the floor totally winded, the pain is indescribable as I fight for breath. By the time my brain starts functioning again I see that Victoria is lying very still on the bed and the two thugs are coming towards me. Jermaine has a small brown bottle and a handkerchief in his hands and Harry holds me down while the cloth is forced over my nose and mouth. It reeks of chemical and I'm retching until I lose touch with conscious thought.

∞

I wake up to the reality of the mother and father of all headaches. Not helped by the fact that my head is bouncing up and down on the corrugated metal floor of whichever van I'm being transported in and all of this is intensified by the fact that I feel very sick. My hands are tied in front of me with a nylon tie, and my legs are similarly bound. Victoria is snoring lightly in my ear. Through the discomfort

I can hear voices and manage to manoeuvre myself to the partition at the front of the van.

"Wow, look at the tits on that." I recognise Jermaine's disembodied voice through the partition.

"Never mind eying up them slags," says Harry Brown. "Keep your mind on the job in hand."

"Piece of cake innit? We just hold onto them 'til Lenny tells us he's got the money"

"Yeah dead simple, so no pissing about then like you normally do. This is too important, we play it straight."

"When we get the money, what do we do then?"

"We get a flight to join Lenny in Thailand, the plastic surgeons are already booked. We all have our appearances changed and Lenny's Ruski mates are going to organise new ID's for us. All we have to do is decide which country to make our new home."

"Where do you fancy then?" asks Jermaine. "I might try the States.'

"Lenny will decide that," Harry replies.

"Why? If we've got three million, that's a million each, we can go our own ways."

"The money's Lenny's, he'll pay us, he's always looked after us."

"I don't need him to look after me. We're the ones holding the merchandise, we're taking all the risks looking after them so we should be sharing the money."

"Alright then, how are you going to contact her boyfriend, had you thought of that? No you haven't. Have you organised a bank account in Switzerland for the money to be paid into? No you haven't done that either. You're just a little gob shite, you haven't got a clue have you so why don't you get out now? Just fuck off if you don't want a new life in the sun."

This seems to take a little of the wind out of Jermaine's sails and silence reigns for a few moments.

"What are we doing with these two when the money comes through?" Jermaine asks. I find his concern a little touching.

"Lenny didn't say."

"That means it's up to us then."

"I suppose so, what do you think?"

"I think corpses don't give evidence," says Jermaine. "Especially if they're never found, in fact people might even think they organised the kidnapping themselves and then run off together with the money."

"I don't know about that, what about the teacher woman?"

"It would just look like she was a part of the plan."

"So you think we should knock these two off then?"

"Well they wouldn't be the first would they?"

"No but we play it by ear till we hear from Lenny. Don't let on to them though, they'll be less trouble if they think we're going to let them go."

"I'm not that stupid."

The van comes to a halt and as the engine is switched off I shuffle back to my position alongside the still comatose Victoria. The bright sunlight pierces my closed eyes as the back door opens but I continue to snore as I feel a blindfold being applied and my mouth being taped up. I'm dragged to the back of the van and then carried up what seems to be two flights of stairs, before being unceremoniously dumped on the floor. A few minutes later they return and Harry wheezes, 'put her on the settee.' I know that when they take the tape off I won't be able to maintain my 'dead to the world' pretence so I let out a groan, not to difficult given the way I'm feeling.

"Here, put these on them now that we're here, before those plastic ties cut off the circulation."

A handcuff is applied to my right wrist and I hear a chain rattling. After more S&M related sounds, the tape is gripped and torn away from my mouth. It feels as if half of my face has gone with it and as predicted I let out an exclamation of Anglo Saxon origin. The blindfold is removed and after blinking I can see that we're in a furnished room that has the window boarded over. Jermaine rips Victoria's tape off and she lets out a little moan. As the blindfold is removed her eyes open.

"Where are we?" Victoria asks in a blurred voice

"You don't need to know that," says Harry. "Just make yourself comfortable. You'll be here for a few days but we won't be far away so don't try anything."

My handcuff is attached to the end of a long chain, this in turn is slid through the frame of a wrought iron double bed and Victoria's cuff is snapped to the other end. The room also boasts the settee that Victoria reposes on, a table and chairs and a television set. Harry and Jermaine leave the room, after closing the door we hear them locking it behind them. While Victoria is still groggy I investigate our predicament. The cuffs and chain are sturdy, as is the bedstead that we're secured to and the frame is bolted to the floor. The chain is very long and allows us to reach the bathroom if we work as a team, but not anywhere near the window.

"I feel awful," groans Victoria.

"You won't feel much better when I tell you what I heard."

Victoria sits up, looking more attentive.

"Go on."

"While they were bringing us here I woke up in the van and could hear them talking in the front. They were discussing what happens if and when Ben pays up."

"He will pay, I know he will, money doesn't mean that much to him."

"It seems that Lenny hasn't left them any directions on what they should do with us when they get the money and Jermaine is of the opinion

358

that they should kill us. That way we can't give evidence against them."

"But then they'd risk facing a murder charge."

"Jermaine seems to think that if they dispose of our bodies efficiently, there will be a strong suspicion that we planned it all and have run off together."

"Yes but Julie can tell the police the whole story."

"They may think that she's part of our plan and it would be her word against theirs. Anyway, apparently Lenny has it all arranged for them to go to Thailand for plastic surgery and new identities. Despite all of that I think Jermaine just hates both of us and it's a good excuse to kill us."

"So we can't afford to hang about," says Victoria. "We seriously need to escape."

"Yeah but we've got a couple of things going for us. It'll take at least a couple of days for Julie to reach Ben and get back and they need us alive in case he asks for proof, as well as that they don't know that we're aware of their plans for us. On the other hand there's no way we're going to break out of these chains. I think we'll have to bide our time for now and be ready if the chance arises. In the meantime we must seem relaxed, not do anything to make them suspicious."

"I'm going to make a start now by having a sleep on the bed," said Victoria. "I feel like shit."

"I might as well join you, it can be our first platonic bed experience."

"Don't count your chickens, I may wake up feeling fruity," and with this reminder that Victoria isn't going to let a little thing like imminent death get her spirits down, we retire.

Chapter 41
Slippery People – Talking Heads

The rattling of a chain wakes me up. It's not Marley's Ghost but Victoria, fiddling with her end of our umbilical cord.

"What are you doing?" I ask.

"Sorry, did I wake you?"

"It's okay, I think I was already awake."

"Look, I've nearly got my hand out of this end," she says and I can see that her hand is much more flexible than mine, almost double jointed. "If I can get some sort of lubricant I could probably slip out of it."

"That's great but stop trying now, if they see your hand's red they might take a closer look and fasten the cuffs tighter."

As I say this, the sound of a bolt drawing back heralds the entrance of Harry, followed by Jermaine carrying a tray.

"It's pizza, best we could manage tonight," says Harry. "We'll get you something proper tomorrow."

"Don't apologise to them," sneers Jermaine "They're lucky to get this."

"They're our guests," Harry replies. "We treat them decent."

"Call this decent?" Victoria jumps in, shaking the chain on her wrist.

"As I remember, you were always partial to handcuffs," Jermaine sneers.

"What do you mean by that?" Harry barks at him.

"Nothing, just something I heard."

"Don't be so modest Jermaine, haven't you told Harry about our little affair? You normally enjoy boasting so much."

"She's lying," shouts Jermaine, lunging towards Victoria but Harry puts out a hand and easily stops him in his tracks.

"Is she?" Harry asks.

"Of course she is, she's just trying to cause trouble between us."

"Of course I am Harry, so how do I know he's got a mole on his willie? Or is it just a lucky guess, ask him for a look if you don't believe me."

"Shut up, both of you, I need to think about this. Come on you, out," he thrusts Jermaine out of the door and the bolt slams into place.

"That was a bit risky wasn't it?" I ask through a mouthful of pizza.

"We need every advantage we can get and having them at each other's throats can only help our cause. Harry's slow but he's very loyal to Lenny and he doesn't like Jermaine much anyway. He'll like him even less when the significance of that little lot sinks in."

"Anyway, getting back to your wrist, we might get something with the food we could use as a lubricant."

"Yes I'd thought that, butter or spread would be just the job."

"Oh well," I say, raising a can of the Coke they've given us. "Here's to sandwiches for breakfast."

∞

We don't get sandwiches in the morning. In fact, it's a nice fry up, which Harry and the driver watch us eat.

"Any chance of some toast?" Victoria asks.

"We haven't got a toaster," answers the driver.

"There's a grill in the cooker," says Harry.

"Bread and butter will be fine," says Victoria, unusually considerate.

Harry grunts and the driver leaves, returning with a plate of white sliced buttered bread.

"You really are an angel," Victoria flutters at him. "Oops I think my boob is falling out, you don't mind if I adjust myself do you?"

While she fumbles with her negligee, in a manner guaranteed to have left Gypsy Rose Lee green with envy, the two men watch transfixed and I surreptitiously fling a slice of bread under the bed. The empty plates are taken out and the door secured. I retrieve our prize and rub the butter onto Victoria's wrist. Her hand slips through the cuff without a hitch and suddenly I'm more frightened now that action's required, than when we were unable to budge. Victoria is already at the window and I join her there, it's only covered with hardboard.

363

"This should come off easy enough," I say. "If we rip up the sheets we can make a rope and climb down."

"I can't I suffer from vertigo, I'll freeze, I'm terrified of heights."

"You'll be alright," I say. "Just don't look down."

"I'm sorry but I can't, you go and summon help, I'll barricade the door until you get back."

"No, I'm not leaving without you. I couldn't live with myself if anything happened to you."

"What then? We can't just wait here for them to shoot us."

Just then, I hear voices in the yard. Looking through the gap in the hardboard, we see the driver and Harry get into the van and drive off leaving Jermaine. The germ of an idea springs into my mind.

"Start tearing the sheets into strips while I pull this hardboard off," I said.

"You're going to go for help?" Victoria asked.

"No, I'm going to try to make Jermaine believe that we've gone through the window, quick wedge that chair under the door handle. The window's nailed shut, I'm going to throw the TV through it and then put our rope of sheets out. You can hide in the bottom of the wardrobe under those old clothes and I'll hide behind the chest of drawers in the corner. I'm hoping he'll think we've gone down the rope and go after us. If he starts to search the room I'll have to try and whack him with my chain, then play it by ear. What do you think?"

"You're either a genius or mad. Anyway I can't think of a better idea and I'm just glad to be doing something instead of waiting around."

As I pull off the last of the covering, Victoria is still tearing sheets. After knotting them together I tie one end to the leg of the bed.

"Are you ready?" I ask.

"Yes, do you want me in the wardrobe?"

I can't believe that she's still capable of joking while I'm so nervous, I can feel the chain that's still attached to my arm trembling.

"Yes."

Victoria lies down in the bottom of the big double wardrobe and I scatter some of the musty smelling clothes over her. I unplug the television set and feeling suddenly very calm, heave it through the window for all I'm worth. After kicking out the remaining bits of frame I almost forget to throw the rope out but after doing so I scurry into my hiding place.

The silence seems to last an age before I hear the sound of running footsteps. The doorknob turns a few times, followed by a loud bang and another and on the third I can see through a gap at the side of the mirror the chair flies away as the door springs open. Jermaine cautiously steps inside, pistol in hand but not looking his normal cool self. He looks around and the reality of the situation suddenly hits him.

"Oh fuck! Fuck, fuck, fuck, fuck, fuck!

Jermaine runs to the window and then has one more worrying look around the room before running out. Thankfully he doesn't bother shutting the door behind him. I check that he's gone before retrieving Victoria from the wardrobe.

"Come on, we may not have long."

Chapter 42
Up Up And Away – Fifth Dimension

I tiptoe down two flights of stairs and Victoria follows carrying her shoes. As we reach the ground floor it becomes obvious that we are in what is or at least was, a farmhouse. The front door is wide open but there's no sign of Jermaine. The kitchen is behind us and we head that way. The back door leads onto a yard that contains a Range Rover and an old Ferguson tractor. The Range Rover is open but there are no keys.

"I don't suppose you know how to hot wire one do you?" Victoria asks but the look on my face betrays my inadequacies. "Have a look in the house for the keys, I'll search in the car but watch out for Jermaine coming back."

I do as I'm told but within a minute or two I hear the sound of a vehicle pulling up at the front of the house, followed by doors slamming and voices shouting. I decide we'll have to try to run and hide but as I return to the yard I'm greeted by the incongruous vision of a beautiful woman dressed in a skimpy negligee while sitting astride the old grey Ferguson, like some exotic agricultural Boadicea. She's furiously hitting the controls and the engine is valiantly attempting to respond. Suddenly it bursts into life and the tractor lurches forward, dragging with it, the trailer that I hadn't realised was attached.

"Jump on," she shouts not stopping, and I manage to throw myself into the trailer as it lurches past.

We head for the drive at the side of the house just as Jermaine, followed by Harry and the driver emerge from the back door. Jermaine chases us as the others head back through the house. He leaps onto the back of the trailer but I'm prepared and picking up a lump of wood from the floor of the trailer, I attempt to separate his head from his shoulders. Unfortunately, hand eye co-ordination has never been my forte but I still make satisfying contact with his shoulder, sufficient to send him toppling over the back and more gratifying, as he gets up his pristine suit is covered in all kinds of animal related substances previously foreign to Jermaine.

Our arrival at the front of the house coincides with Harry, who runs towards us. Victoria returns the compliment by heading straight for Harry, causing him to decide that discretion may well be the better part of valour. He retreats colliding with the driver coming out of the front door. As we roar past at a respectable twenty miles an hour, I scramble to the front of the trailer.

"How fast does it go?" I shout, as we head up the single-track lane that leads from the cottage.

"This fast," is the reply.

Just then the van appears behind us, Jermaine is hanging out of the window gun in hand, like a modern day remake of The Sweeney. Fortunately he's unable to fire, due to being hampered by the hedgerows in the narrow lane but it will only be a matter of time before the road widens and we'll be sitting ducks.

I realise that Victoria is shouting at me.

"Climb onto the tractor and see if you can release the trailer."

I recognise the type of connection as I'd helped my Dad with a similar one on his caravan many times. The only difference being that his was perfectly greased and maintained whereas this one is stiff with corrosion. The situation is also slightly complicated by doing it hanging off the back of a speeding tractor on a country lane, while someone tries to shoot me. I resort to the 'Brummie screwdriver,' also known as lump of wood and after four lusty blows the trailer leaves the mother ship before attempting to dock with the front of their van.

"Only just in time," shouts Victoria, as the road does indeed start to widen. "That's only stalled them though they'll soon be after us again."

"I was hoping we might see some houses but we seem to be in the middle of nowhere."

"Look! Over there," shouts Victoria.

In a field about a mile away is the incongruous sight of a multi- coloured hot air balloon, looking as if it's ready for take-off.

"How do we get to it?" I shout.

"I'm not too sure how to stop this thing but I'm pretty certain it will take more than a few fences and hedges to do the job."

With that we smash through the middle of a five bar gate before steering a course directly for the balloon. We're halfway across the field when the van comes through the same gate. Instead of bearing down on us however, they're struggling to make any headway at all as their back wheels slide from side to side in the mud. We crash through another two fences and a hedge before entering the field with the balloon.

"I'll steer to one side of it, get ready to abandon ship."

We hit the ground together, not only too scared but too pumped with adrenalin to injure ourselves. I don't know what I look like but Victoria's hair is standing on end and her very expensive negligee is plastered in mud. Five people are in the basket, one of them, a man wearing a striped blazer and straw boater along with what appears to be two young couples in their twenties.

We run over and Victoria shouts. "You must help us, there are people trying to kill us."

We start to climb in when Stripy Blazer puts his arm out to stop her. "That's impossible," he says. "I'm only licensed to carry four passengers."

At this opportune moment, the van, which has failed to negotiate the hedge, disgorges its load. The three start running towards us as I'm attempting to push Victoria into the basket while struggling with Stripy at the same time. A shot rings out and what sounds like a supercharged hornet whizzes past us.

"What was that?" shouts Stripy.

"They're shooting at us," replies Victoria.

"Oh my God! Release all the ballast ropes," he shouts, while opening the gas taps with a deafening whoosh, as suddenly we're airborne.

More shots ring out from the ground.

"Will it affect the balloon if they hit it," I ask.

"No, a hole the size of a swan wouldn't. I can replace the hot air quicker than we lose it."

One of the men in the balloon is laughing. "Where's the cameras then, this is 'Game For A Laugh' ennit? Or one of them programmes, I know your face from off the telly."

"You're the one from the murder case aren't you?" asks a blonde girl. "The man who got off."

"That's right and I'm the one that he murdered," says Victoria.

As we soar out of gunshot range, we tell them the whole story. It turns out that they've paid for a morning balloon flight and we've hijacked it.

"We're so sorry we've ruined your day out," says Victoria.

"Don't worry about it," the blonde girl answers. "This has been much more exciting, something we'll be able to tell our children and grandchildren about. Anybody can go on a boring old balloon ride."

Stripy looks a little crestfallen at this, but says nothing.

Chapter 43
Our House – Crosby Stills And Nash

Stripy is in radio contact with the local airfield and after landing safely we tell our story to the Authorities. It turns out that Julie didn't trust Lenny and went straight to the Police before contacting Ben. Ben had flown over immediately and made the ransom money available if it was needed. Harry, Jermaine and the driver, who it turns out is called Dave, were arrested at Luton Airport and await trial. Lenny is still on the run.

My three confirmed bachelor mates hold a triple wedding to their respective partners, Sue, Emm and Kim. I was surprisingly awarded the honour of being best man three times over and Julie was maid of honour to Sue. I remember the wedding but very little of the ensuing celebrations. Lyndsey and Violet are too busy with their Mexican enterprise to consider leaving the country or indeed to have second thoughts about starting a family at the moment and if they do they have said they could only consider the turkey baster now that I'm spoken for, I'm pleased and relieved on both counts. Victoria and Ben return to their South Pacific idyll but not before witnessing one more momentous event in my life. Julie and I tie the knot in a Register Office before honeymooning on Ben's island.

It's been an unbelievable journey from my former life where although I was content I wasn't really going anywhere. I've passed through the exciting but worrying months with Victoria and into the depths of despair I experienced while being a fugitive, a prisoner, reprieved, and finally a hostage again. I have emerged at the end of it into a new kind of fulfilment, one that's even scarier in its own way. I've much more to lose now but it's well worth all of that extra worry. Life's good, I've got real friends and I've got Julie. I've moved into her cottage in Blakedown and my arm should be black and blue from the hypothetical pinching it's received. I've learnt to forget the past, ignore the future and live in the here and now. The here and now is pretty damn wonderful.

14949091R00218

Printed in Great Britain
by Amazon.co.uk, Ltd.,
Marston Gate.